HOW TO
SAVE A
LIFE

Emma Scott

Cover design by First Edition Design Publishing
http://www.firsteditiondesignpublishing.com/

Interior formatting by That Formatting Lady
http://thatformattinglady.com/

SUGGESTED
SOUNDTRACK

Everybody Knows, Concrete Blonde
Heat Wave, Martha and the Vandellas
Creep, Radiohead
Hurt, Christina Aguilera
Smokey Joe's Café, The Robins
Josephine, The Wallflowers
The Story, Brandi Carlile
Silent all These Years, Tori Amos
The Way, Fastball
All I Ask, Adele
Crazy, Patsy Cline
How to Save a Life, The Fray

ACKNOWLEDGMENTS

I'd like to extend a tremendous thank you to my formatter, Angela Shockley: You graciously rearranged your schedule to accommodate my craziness and ensure this book made deadline (by the skin of its teeth). You went above and beyond what any formatter should put up with and I am in your debt.

Thank you, Erin Thomasson Cannon. Your constant support and encouragement is the fuel by which I've made it to *The End* of five novels.

Thank you to Elaine Glynn and Jennifer Balogh-Ghosh for the playdates that kept my kids from mindless boredom while I typed and typed, and gave me time I wouldn't have otherwise had, and for your support and friendship.

Thank you to my beta readers, Dawn DeShazo Goehring and Priscilla Perez. Your input and encouragement mean the world to me.

Thank you to my fantastic PAs; Melissa Panio-Petersen for keeping my page alive when I was buried up to my neck in the book, and for being there whenever I needed something, be it a teaser, a graphic, or just your friendly ear. And Nathalie Raven for keeping my schedule, for remembering everything I was too frazzled to keep in my head, and for being there for me from the very beginning. Love my team!

And to Suanne Laqueur. There are not enough words to convey what you mean to me. It has been one of the greatest privileges of my life to be the beneficiary of your artistry, your editorial genius, and your emotional ballast when I was sure I was sinking and taking this book with me. And above all else, for your friendship. You so much.

DEDICATION

For Mom,
Who knew I wanted to write before I did,
And who believed in me even before the first word was set down.
With all my love,
J

PART 1:
SLEEPWALKER

Yet it is in our idleness, in our dreams, that the submerged truth sometimes comes to the top. ~**Virginia Woolf**

CHAPTER

1

JO

Good morning Karn County! It's going to be another scorcher today with highs in the low- to-mid 90s. This heat wave shows no signs of lettin' up, with those high temps continuing through 'til next week and beyond. So here's a little a "Heat Wave" for your heat wave, brought to you by Martha and the Vandellas, and your oldies station, KNOL.

Heat wave was the goddamn truth. It'd been hot as hell since we rolled up from Missouri yesterday and the cab of the semi was stifling. Gerry didn't like to keep the AC on for too long for fear of overheating the engine. I had my bare feet kicked up on the dash and my face practically hanging out the window like a dog, desperate for a breath of wind.

I wasn't a fan of the music jangling out of the radio, but the choices around these parts were oldies, God, or country. Oldies were the best of the bunch and all three were better than silence. Gerry didn't talk much while he drove but to answer some other trucker on his CB now and then. Mostly, he just pointed the semi-truck down an almost straight line of road, across the flat horizon of Iowa.

Martha and her Vandellas wondered how love was supposed to be. I wondered if this was all Iowa was supposed to be: miles and miles of corn. As if a vast ocean were drained of water and all that remained were the swaying forests of seaweed. We passed some farms—satellites orbiting tiny towns— and telephone poles measured the stretch of highway at twenty yards apace, stretching up to the cloudless sky. I stared at the flat nothing of green below and the blue above, searching for some kind of interesting for my eyes to land on. A sign came up on my side.

Planerville
Pop. 1,341

"That us?" I asked.

"Yep," Gerry replied, his eyes on the road and his belly protruding almost to the rim of the steering wheel.

That exchange was the most we'd said in an hour. Not that we had anything to say to each other anyway. Nothing to say. Nothing to see. Going nowhere. Another tiny town, another high school—my third this year alone. *And my last,* I prayed. Surely Gerry wouldn't be transferred again before June. There were only a few weeks till the end of the school year and then I'd be done being the perpetual 'new girl.'

Gerry Ramirez was my mother's cousin. The only family I knew on her side. When my mother killed herself five years ago, he'd come all the way from Florida to take care of me.

He was a long-haul trucker; addicted to the road, and not cut out for raising kids, never mind a teenage girl. For my mother's sake, he put a roof over my head, even if he didn't stay under it but a few days out of every month.

I was the ultimate latch-key kid. If any of the schools I'd been bounced around to had known how much time I spent alone, they'd haul me in for truancy. Gerry would get in trouble for child neglect. But I never let on my situation to anyone. Why would I?

It was either live with Gerry, or remain with my dad's side of the family in Fayetteville, North Carolina. They would've tossed me to the street, pronto. When it came out what Uncle Jasper had done to me when I was thirteen, it had been like a bomb dropped into their make-believe, happy crappy world. My mother ended her life, Jasper went to jail, and the Clark clan never forgave me for any of it. And my dad wasn't there to defend me. Or protect me from his sicko brother in the first place.

My dad's name was Vincent and that's pretty much all I knew of him. His name and that he died serving in Afghanistan when I was two. I didn't know what kind of father he would have been had he lived. Maybe shitty. Maybe okay. Or maybe he would have been the best father ever. If some asshole militant hadn't chucked an IED into my dad's patrol, our family would still be whole, Mama would still be alive, and I wouldn't be scarred up, inside and out.

But whether bombs dropped in distant desert warzones or in small towns in North Carolina, the carnage was much the same. Shit happens. Sometimes a lot of shit. Sometimes more than a girl can fucking handle. All this moving, from place to place, town to town. It felt like running away when I really wanted to plant myself somewhere solid and recover. Heal.

I touched my left cheek under the wall of dark hair I kept over it at all times. The texture of my skin changed under my fingertips.

Planerville, Iowa, population nothing, appeared on the horizon.

"Don't look too bad," Gerry said.

"Looks great," I said. For a few weeks, anyway. When I turned eighteen this June, Gerry's duty to my mother would be fulfilled. I'd be on my own, and then what?

Some people laugh at a situation and say, "Story of my life." I didn't have a story. Just a question.

And then what?

We arrived in Planerville on a Saturday, which gave me two days to explore before I started school on Monday. The dingy little two-bedroom Gerry rented felt like the same house we'd always lived in. It could've been airlifted straight from our last town: white walls that smelled like fresh paint, carpet that smelled like cigarettes, and boxy rooms. No personality. Gerry had no intention of settling in and making it our own. I thought he was a sadistic gardener in a past life—just tearing everything out by the roots so nothing ever had a chance to grow. After our fourth town, I didn't even bother unpacking.

Sunday afternoon, with the sun beating at my back, I biked to downtown Planerville. One bank. One auto shop. One grocery store. A pizza place and a sporting goods store. That's it. I'd later find out that all the action took place up in Halston, about a ten-minute drive north. I could see why.

I wrote poetry, and I usually wrote a few verses about whatever new town Gerry dragged us to, pinning down first impressions. For Planerville, a plain piece of blank paper would've sufficed.

Only one point of interest: the town had put up a new aquatic park last year. I rode by it on my bike, and it was no Raging Waters, that's for sure. Only three slides—none of them huge or scary—a lazy river, a pool. One of those shallow areas with sprinklers and mini-slides where toddlers splash around, pissing in the chlorine to their hearts' content. High bars kept people out after closing at 5pm and the whole thing shut down in winter.

While I had zero intention of ever swimming there during business hours, it looked like a good place to hang out at night, dip my feet. Maybe scratch out a poem. I made a mental note to test the security features of Funtown Water Park sometime soon.

As the sun was beginning to drop and the bugs began their twilight symphony, I biked to Wilson High School. It became immediately apparent this was a *Friday Night Lights* situation. Football was life in Planerville. The field was newer by a good ten years and better maintained than the shabby brick buildings of the school proper. I had images of raging pep rallies, marching band fight songs, and the entire fucking town cramming the perfectly maintained stands. Jocks were kings, the cheerleaders queens.

With football season long over now, the tiny school populace was desperate for the next big distraction. It was the end of May, so that meant prom, probably.

Or maybe the new girl in black, hiding behind a wall of hair, and who had a penchant for screwing boys she didn't give a shit about and who didn't give a shit about her. Uncle Jasper had ruined me; no guy would ever consider me girlfriend material. Those were the cards I'd been dealt and so I played them the only way I could. On *my* terms.

I mentally prepped for my first day at Wilson High School (population: 311), ready to take on the mantle of class slut or freak.

Turned out 'slut' was available, but the title of 'freak' already belonged to someone else.

4

I didn't even make it to lunchtime before I'd heard all the dirt on some poor schmuck named Evan Salinger. Without speaking to a single person directly, I learned Evan had been a foster kid. A weirdo. A loner. There'd been some kind of incident here at school three years ago. Something about him having a major breakdown in algebra class. I didn't have the details, but that breakdown had landed Evan Salinger in a mental institution, and permanently awarded him the name "Freakshow."

As resident freak, I half-expected Evan to wear the title as I would have: dark clothes, long hair from behind which to hide and observe, maybe some emo eyeliner if he was really feeling it.

As it turned out, I sat next to Evan in Western Civ—my last class for the day. I didn't even realize it until the teacher called on him to answer a question. He sat to my left, and the hair covering that side of my face had blocked him from view. I turned and nearly choked on my contraband chewing gum. No black clothes or emo makeup or stringy hair. Not this guy. Evan Salinger was, to put it mildly, fucking gorgeous.

He wore his blond hair long, like Leo DiCaprio in his *Titanic* era, but Evan was bulkier than young Leo. I only saw him at profile, but Evan's biceps stretched the sleeve of his t-shirt quite nicely, and his shoulders were broad and looked strong, even if all they did was hunch him over a book. He was tall—his knees bumped the underside of his desk—and when he looked up to answer the teacher's question, I caught a glimpse of striking, sky blue eyes.

Gorgeous.

Impossible, I thought, this guy could possibly be the same notorious weirdo the school populace couldn't shut up about. I would have cast him as the quarterback for the Wilson Wildcats. Or captain of the local 4H. Class president. This guy was Prom King, not Freakshow.

From behind my half-wall of hair, I took in Evan's clothes, searching for clues, but I found nothing to support the whisper brigade. He wore faded jeans with his plain t-shirt, and work boots. The jeans were smudged with what looked like faded motor oil stains. This at least made sense: I'd heard he was the adopted son of Harris Salinger, who owned the town's mechanic and auto-body repair shop. The Salingers lived in a big white house on Peachtree Lane and Mrs. S drove a Lexus.

Evan's adopted family had money—another thing he had going for him. Obviously, his position on the lowest rung of the social ladder could only come down that stint at Woodside Institution. I hoped that wasn't the case, but what else could it be? In a school of only three hundred kids, that sort of history would kill Evan's chances of ever being named anything but the local mental case, never mind Prom King.

Wilson High, I quickly deduced, was isolated as hell. Its kids so bored with each other, you couldn't pass gas without everyone whispering about it.

And *goddamn*, they sure whispered about Evan Salinger.

When Mr. Albertine called on Evan to answer that question about the Roman Coliseum, the entire class seemed to flinch all at the same time. The air tightened, and then everyone—and I mean, *everyone*—swiveled in their chairs to hear Evan's reply.

I expected him to bust out in some operatic aria. Maybe stand up, raise both middle fingers to Mr. Albertine and tell him to shove the Coliseum up his ass. I was kind of hoping he would. I mean, if you were stuck with a shitty rep, why not make the most of it?

Evan, still hunched over his book, answered the question correctly in a totally normal, sort of deep, sort of gravely, (okay, sort of sexy) voice. The other students stared a moment more, some narrowing their eyes at him, all suspicious-like, as if to say, "What are you playing at now, Salinger?" Then one by one, went back to minding their own business.

Not me. I kept staring. For all his hard angles and masculine ruggedness, there was some intangible softness about him too. I don't know how or why I could possibly know this at first glance, but to me Evan looked like he'd spill the deepest secrets of his heart to the first person to show him any kindness.

He's sort of beautiful, I thought.

I was jolted out of my reverie when Albertine called on me to answer the next question. I tucked my gum into the corner of my cheek. "Didn't catch that, sorry?"

The whole class turned around again to get a load of the new girl with her torn black tights, purple skirt, black T-shirt and boots. My ear caught a few snickers. The *actual* quarterback of the Wildcats, Jared Piltcher, gave me an appraising glance from the next row.

Albertine repeated the question, I bullshitted my way through an answer, and still I felt Jared's eyes on me. He fit the bill for masculine hotness too, but he lacked that intangible quality I'd noticed in Evan. Jared was barricaded behind his popularity and good looks and his star status. You could talk to him for days and probably never get through all that posturing to the real him.

Which made him the perfect candidate for my purposes.

I trapped Jared's gaze with the eye not hidden behind my hair and ran my tongue over my upper lip. Slow, like I was tasting something good. His eyebrows shot up, and then he laughed quietly to himself, shaking his head. He gave me a final, questioning look. I nodded once. He coughed and turned to face the front of the room again. Did he adjust his crotch to quell a burgeoning boner, ladies and gentlemen? I believe he did. Under the bleachers or behind the gym, or in some abandoned corner of the library, we'd meet up and I'd start building my own reputation.

I slouched back down, making sure the wall of hair over the left side of my face hadn't moved and the class dragged on. A sense of warmth fell over me, a ray of sunlight from the window maybe. Except that I wasn't sitting near a window.

I glanced at Evan Salinger. He wasn't looking at me; his head was down, eyes on his book, but even so. It was *him*. I could feel him, if that makes any sense. Which it doesn't. I know it doesn't, and I knew it then. But it felt like Evan Salinger was observing me without looking.

"Stop that," I whispered.

"Sorry," he whispered back immediately. He wasn't confused by my request. He'd known what I meant, which was fucking odd since *I* hadn't known what I meant. And then it was as if something got shut off. A beam of light dimmed by a passing cloud. I shivered, and that feeling of Evan's attention on me was gone.

Okay, so that was weird.

Was this part of his freakshow reputation? He had a strange vibe, no doubt. Not explainable and likely a product of my imagination. But not terrible. Not when I really thought about it.

Not terrible at all.

CHAPTER
2

JO

The next morning, before second bell, I lured Jared Piltcher to the bleachers behind the gym and let him reach up my shirt until his hard-on was obvious against my thigh. He kissed like he was trying to eat my tonsils, but I managed to keep my hair over my left cheek. He wasn't interested in my face anyway.

"I have a girlfriend," he said as the bell rang. "I'm taking her to prom. Just so you know."

I shrugged. "It's cool. Our little secret."

"Cool. So...after lunch?"

I shrugged again. "We'll see."

First rule of showbiz: always keep them wanting more. And this was all an act. *I* was an act. A facsimile of a human being, playing the part of a seventeen-year-old high school girl. And like my part required, that day at lunch, I sought my people. I found the table populated by boys and girls dressed in black, sporting emo hair and makeup and I sat among them as if I had been doing so every day since the start of the school year.

I plunked myself next to Marnie Krauss—the alpha bitch of the misfits, and across from her second-in-command, Adam Lopez. Adam was the only uncloseted gay kid in the whole school, maybe the whole town.

Adam gave an affronted huff, drawing his chin in and raising his brows. "I'm sorry, have we met?"

"So glad you could join us," Marnie said, her voice drawling. The look she exchanged with Adam was so loud, I could hear it.

Is she for real?

I know, right?

"Jo Clark," I said. "I'm new."

"Obviously." Marnie narrowed her eyes at me. "What's your story?"

"I heard you guys run an underground 'zine."

Marnie perked up, her expression brightening momentarily before carefully morphing back to blasé. She was the editor-in-chief of *Mo Vay Goo,* one of the school's monthly circulars. I'd rescued a copy from the hallway trash not ten minutes before.

Mo Vay Goo was a play on the phrase mauvais goût, meaning *in bad taste.* It was an angsty little number, full of angry rants against The Man and existential editorials. I expected it to be puerile and kind of silly, but it was actually pretty good. Plus, I wasn't a fan of sitting by myself at lunchtime.

"Yeah, I'm the editor," Marnie said. "Your point?"

"I'd like to contribute," I said. "I write poetry."

Adam Lopez sniffed. "Honey, we're a *serious* mag."

"I don't write fluffy shit." I turned to Marnie. "If you want a sample first, I'm happy to provide."

Adam looked inclined to protest but Marnie's eyes were on me and the hair I kept over the left side of my face. She tapped her teeth with a black-chipped nail. "New content is never a bad thing."

"How do we know she's not just trying to get in to fuck us up?" Adam said.

I snorted. It was cute they thought anyone cared enough about their 'zine to crash the party. "Do I look like I'm running undercover for the pep squad? I said I write poetry. Much of it in bad taste."

Marnie crossed her arms. "That's cool. But we're not interested in poems about purple clouds of sadness or how your life is a dark house with no doors."

"We want art," Adam said. "Not imitation Nick Cave lyrics."

This was encouraging. Maybe *Mo Vay Goo* was up my alley after all. I glanced around at the table. Six other kids in black with jagged haircuts, some with chunks of chalk-coloring, all stared at me. My people. Or they would be once I initiated myself into their circle. *Just do it,* I thought. *Like tearing off a Band-Aid.*

I sat up straight and lifted the hair hiding half my face. The cool air hit my cheek, and I felt naked. Exposed. My left eye blinked at the sudden infusion of light. The whole table got a good look for three excruciating seconds, then I dropped the curtain.

Adam whistled low between his teeth. "Jesus. What happened, girl?"

"Car accident," I said. "I was thirteen. Killed my mother, left me this beauty of a souvenir. I don't talk about it. I write poems about it." I looked to Marnie. "No fluffy shit."

"Yeah." She nodded, her eyes wide as she took in my cheek where my scar hid. "No fluffy shit."

I was in. Insta-friends: just add tragedy.

That night I ate my dinner sitting cross-legged in one of the old Laz-Y-Boy chairs stationed in front of the TV. Gerry sat in the other, watching baseball with a bucket of KFC on his lap. He'd offered me some—thereby fulfilling his guardianship duties for the evening—but I wasn't a fan of the greasy stuff. Only the best BPA-filled ramen and a Diet Coke for me.

"I've got a long haul coming up," Gerry said, never taking his eyes off the tube. "Week and a half. Maybe two."

"Okay."

"You'll be fine?"

"Sure."

Like I had a choice, anyway.

That night, I stood at the mirror of my own bathroom and tied up my hair from my face. My scar stood out brilliantly under crappy fluorescent lighting. A ragged seam that started just under my left eye and stretched in a perfect, if shaky, line to my jaw. A lightning crack of shiny white.

I'd told the gang at school it was a car accident, and they bought it. And why not? I'd given no reason why they shouldn't believe me. And 'car accident' was much more humane than telling them the truth: that I'd taken a three-inch long screw and carved that narrow trench myself. To stop my uncle's thrice weekly nocturnal visits.

Jasper had told me not to tell—never to tell—so I showed them instead.

A horrible mistake. It stopped Jasper but it killed my mother. I cut my cheek with a screw, but I may as well have dragged it across my mother's wrists for her. She took one look at that bloody rent in my cheek, heard why I'd put it there, and lost it. She wasn't all that mentally strong to begin with. She held on for three days, wailing and crying behind her closed bedroom door, until my Uncle Jasper was hauled off to jail. Then my mom checked out.

I spread cold cream on the scar like I used to do with all kinds of "scar-diminishing" or "blemish-reducing" lotions they hawk on late-night infomercials. Nothing worked and unless I suddenly hit the lottery to afford some plastic surgery, nothing ever would. I had done a thorough job of wrecking my face. And destroying my mother. And ruining my life. All in one shot.

Ugly thoughts and memories. They always rose up when I showed anyone my scar. An aftereffect or PTSD, or something. My hands were shaking by the time I finished washing my face and brushing my teeth.

I lay on my bed and pretended I was floating on a lake somewhere remote, with beautiful, jagged mountains surrounding the water that was as placid as ice. It worked; my blackened and bloody thoughts began to scatter like oil over water, taking me to sleep.

Just before I slipped under, I thought of Evan Salinger.

We were back in Western Civ and he was doing that thing again, where it felt like a beam of warm light had fallen over me. I started to tell him to stop, but he faced me in his chair and looked at me with those sky blue eyes head-on. I felt my breath catch, suddenly wanting to be the object of their clear, warm gaze.

He smiled at me as if I weren't ugly and carved up and ruined by my predatory uncle.

"Good night, Jo."

I tried to say goodnight back, but I'd already slipped off to sleep.

Chapter 3

JO

The bell rang and my AP English class started clearing out. Ms. Politano called me back. She was a younger teacher, with her hair always in a messy bun and her clothes more bohemian than what I pictured for a teacher in Middle America. She looked like she belonged in a library in Seattle, always with a book under her arm and reading glasses sliding down her nose.

"So, Jo," she said, smiling brightly. "Short for Josephine. Like Jo March from *Little Women*."

I nodded. "That was my mother's favorite book."

"Mine too," Ms. P said. "You couldn't have a better namesake in my humble opinion."

My lips twitched as I tried to muster a polite smile and failed. Ms. P didn't let my lack of answer throw her.

"Since the school year is nearly over, I'm having a hard time determining how to grade your progress," she said, smiling kindly. "I've received your work from one of the two schools you attended previously, but it's not really enough to get a full picture of where you are. Academically-speaking."

I shrugged, though my guts started to roil. "Okay. So?"

Ms. P perched at the edge of her desk. I could see her take me in: the hair over my face, the dark clothes, the defiant stare. Her smile turned patient. "Without a broader scope of work, I'm at a loss as how to grade you."

"I need to graduate. I *have* to graduate."

"Of course," Ms. P said. "But time is running out. I can't test you. We're doing literature analysis, and we're already halfway done with *As I Lay Dying.*"

As I Lay Dying. I'd read it. I'd read a lot on the road. That one was a novel where the main character is a dead mother. You could say I was intimately familiar with the material.

"I can catch up."

Ms. P's warm smile was starting to get on my nerves. "I have no doubt you can," she said. "But that, plus the end-of-year course work isn't going to be enough. There are simply too many holes in your school year."

"What are you telling me? I have to go to summer school?"

"I don't see how it can be avoided."

Ms. P smoothed her knee-length knit skirt, like we were pals, shootin' the shit. Equals. I hated when teachers pretended to be equals, especially when they held my entire future—fragile as it already was—in the palm of their hand.

Ms. Politano didn't seem all that bad, but she could royally fuck up *my* life if she didn't let me graduate.

I gnawed my lip. "What if I did some sort of special project? For extra credit?"

"I was thinking along those lines as well. But it would have to be pretty spectacular."

I had thirty poems in a collection at home. Twenty of them were okay, ten were pretty good. I hadn't intended to use them for something stupid like school, but if it meant graduating or not graduating, they'd be my sacrificial lambs.

"What about a poetry project? I have a bunch I could show you and maybe you could assign me a few more?"

Ms. P's face lit up. "You write poetry? Wonderful. Earlier this year we did a whole unit on love poems and sonnets. Keats, Shakespeare, Elizabeth Barrett Browning… Maybe we could focus your project on that."

I struggled to keep my lip from curling. "Love poems aren't really my thing."

Ms. P laughed. "Can't make it too easy on you, can we? Bring me what you have tomorrow and we'll see what we can work out. Sound good?"

It sounded better than not graduating, but I didn't have much hope this project would satisfy Ms. P. She was a dreamy-eyed romantic. My stuff about suicidal mothers, dead fathers, and pervy uncles wasn't going to float her boat. Then I'd be royally screwed.

What did I know about love? Jack and shit, that's what. What little I'd known had been ripped away, leaving only a gray haze of distant memories that were growing fainter by the day. My mother…She'd been my whole world—vibrant and full color, and now I could hardly see her face.

I rubbed an ache over my heart as I left Ms. P's class, and braced myself for summer school.

Later that day, I was walking down the hall with Marnie and Adam. Evan Salinger walked ahead of us, his nose in a book. He wore a blue and black plaid flannel over a worn t-shirt, jeans, and his work boots. The jeans were streaked with engine grease but they made his ass look damn fine.

Jared Piltcher, now my recess make-out buddy, leaned against his locker with a few friends from the football team. A wall of beef in denim and letterman jackets. They elbowed and jostled one another as Evan approached.

"Uh oh, hold up," Adam said, drawing me aside.

Marnie pursed her lips. "In five…four…three…"

As Evan passed the guys, Jared knocked the book out of his hand.

"Blast off," Marnie muttered.

"Knocking books," Adam said. "How original."

Neither he nor Marnie made a move to help Evan. They just watched. So did the rest of the hallway population. So did I.

Evan knelt to gather his book. "Fuck off, Jared."

"It's alive! Alive!" Jared laughed while Matt King, a linebacker, stuck his arms out like a bad Frankenstein's monster, moaning and goose-stepping. Another jock put his fingers to his temples and made a *zzzt!* sound, then convulsed as if electricity coursed through him.

I leaned toward Marnie. "What's this bullshit?"

"Evan spent time at Woodside," she whispered. "The mental institution up in Halston."

"Yeah, I heard. So?"

"So you see that scarecrow-looking creep tagging along with the jocks?"

I looked and noticed a scrawny stick of a guy with a pinched look on his face, and the curved handle of a cane clutched in his bony hands. The runt of the litter.

"I see him."

"That's Shane Salinger. A senior, like Evan. He told everyone Evan had ECT at Woodside."

"ECT... You mean shock treatment?"

Marnie nodded.

"Is it true?" I asked.

She shrugged and smiled dryly. "That's the majestic, terrible beauty of a rumor. It doesn't have to be true for it to spread."

Evan walked out of the hallway, head up, eyes forward. Shane Salinger laughed along with everyone else, twice as loud. "Ha! Good one, guys!"

The jocks ignored him, and Shane inched his emaciated body—it was obvious he was suffering some degenerative disease—closer to the huge dude standing beside him. Like he was taking shelter. The big guy had the same straw-colored hair as Shane but was ten times as brawny, with pimpled skin and dull, flat eyes.

I nodded my chin at him. "Who's that?"

"Another Salinger brother, Merle," Adam said. "A junior. Shane's a tag-along, trying to run with the big dogs, but Merle *is* a big dog because he's good at football."

Marnie nodded as we resumed walking. "The only thing keeping Shane from joining us at the bottom of the food chain is Merle. That, and the rumors he coughs up about Evan. Keeps the lugheads entertained."

I frowned. "Why does Shane talk shit about Evan? Isn't he their brother?"

"Officially adopted." Adam shrugged. "But so what? Not blood. Shane hates Evan. Like, seriously hates him."

"Seems like lots of people do," I muttered to myself. I walked another step and realized Marnie and Adam had both stopped and were staring at me with mild alarm. I glared back.

"What?"

"Do *not* go there," Adam said. "Evan Salinger is yummy, I will give him that. A strong, silent type. But then you get in his space..." He shivered dramatically.

"He's hot, I'll admit," Marnie agreed, "if a little white-bread for my tastes, but there's something...*off* about Evan."

"Aren't we all?" I muttered.

Marnie didn't seem to have heard me. "You ever walk under a field of electric lines? Where you can hear them humming, and the hairs on your arms stand on end?"

I fixed them both with a dubious, one-eyed stare. "Yeah?"

"Try standing next to Evan sometime," Adam said.

Marnie nodded. "He gives me the creeps. And he's social poison, to put it mildly."

"Why?" I snapped. "Because he was in a mental institution for a little while? Is the whole fucking school so backward that they're going to pick on him for that? For *years*?"

Adam put his hand on my shoulder and said seriously, "Your concern is cute. But misplaced."

I brushed him off.

"It was kind of a big deal, what happened to land him in there," Marnie explained.

"So what happened?" I asked impatiently. "Something about Evan having a breakdown in class?"

They exchanged looks.

"Something like that," Marnie said.

"Oh, if it were only that simple," Adam said with a dramatic sigh.

I tried not to roll my eyes with impatience. The bell was going to ring any second now, and I'd be left with a goddamn cliffhanger. "So what *happened*?"

"A few months after the Salingers officially adopted Evan—three years ago, or so—there was a factory shooting up near Jefferson. Six people dead, thirteen injured."

My eyes widened. "Evan was involved in a *shooting?*" *That would explain a lingering bad rep, and then some.*

"Not directly," Marnie said. "But the morning of, Evan started freaking out, screaming and yelling for help; shouting at someone to stop doing whatever horrible shit they were doing. Someone only he could see. And all this right at the *exact* same time as the shooting."

Now I did roll my eyes. "Seriously? A coincidence…"

"You would think. Except Evan seemed to know it was happening before anyone else heard about what was going on in Jefferson. It's not like the news was on. No one knew shit. Except for Evan. He *knew.*"

I crossed my arms. This all smelled like so much rumor-mongering bullshit, but I played along. "So he's psychic or something? How did he know?"

"That's the kicker," Marnie said. "They asked Evan a hundred times and kept saying he saw it *in a dream.*"

Adam shook his head. "The cops came and they hauled him off to a doctor, and apparently Evan told the doc a whole lot more stuff he'd 'seen in a dream.' Stuff that wasn't really possible for him to know."

"Stuff like what?"

First bell rang.

"To be continued," Marnie said, and put her hand on my arm. "Until then, remember: Social. Poison. You start associating with Evan Salinger and even we can't help you with the fallout."

Adam nodded solemnly and the two of them headed off to their next class leaving me standing there with a hundred more questions.

I sighed. Fucking cliffhangers.

I walked to my next class, and recalled what Marnie had said about standing next to Evan. Like standing under power lines.

It's not like that, I thought. *Not an itchy buzz but a warm ray of light…even when he wasn't looking at you.*

CHAPTER 4

JO

All through Calculus, I didn't stop thinking about Evan. Since I was thirteen years old, I'd gotten really good at not giving a shit about other people. But I sort of felt bad for him. Not for being institutionalized, but because he'd needed to be. He'd hit some kind of breaking point, I guessed. I could appreciate that. I'd been there too, and wore the scar to prove it.

That afternoon, while Jared was fumbling his way up my skirt behind the bleachers, I asked him about Evan.

"What?" Jared stopped, blinked at me. "What *about* him?"

"Why do you guys rag on him so hard?"

"He's a freakshow, that's why."

"Seems pretty normal to me."

"He's a mental case and shouldn't even be allowed at school." Jared was intent on his prize, like a little boy rummaging in a cookie jar. "He's a liar and a lunatic."

Jared's enthusiasm was getting rough and it was unspooling a sickening sensation in my gut.

"The fuck do you care, anyway?" Jared said, grabbing at me hard.

"I don't," I said, and bit down on his neck, harder.

Jared tore away from me. "What the hell?"

My terms. My call. Always, my call.

The mantra repeated in my head and I made *my* hand reach for Jared, not the other way around.

"You need to chill," I said, and *I* reached for the zipper on his fly. Me. Because it was my fucking choice.

Jared eased back toward me. "I just don't want a hickey. Laney will see."

I slipped my hand down his pants. "I'll try to be more gentle."

"Good."

He tried pushed me down to kneeling but I was already on my way.

I left the field at quarter to four. The sun was sliding toward the horizon, and the school was empty as I made my way to the bike rack. Mine was the only one there beside some rusted junker someone must have abandoned.

I unlocked my bike and was about to climb aboard when my stomach suddenly heaved. I nearly puked right then and there.

Jesus, calm down!

That had never happened to me before, and there had been a lot of *before* over the years. A lot of sneaking off; a lot of bleachers or storage closets or backseats of cars. So why was my body suddenly in revolt?

I sucked in several deep breaths, reminding myself why I did that shit with guys like Jared Piltcher in the first place. Because I wasn't a victim. I got to say who and when and how much. Just like goddamn *Pretty Woman*.

I biked to the nearest corner grocery and bought a Gatorade and a tin of Altoids. I drank half the bottle and chewed up three mints before continuing to my house. I was calmer by then, my stomach had settled down.

Gerry was at work; the house was silent. I wended between unpacked boxes of our meager belongings to my bedroom. I shut the door, sat at my desk overlooking the neighbor's chained-in yard and pulled out my notebook.

I had an idea for a poem. A couple sentences I might be able to work into something. I had to write it down before it fled my brain or burnt up in shameful memories.

My body is not my own
He showed me that
In the secret nights
private parts
now
Public property
And a lesson learned:
Give it away before they
take it
so you can pretend
it doesn't
hurt.

CHAPTER 5

EVAN

If I never heard the sound of spoons and forks scraping against bowls and plates, I'd die happy. That was the background music to almost every breakfast, lunch, and dinner at the Salinger household. Every meal, scrape, scrape, scrape. The soundtrack of a family with nothing to say to each other. But for little Garrett. His little voice was like a flute piping up amid the scraping. Tonight's dinner was no different.

Norma sat at one end of the table, lips pursed, surveying the scene and eating in silence. Harris sat at the other, shoveling in his food like you shovel coal into a furnace: for fuel only. A newspaper lay opened beside his plate. On the sides of the table, Merle and Shane sat beside each other, Garrett and I across from them.

"Hey, Evan, you want to play catch with me tomorrow after school?" Garrett asked. His sweet round face looked up at me with unabashed affection. It made my chest ache. My nine-year-old little brother was the only human being in Planerville who didn't look at me like I was a leper.

"Sure, buddy. You got it."

"I need you at the shop," Harris said without looking up from his beef stroganoff or his newspaper. "Right after school."

Shane, across from me, shot me a death glare, then turned to his dad with a whine. "I thought it was my turn to take a shift. You said so last week."

Harris's eyes darted between Shane and me, then back to his food. "It's a busy week. I need Evan."

"Sure," I said.

Shane's silent storm of rage blew over me. There was nothing I could do about it. Harris's rule was law, but that wouldn't stop Shane from seeking retribution.

Beside me, Garrett slumped. I wanted to ruffle his pale blond hair. "Next time, buddy, okay?"

He brightened immediately. "Okay," he said, and began prattling on about the science fair at his elementary school.

Shane sat in sulky silence, like a petulant little kid, arms crossed over his narrow chest. He had multiple sclerosis, the relapsing-remitting kind, now in relapse. It left him skinny, weak, and living in fear of its eventual return.

It was terrible watching the disease take a physical and mental toll on my adopted brother, and it pissed me off that our parents only gave him treatment for the physical symptoms. Shane took out his unchecked rage and fear on me, casting me as the interloper out to steal his future at the auto shop with my strength and health. Worse, he made my life a living hell at school. I tried to remember how scared he must be. He was fighting a battle he couldn't win. I hated he had to suffer it. But I guessed after the fallout from my little stint at Woodside Institute, the Salingers weren't about to have two kids who required mental health care services.

As if shit weren't hard enough for me since Woodside, Shane used Merle for a bodyguard and attack dog. Shane channeled his rage right into Merle. Merle—one year younger than us, but a good five years behind mentally—was more than happy to oblige. Whatever Merle lacked in brainpower, he made up for in muscle. Shane liked to sic Merle on me right before school, or right after. Before work at the shop so I'd show up with blood on my shirt or a shiner that didn't look good in front of customers. Harris hated that.

I watched Shane elbow Merle and the big guy nodded, shoveling food into his immense bulk. My hackles went up immediately.

"Boys, dishes," Norma said.

On cue, we all stood up, the parents to the TV room, leaving us boys to clean up.

Merle pinned me against the pantry as soon as Norma was out of sight. He jammed his thick forearm under my chin, pressing hard against my throat. Shane sneered at me over his shoulder.

"You think I'm blind? You think I can't see what you're doing? That fucking business is *mine*. And Merle's. We are the *sons* on the sign, not you."

I shoved Merle off of me and stood ready, my muscles coiled, and my nerves jumping, ready to defend myself.

"Let it go, Shane," I said. "Just fucking drop it."

I tried to push past them, to end it there, but Merle grabbed the front of my shirt and shoved me back. I tore his hand loose and we stared each other down. There was nothing in Merles' piggish eyes but dull hate, put there by Shane. Garrett stood behind us, in the center of the fluorescent yellow kitchen, shifting his feet from side to side and worrying his lower lip.

"I don't want to fight," I told Shane. "And I don't want the business. After graduation, I'm out of here."

"Goddamn better be," Shane spat. "I'm counting the seconds."

He turned to leave, leaning heavily on his cane as he left me to clean up the rest of the kitchen with Garrett. Merle followed slowly, disappointed at the lack of bloodshed.

They let me off too easy this time. Usually it came to blows with Merle, who behaved like a dog itching to get off his leash. As if only Shane's word kept him from killing me.

It sounded ridiculous, but it didn't *feel* that way, not when Merle and I were down in it. Our fights didn't feel like brotherly scuffles, but life and death.

"You want to know what I think?" Garrett asked, putting away the dishes I dried. "Shane is scared."

"Of what?" I asked.

"Of you."

I tensed up, wondering if he were going to bring up the factory shooting. Like Voldemort's name, I didn't say it out loud; didn't dare even think about it too hard in my mind. But no matter how I tried to pretend it never happened, or how many years I put between those fucking horrible days and myself, it was still *right there*, in my face or on the minds and mouths of everyone in this damn town.

"He's worried Dad is going to give you the auto shop," Garrett said. "Put it in your name."

"Don't talk like that," I warned, glancing around. "Shane hears you talking like that and he'll give you hell." I felt sick just thinking about it. The only thing worse than Shane sic'ing Merle on me was the idea he'd do it to Garrett.

The little boy nodded. "My teacher says bullies are scared. When they're scared, they get mean."

"They're mean anyway." I wanted to reach out to Garrett. Hug him tight. I held back. Since Woodside, no one touched me and I didn't touch them, as if emotional breakdowns were contagious.

After the kitchen was cleaned up, Garrett joined Harris and Norma watching TV in the den. The laugh track of some sitcom blared. Merle was in his room, probably playing Grand Theft Auto. Shane was in his room, doing whatever he did before bed. Lay around hating life, I guessed. He was a bright guy but didn't study any more. I guessed he figured there was no point—the disease was going to get progressively worse. But it was horrible to think about him giving up already. I caught myself on the way to my room, wanting to stop and talk to Shane. To call a truce at least. Or let him know he didn't have to hate me.

I paused outside his door then kept going. Maybe he did need to hate me. Maybe lashing out at me was better than keeping it in, letting it eat away at him as much as his disease did.

I went up to my room that overlooked the street. I had to step around stalagmites of books to lay down on my bed under the window. My room and sanctuary. Bed, desk, chair and dresser. Books stacked all over. Books were my escape until money and time made actual escape a reality.

Books and that water park they'd built last summer.

We'd visited as a family when it first opened and I'd hated it. The noise, the crowds, the churning water. I swam in the smallish pool with fifty other people and thought I was drowning. But alone, at night, when the water was still and quiet…then it was perfect. I don't know what drew me there the first time, but once I started sneaking over at night, I couldn't stop.

Through the window, I watched the night deepen. I waited.

By nine in the evening, the house was quiet. Norma and Harris were early risers. They never checked on me. I slipped downstairs and out the back door. Past the detached garage, down the gravely drive and out into the street.

I half-jogged to Funtown Water Park through a night thick and stifling with heat. I hit the perimeter and scaled the fence easily, having done so nearly every night for the last four months.

The park was empty. The three slides—short, medium, and tall—were shut off. The stand of water guns, sprinklers, and spraying arches was quiet. All the bored teenagers who worked there had cleared out. As winter came on, it would be closed permanently, and maybe locked up tight. That thought used to curl my guts, until I reminded myself I'd be long gone by winter.

I headed to the northeast corner, to the rectangular pool reserved for adults to dip in and where private lessons were sometimes given. It was only fifty feet long, and nine feet deep at its deepest, but that was enough for me. I kicked off my boots, stripped off my socks and jeans. Wearing just my boxers and t-shirt, I jumped in.

Cool water slipped over my skin. I felt calmer, at peace. I swam to the deep end, weightless. I held perfectly still and emptied my mind, while huffing a few deep breaths, sucking air deeper and deeper. When I couldn't hold any more, I slipped under.

The underwater lights cast faint glows in the dimness, turning the water a greenish hue.

I pushed the breath in my lungs down deep, where my body took what it needed, molecules at a time. I held very still, waving my arms only enough to keep me under.

Under the surface, I closed my eyes. I don't know what prompted it, but an old memory—my oldest memory—played out like on a newsreel or home movie.

The man was huge, tall like the tallest tree. The boy was small—maybe three years old, staring up at the man, unblinking.

The man put his hands on his knees and bent low, a confused smile on his face. "Where'd you come from, little man?"

The boy's words burst out on a current of barely restrained sobs. "Are you a fireman? Mama said to find a fireman. If you ever need help, that's who you ask."

"*I am a fireman. Just not in uniform yet.*" *The man's eyes took in the boy's dirty overalls, his mussed hair, and the note pinned to his shirt. He hoped this wasn't what he thought it was.* "*Where is your mama now?*"

The boy's face crumpled into tears he tried to hold back. "*I don't know. I think she said goodbye.*"

The man straightened and looked around, praying this wasn't happening, that the kid's mom would coming running up, calling for him, thanking God he was all right, she'd been worried sick...

The man unpinned the note from the boy's shirt.

Take care of him, please. Please.

His heart sank. He called over his shoulder. "*Harry? Better call Gloria at CPS. We got a safe haven situation here.*"

Another, bigger man came out of the garage, his face twisted in alarm. "*No joke?*"

"*No joke,*" *said the first man. He handed the note to Harry, and then knelt in front of the kid. He wanted to hug him and tell him it was going to be all right, but that was a lie. He laid his heavy, thick hand on the boy's shoulder.* "*You ever seen a real firehouse, kid?*"

"*No,*" *the boy said, wiping his nose on the back of his hand.*

"*Well, come on. I'll show you. Grand tour. Get you warmed up too and maybe something to eat?*"

The boy nodded and took his hand, squeezing hard.

The man held on tight, waited until he could speak again. "*What's your name, kid?*"

"*Evan.*"

My chest constricted and my mouth opened, ready to suck in a lungful of water. I pushed to the surface, gasping. By the time I was done wiping the water off my face, the memory retreated. The deep, hollow pain remained.

I drew in more air, my lungs greedy. That was a good sign, at least. *That had to be longer than three minutes. Had to be.*

I had no way of timing myself. My cell phone was old and I was paranoid of bringing it near the edge of the pool. If it got ruined, I'd have to buy another, and I needed every dime I had to get the hell out of Planerville.

I sucked in air, treaded water, and let the memory of the firehouse fade out. I couldn't look back, only forward.

Only a few more weeks and I'd escape this town and everyone who knew me. I'd go somewhere and live by a lake or an ocean or a river, alone, and never feel like this again. No one would know me. I'd start over. No freakshow reputation, no stints at the local mental institutions, no accusing or suspicious or hateful eyes. I'd start over. I'd be new, somewhere else.

I'd be free.

CHAPTER

6

JO

I dropped off my poems with Ms. Politano in the morning and then came to her room just before lunch to hear the verdict. She looked up at me as I entered and smiled in a way that freaked me out. I could handle—and expected—teachers to focus on the content of the poems, not so much my actual talent, or if I had any in the first place. Teachers are required by law to report child abuse when it's suspected. I always had to explain it was five years ago and the key players were all dead and gone.

Ms. P had me pull up a chair to her desk at the front of the class, my poems fanned out before her. Some pages were wrinkled and stained with age and tears. Some were newer. "The Guillotine"—an ode to my scar—was front and center.

"Jo," she said in a quiet voice, "I've read your poems and I'm impressed. Very impressed. Survivors are worthy of tremendous admiration and you have mine."

I started to sit back, to sigh, to roll my eyes, but she held up a hand.

"You have my admiration because your poems are exquisite windows into the incidents of your past. The ferocity of them, the..." She fought for the right words. "The tenacity of your spirit. It's all here. I felt everything you sought to make a reader feel with your words, and that is the hallmark—in my estimation—of great poetry."

I tucked my hair behind my right ear. "Uh, okay. Thanks. Does this mean I can graduate?"

I needed a diploma more than I needed compliments. But I had to admit, it was kind of nice to hear my poems didn't suck.

Ms. P sat back and folded her hands on the desk. "It means I think I've come up with a project that will satisfy the academic holes in your file. Earlier this year we studied romantic poetry. Keats, Browning."

"Yeah, you told me that already," I said, probably bitchier than I was aiming for.

Ms. P only smiled. "I'm going to assign you some reading, but your primary assignment is to write your own take on a love letter or poem."

"A love letter? To whom?"

"Anyone you choose." Ms. P leaned over the desk. "You have revealed a very personal pain here, Josephine. These poems are raw, honest, and frankly, hard to read. But they are also very similar in theme. I can see your facility with this subject matter, difficult though it is. What I'd like to see is something different."

"Different," I stated.

"Yes, I think it would be good for you to stretch your abilities. Venture into new territory."

"I don't love anyone, Ms. P," I said flatly. "Not anymore. What I need is to graduate. So if you want a love letter, I'll write one. I'll write a hundred if that's what it takes. I can fake it. Because if you're trying to steer me toward better times or sunnier days in my life, forget it."

A short silence passed.

"Am I right to assume you've seen your share of counselors over this material?" She tapped "The Guillotine" with her fingers.

"You could say that."

"And was anyone able to offer you some relief?"

"A little," I admitted. "But I always move before anything earth-shattering happens."

"And you aren't seeing anyone now?"

"I called before we moved here. I was told the guidance counselor was up to her neck in college application assistance."

I strained to sound casual. God, why did I tell her I'd investigated a counselor here? Why was I leaning forward in the chair across from Ms. P as if I were freezing to death and she was a roaring fire?

"Perhaps," she said, "as part of your poetry assignment, we could have you come to my office once a week or so."

"What for?"

"We could discuss your poems. Analyze them, maybe. From a literary standpoint, only."

I wasn't stupid. I could hear the words behind the words and the old defensive part of me wanted to tell her to mind her own business. Stick to being an English teacher, not some armchair psychologist.

But the broken pieces in me that faintly cried to be put back together were reaching for whatever it was she was offering. I was like Charlie Brown running to kick that football, each time thinking *This is it! Finally!* And that bitch, Lucy, always pulled it away. You'd think after so many times Charlie Brown would wise up, but no. I'm like him. I see the ball. I see help held out in front of me and I want to run at it full speed, my heart in my throat and hope choking my breath, because deep down I need it so badly.

But Gerry moved us too often, too quickly. He pulls the balls away and I'm left lying flat on my back, the wind knocked out of me and having to pick myself back up and start all over again.

It was too late in the year to be cozying up with Ms. P. Too late by half.

"If you want to help me, then let me graduate. I'll write the love poem, okay? But that's all I can do right now. I'm just...tapped out."

The bell ending recess clanged. I rose and shouldered my bag. Ms. P gathered my poems in a folder and handed the folder to me, her eyes soft with disappointment. And concern.

"I look forward to seeing what you come up with."

"Me too."

I was curious myself. Writing a love letter or poem was like climbing up into a dusty, dark attic; cobweb-strewn and dust-choked. A cramped space where nothing had been touched in years. Gray and disconnected.

At lunch, I sat with the staff of *Mo Vay Goo*, but I didn't eat or participate in the conversation around me. My one-eyed gaze roved and landed on Evan Salinger. He was at his customary spot, on a bench against the exposed brick wall of the cafeteria. A window above him streamed light over his blond hair, more than enough to read by. He was nose-buried in a book, as usual, absently eating a sandwich from a sack lunch.

He was beautiful, sitting under that beam of light. His hair fell in his face as he bent over his knees, and I watched him absently brush it out of his eyes. Not for the first time, it struck me how seriously miscast he looked for the role of School Freak.

I shot a glance at the table of popular kids, the jocks and the cheerleaders, the pep squad and the 4H rancher boys. On the surface, Evan Salinger belonged with them. I could easily imagine him talking and laughing in their ranks, his arm slung around some girl. Both of them likely to be nominated for Prom King and Queen.

It just didn't make sense he was cast adrift from the islands of safety known in high school cafeterias all across the country as the lunch tables. Evan had no island. Even the geeks shunned him. My people, the misfits, shunned him. If anyone was going to take him under their wing, it should be us, if for no other reason than to give the finger to everyone else. But Marnie warned me I'd be S.O.L. to throw him a life preserver.

I wondered idly if it were worth it.

At my table, Adam talked about *The Voice* and who he thought was going to be voted off that night. Marnie chatted about prom and how fucking stupid it was, but of course she was going to go. We all knew she was secretly excited about it ever since Logan Greenway asked her to go with him.

I tuned them out, consumed by Evan Salinger. I wanted to know what he was reading. I tried to get a glimpse of the book's spine, but I was too far away. Then Evan looked up as if someone had called his name. I froze while he looked around, some stupid part of me clamoring for him to look my way.

Then he did.

And he smiled.

My damn heart stopped beating. I felt hot all over, and was trapped by Evan's smile, by his eyes that watched me with a gentle curiosity. A "Hi, how are you?" kind of look that would have put me at perfect ease if it hadn't turned me completely inside out first.

I stared back for a good three seconds, wrapped in the warmth of his attention, then broke free with a flinch. I looked away, hiding behind my hair. When the heat flush drained out of me, I glanced through my wall of hair to where Evan had been sitting.

He was gone. The beam of light was empty and all that remained were dust motes, dancing.

I'd made plans with Jared to meet him after school behind the bleachers. And by "made plans with" I meant he shot me a questioning glance in Study Hall, and I nodded. But when the time came, I wasn't feeling it.

"Sorry, I'm not in the mood today."

And Jared, bless his little heart, looked at me all perplexed-like, as if he couldn't fathom what possible difference my interest made. But he wasn't all bad. He was cheating on his girlfriend and he was evil to Evan Salinger, but he backed off when I told him no.

He sighed and adjusted his crotch. "This was a giant waste of time. I could've been out with the guys at Spinelli's."

"Sorry."

He cocked his head and a mop of unruly brown hair fell over his eyes in a way most girls at Wilson found adorably scruffy. He looked at me hard, probably for the first time since we'd started meeting out there.

"You know, you're sort of lucky I'm even giving you the time of day."

I arched my visible eyebrow. "Is that a fact?"

"I mean, you're really pretty. The one side of your face? You'd be so hot without that scar. What happened, anyway?"

I spun the Wheel of Tragedy. It landed on Earthquake.

"I was visiting family in San Francisco. Earthquake country. I was standing by a huge window when a 6.5 hit, and the window shattered all over me. Wrong place at the wrong time."

Jared whistled low between his teeth. "Damn. That sucks."

"Yeah," I agreed. "It totally did."

Once again, talking about my scar dredged up the horrific memories of how it got there. Jasper, the screw I dragged down my skin, his arrest, and then my mother.

I was the one who found her in the bathtub. My cheek, bandaged now and tight with itchy pain, woke me up in the middle of the night. I shuffled out of my room toward the bathroom to pee. I was holding my favorite stuffed blue whale even though I was too old for stuffed animals, and sleepily pushed open the bathroom door.

I couldn't see her all at once. Not as a whole. Only flashes, like blood splatter on a white tile. My brain broke it down, reorganized it into a few words reminiscent of a poem we'd been studying in school that month.

> *So much depends upon*
> *her*
> *eyes glazed by vacancy*
> *And white skin*
> *submerged*
> *in red water*

A snapshot of sixteen words. Words, poetry…they would forever be my coping mechanism when counseling was sporadic or nonexistent. A consolation prize: to find my artistic passion at the hands of terrible tragedy. My mother's death cleaved my life in half. The chasm left behind was so deep and wide, I couldn't even see the shore of my past. Shrouded in black and gray mist, it was lost to me. She was lost to me, and so were all of our happy memories, before Jasper. They were trapped there on the other side.

I could've jumped into that chasm with my mother, but I chose to keep walking.

I can't say it always felt like the right choice.

I got dressed, laced up my boots, grabbed my notebook and slipped out the window. I knew it was safe to sneak out. It would be a frosty day in hell before Gerry even *thought* about coming into my bedroom to check on me at night. He was probably snoring on his chair in front of the TV, another bucket of KFC tipping out of his lap.

I headed east toward the edge of town, where the new water park had been built. The night was sticky and thick. The streetlamps pushed the dark away in halos of pale yellow. Moths battered themselves against the bulbs. The cacophony of locusts or crickets or whatever bugs infested this part of the county at the tail end of spring was relentless. But they were the only sound. No cars drove by. It was only nine o'clock but Planerville had gone to sleep.

Once at Funtown, I climbed a high fence of chain-link draped in green canvas and dropped to the other side. The slides and sprinklers were shut off, but the park remained well-lit. New lamps and floods were set up at intervals and left on to deter trespassers. Such as myself.

I passed the tube slides, rising and coiling up like snakes. But they didn't freak me out or anything. The memory of my mother in the bathtub faded. Instead, I recalled a vague memory of going to Tybee Island with her when I was four. The memory was grayed out, like a piece of moldy bread, but it was infinitely better than the bathtub.

We made sandcastles, or played in the mud. I can't recall, but I can hear echoes of her laugh. Her laugh sounded more like a kid than a grown-up, and even then—to my four-year-old observation—her eyes looked a little loose in her head. Everything about her was loose and kind of jangly. Nerves, she told me when she was happy.

We moved a lot in her endless quest for solid employment, and when she was happy, she'd shout and dance me around whichever tiny shabby apartment we happened to be living in. "The light's flipped on, Josie!"

Other times the light was off, and Mama stayed in her bed, sleeping. For days. I'd come to her and she'd peek her tangled head out and smile.

"Is the light off, Mama?" I'd ask in a tiny, fearful voice, and she'd nod and pat my cheek.

"Yes, baby. But just for a little while longer. Be a good girl, and let Mama sleep?"

I'd eat cereal and watch cartoons on TV until the light came back on and Mama was back, and I was happy.

I don't remember happy. Like I said, it's all grayed out. I know the feeling was there, but I can't call it up, and so I keep walking.

I meandered through the water park with no intent, until I saw the swimming pool at the northeast corner, partially enclosed by a wrought-iron fence. Lounge chairs were set up around it. Perfect place to lay back, and write in my journal. Maybe finish the poem I'd started for *Mo Vay Goo*. I was in the mood to write about my mother. If Marnie wanted dark, she was in for a fucking treat.

I was about twenty yards out when I heard a splash and saw a dark shape in the pool. Some guy was swimming.

Fuck. Way to ruin my night, asshole.

I nearly did an about-face. I thought I saw some loungers near the baby wading pool. I'd wanted to write in peace. Alone. I wasn't a fan of being along in the dark with strange men.

But instead of walking out, I drew a little bit closer. Underwater lights in the pool showed me that the swimmer was a young guy, blond...

I stopped walking. It was Evan Salinger. He treaded water in the nine-foot deep end, and he was dressed. Or at least it looked it from where I stood. I could see the white cotton of a t-shirt clinging to his shoulders.

He didn't see me. He looked straight ahead, in profile, sucking in deep breaths, one after the other without exhaling. And then he went under. Straight down, waving his arms to get to the bottom, and then gliding them from side to side to stay there.

Marnie's warnings about associating with Evan meandered in and out of my head, but mostly I was just curious. Why the hell would he be swimming fully clothed? Maybe he was nutso after all. But I was tired listening to rumors, so I crossed my arms and waited.

A minute passed.

I pulled out my phone and stared at the clock. 9:23p.m.

At 9:25—when he'd been under for two solid minutes—my feet shifted from side to side, and I gnawed my lip mercilessly.

What the fuck is he doing?

At 9:26, panic danced along my nerves. Evan made no signs he was coming to the surface any time soon. I rushed to the edge of the deep end, waving my arms and stomping my feet.

"Hey! *Hey!*"

Nothing. Just the slow waft of his arms beneath the surface, like seaweed in a soft current.

At 9:27—*four* minutes since Evan had gone under—I tossed my phone onto the rubbery slats of the nearest lounger where it promptly bounced off and hit the concrete. I chucked my journal next and dove into the water. Clothes, boots and all.

Evan jerked in shock as I gripped him by the shoulder. I got mostly shirt, but managed to get him around the waist with my other arm. I tried to push off from the bottom but it wasn't like how it is in the movies. I didn't effortlessly rocket to the surface with my drowning victim. My boots were like little anchors pulling me down and Evan was like a damn boulder. I struggled to push him up and only succeeded in pushing myself deeper as we got tangled up in a flurry of confusion. Finally, Evan kicked to the surface. We came up together, gasping together, face to face, my hand still twisted in his shirt.

The world fell away as we held each other with our gaze. We were so close. Close enough for me to see the gemstone facets of his sky blue eyes. Close enough to smell the minty sweetness of his breath as he gasped for air. Close enough to see the water streak from his hair and down his cheeks like tears. Close enough to kiss him, if I wanted, or slap him for scaring the shit out of me.

I thrust away from him with a splash, back-pedaling toward shallower water. My heart thudded from exertion, laced with adrenaline and the strange, exhilarating thrill of being in Evan's space. It was like what Marnie had said: electric lines humming, making my skin break out in gooseflesh. She'd made it sound unpleasant, but it was the exact opposite. I felt warm. Warmer than the pool water should have allowed.

Evan stared at me. A faint smile spread over his face, his eyes warm and full, looking at me as if we'd planned to meet here but he was surprised I'd actually shown up.

Then I remembered that he'd been trying to drown himself, and I went cold all over.

"What the hell?" I seethed, moving toward the shallow end, my booted feet clumping awkwardly over the pool floor. "You can't *do that*. You can't leave your dead, bloated body for some stay-at-home mom and her toddler to find tomorrow morning. For some *little kid* to walk in on. That's all kinds of fucked up."

"What...?" Evan shook his head, confused. "No, I—"

"If you're going to kill yourself, do it somewhere else." I climbed out of the pool. A torrent of water rained from my clothes. My boots were heavy with it. Probably ruined. *Goddammit.* I sat on one of the loungers and tore at the laces.

Evan remained in the center of the deep end, treading water easily. His longish hair was slicked back from his face and gleamed with gold threads in the lamplight. His eyes were the same color as the pool water would be at midday.

"I wasn't trying to kill myself," he said quietly.

"No?" I snapped. "Sure as hell looked like it to me."

"I was just holding my breath."

"What the hell for?"

"To see how long I could do it." He cocked his head. "How long was I under, do you think?"

"Are you fucking kidding me?" I held up one boot and emptied it over the cement.

"Just curious," he said, his tone distant now, retracted. Like he'd been holding out his hand to me and now took it back. "Sorry about your boots, Jo."

"Forget it," I muttered, then whipped my head up. "How do you know my name?"

He sighed, and suddenly looked exhausted, as if suspicion was a lead weight he carried around his neck. "You sit next to me in Western Civ."

"Oh, right," I said quickly.

"I'm sorry I scared you. I didn't mean to."

"Yeah, well..." I didn't have words to finish my thought, mostly because I felt like I should apologize to *him.* I couldn't imagine what for. He was the one who scared the hell out of me, wrecked my boots, probably cracked my cell phone, and ruined my night.

A silence stretched between us and I felt my anger dip a little. "Four minutes," I said, taking off my other boot to empty it.

Evan brightened. "Really? I was under for four minutes? Holy shit, that's long."

"Uh, *yeah*," I said dryly. "It's Houdini-long. Is that what you're training for? Join a circus or a frea—"

Freakshow.

I'd caught the word before it could escape but it hung between us loud and clear anyway.

Evan's expression darkened and he turned away. I immediately and in all ways felt like total crap. Which made my hackles rise. I didn't need this kind of aggravation in my life. But there was something about Evan that made being pissed at him feel ugly and wrong.

I wrung out my hair over the side of the lounger. "Why don't you buy a water proof watch and time yourself?"

"Not in the budget at the moment."

"You work at your Dad's auto-body shop, right? He doesn't pay you?"

It occurred to me I was being insanely intrusive into business most definitely not mine. Not to mention the abuse Evan suffered at the hands of his brothers could very well—and most probably—carried on all the way up the family food chain to Ma and Pa Salinger. Or *started* there and filtered down.

To my relief, Evan nodded and said, "Yeah, he pays me. But I'm saving up for something else."

"What's that?"

"Getting the hell out of here."

Evan turned his gaze to the water park, to the town beyond, and whatever horizon he was seeing in his mind. I found my own eyes following, but I couldn't see past the bars around the pool area.

"Where would you go?" I asked, one dripping boot upside down in my hand.

"Anywhere. No, the Grand Canyon. I'd go to the Grand Canyon. Ever been?"

"No."

"Me neither."

A silence stretched between us. I got the impression Evan wanted to talk more, but didn't. This conversation appeared to be over, and I tilted my chin down, frowning.

"So. Anyway. Four minutes is really long. Congratulations. I gotta go."

I stripped off my socks and stuffed them into my boots. Walking home barefoot was going to suck, but not as much as squelching home in heavy, sodden Doc Martens. *Next time, I bike it.* But was there going to be a next time?

Evan said nothing and I thought he'd continue to say nothing, but as I turned to go, he glided to the edge of the pool and rested his arms on the concrete.

"Thanks for saving me, Jo."

I stopped, jolted by his choice of words. "I didn't *save* you. You weren't drowning."

"True. But you didn't know that."

I turned and looked at him again. His smile was back. Words ordered themselves in my mind the way they did when I was contemplating a new poem.

A smile with a burden: sad, hopeful, heartbreaking.

I shut that train of thought down, pronto. No poems, no fluff. Going soft over a cute guy with a sad smile was not in the schematics.

"Yeah, whatever," I said finally, the two most unpoetic words in the English language.

His smile only widened. "Goodnight, Jo."

Just like in my dream. Same tone of voice and everything. Same warm water feeling washing over me. I gathered up my not-cracked cell phone and my journal and I left without looking back.

CHAPTER

7

EVAN

I got home from the pool after midnight through the side door. I stripped off my shirt and dumped it in the laundry. Norma never asked why my clothes reeked of chlorine. I think it was a concession she made to me. As if she knew I needed whatever I was getting at the pool. So long as I didn't get caught for trespassing (or let anyone at school know about those visits), she didn't ask questions.

The house was dark and silent but for Harris's snores—like ripping linen—coming from the bedroom at the end of the upstairs hall.

I closed my bedroom door and a strange feeling crawled up my skin. *Someone's been in here.*

I flipped on the overhead bulb and scanned the room. Everything looked the same as when I left it. I inhaled through my nose, as if I could catch a remnant on the air. A telltale waft of someone else's skin cells hovering in my space. Nothing. Stupid to even try. But the feeling wouldn't leave. I almost checked the lockbox on my dresser. Or my under-the-table pay from Harris that I kept under a loose board under my bed. But I shook off the urge.

This is the kind of shit that gets you in trouble, I told myself. *No one's been here. Act normal. Go to sleep.*

I crawled into bed, thinking sleep would be impossible after a night like this. But I must've slipped under quickly because the next thing I knew, my old digital alarm clock went off at 6 a.m., waking me from a vivid dream. A normal person's dream. A good one. One of the best I'd had lately.

Jo Clark. At the pool. The moment when she tried to pull me from the water. She thought I was drowning myself and tried to save me.

Me.

We were face to face and the water had pushed her hair back. The jagged line of a terrible scar was visible in the moonlight, white and shiny and almost blue-ish. Translucent. But it didn't mar her. Not to me. She was too beautiful. Pale skin. Large, dark eyes fringed by long lashes and framed by dark brows. And her mouth…

Damn.

In my dream, her mouth was parted slightly in surprise, her lips open and inviting. Instead of being pissed at me—like she had been in real life—she was happy to see me. That beautiful mouth widened into a heart-stopping smile and her dark eyes lit up. She was about to say something to me, and I was sure whatever it was would make my entire waking day. Then the damn alarm went off and Jo vanished as I opened my eyes to the sloped ceiling of my bedroom.

A good dream, but it would never happen. Josephine Clark was closed up like a metal safe. Iron chains wrapped around and a padlock the size of a shield. She'd never smile like that—so open and free, and certainly not at me.

Even so, there were worse ways to wake up in the morning than with a dream where a pretty girl is happy to see you.

"And she saved me," I murmured, smiling faintly.

That wasn't entirely true either. Like Jo said, I hadn't been drowning, but most days in the Salinger household felt a little like that anyway. Suffocating. Restricted. I was trapped between who I was and who they wanted me to be and it was crushing the life out of me so I could hardly breathe.

I sat up on my small bed, in my small, book-filled room. Outside the window overlooking the front yard and street, the sun was struggling to rise over Planerville.

Is this where I'm from?

Is this my home?

Is this my family?

42

I didn't know who or what I was asking. Maybe the same unknown place within me where the dreams lived. The answer was always a definitive *No,* on all counts, but that offered no relief. I'd read that adopted children, no matter how wonderful and loving their adoptive parents are, still seek their birth parents because *family*. Tribe. Belonging.

I got dressed and went downstairs where breakfast was underway. I could tell by the sounds before I even arrived at the kitchen. Spoons scraped against oatmeal bowls, making my teeth ache.

Four minutes, I thought to distract myself. *I was under for four whole minutes.*

That was a record. I'd been going to Funtown since it opened last year, to submerge myself under the quiet water, but mostly to hold my breath. I don't know how or why it became important, but I felt like a long distance runner training for a marathon. But that wasn't quite right. I didn't know what I was training for. Only that the need to stretch out the minutes, to stay under for six, seven, maybe even eight minutes… It burned in me the way champion runners yearned to run faster and faster. I couldn't see the finish line that my 'training' was taking me to, only that I was going to get there. I *had* to get there.

But four minutes? I smiled to myself. I had no idea. I wondered how long I could have stayed had Jo not jumped in. My smile widened.

She saved me.

That idea wouldn't stop echoing my head, either. Like a song that gets stuck on repeat, only not annoying. Not annoying at all. I wasn't used to anyone giving a shit what I did.

Shane snorted over his food. "Look at Evan smiling like a dope," he said to Merle. "He looks retarded."

A strange choice of words, given that Merle probably had an IQ hovering in the low 70s. I glanced at Norma. She seemed not to have heard. Or heard and didn't care. I should have known better. After three years living here, it was clear she was oblivious to her sons' shortcomings. I'd get no help from her. Not that I ever did.

Merle snorted a laugh and the two exchanged knowing looks. Shane's hands twitched even more than usual this morning, and a squealing laugh erupted out of him seemingly from nowhere.

And they call me *the freak.*

Aside from Shane's occasional giggle, the clatter of spoons on bowls continued until Garrett woke up enough to jabber nonstop about his science project. Norma nodded and smiled thinly, but no one else listened. Breakfast finished, we set off for school.

Shane and Merle headed toward their shared truck, a shiny black F150. It was used—given by a grateful customer of Dad's—but a free F150. It had cost them nothing. I drove a truck too: a beat up old Chevy I'd had to buy with my own money. Money I needed for escaping Planerville after graduation. But I needed the truck too, to take me to the Grand Canyon, so I didn't complain.

I noticed Shane and Merle walking with their heads bent, snickering. Just as we reached the garage driveway, they turned. Shane held a piece of paper in his scrawny claw of a hand.

My heart dropped to my knees and my breath stuck. The paper was old and yellow, frayed at the ends and torn into a triangular shape. Hardly more than a scrap. The handwriting on it—a neat, flowing script—was just visible from where I stood some feet away as a few blue loops. But the words written were emblazoned on my heart forever.

Take care of him, please. Please.

"Give it back, Shane," I said, my hands balling into fists.

"What for?" Shane dangled it in front of him while Merle stood close, watching me, ready to act. And goddamn, I was ready to charge at him and beat the hell out of him for that paper. Garrett watched the exchange with wide eyes.

"You know what for," I said, fighting for calm. "Give it back. You have no right to dig in my stuff…"

And that's when it hit me. The strange feeling from the night before. They'd been in my room. He'd found the little wooden chest that held a few keepsakes—baseball ticket stubs, my favorite marble from when I was a kid.

And that note.

The chest was always locked. I kept it locked. How…?

Shane's smarmy smile was like a rash across his face as he dangled the note in front of me. At a safe distance. "What'll you trade me for it?"

I'll let you keep your nose intact. "Nothing. It's mine, Shane. Give it back, now."

"We'll be late for school," Garrett said in a small voice.

Shane lifted his other hand to rest under the first, and in it was a small green cigarette lighter. I choked on my breath and felt my muscles tighten.

"Don't you dare…"

"Oh, do I have your attention now?" Shane sneered, though he was nervous. Both hands trembled and he inched closer to Merle. "I'll say it one more time: what will you trade me for it? Make it something good or else…" He flicked his thumb along the lighter. It made a small metallic scape and a spark.

My guts recoiled. "What do you want?"

"Make me an offer."

"Come on, Shane," Garrett said. "Give it back."

"Shut up, Garrett." Shane's eyes never left mine. "Well?"

"My pay from the shop. Two weeks' worth," I said, hating myself but needing that paper more. "Three," I added when Shane shook his head.

"I changed my mind," he said with an exaggerated shrug. "I don't want anything after all. And Garrett's right. We're going to be late for school."

For half a second, hope flared in my heart…until Shane's thumb flicked the lighter again and a flame licked up. He touched it to the corner of the paper that blackened and curled immediately.

"No!"

I surged forward, intent on the note, and ran into the brick wall of Merle. His fist buried itself in my gut, and I gasped, bending in half while reaching for Shane. As if in slow motion, I watched the flame eat the paper, consuming its way mercilessly toward the writing.

Take care…

"*No! You fucking asshole! Stop!*" I screamed, struggling in Merle's grip. I elbowed him in the jaw in my frantic grab for the paper, but it was too late. Shane had to drop what was left before the flame touched his fingers, and the fight went out of me. Merle drove his own elbow into my back. Pain radiated from under my right shoulder blade and I fell to my hands and knees beside the charred remains. Then Merle's boot came down, squashing and scraping the ashes of the note into oblivion.

I stared at the smudge left behind. "*Why?*" I managed to rasp.

"You're too old for that baby shit," Shane said as he and Merle headed into the garage and climbed into their truck. "Grow up, freak. Your freak parents didn't want you. Get over it already."

They backed out of the garage next to where I sat on the driveway, staring at the ashy smear on the cement.

Shane rolled down his window. "You're welcome!" he called as the truck backed down the drive.

Rage, and a grief that sank deep into my bones, consumed me. My hands made fists again, my left one closing around the crushed limestone that lined the driveway. I got a handful of small rocks, stood up, and hurled them at the retreating truck. The hail of rock against metal sounded like gunfire. Even from where I stood, I could see the nicks they left in the black paint of the truck. It screeched to a halt, and Merle and Shane climbed out, both wearing expressions of shock.

Beside me, Garrett cowered. "Oh, no…"

"Oh, that's it. You are dead. *Dead.*" Shane gaped at me, running his bony hand over the white ticks on the truck's rear fender, like little chalk marks on a blackboard. "Dad's going to kill you for this."

Merle, to whom the car was a source of pride, took one heavy-lidded look at the damage, his piggish eyes widening. "*I'm* going to kill you," he grunted.

I made a beckoning motion. "Come on, then," My heart pounded until I thought it would explode. "Come on, fucker!"

Merle was always itching for a fight. He didn't hesitate, but charged at me like a bull.

I was ready for him, burning up on the inside, the image of that scrap of paper curling and blackening to ash in the red haze of my vision. Merle came at me swinging. I ducked and managed a right hook to his kidney, putting my entire weight behind it. I felt the strength of my punch all the way up my shoulder. It would have ended the fight with anyone else. Merle only grunted and thrust his forearm up, catching me under my nose. Blood poured, but I hardly felt the pain or heard Shane's cursing and Garrett's cries. I grappled with Merle, our fight turning into a scuffle of half-cocked punches and scraping feet over cement.

I was losing. Merle found more openings in my defenses than I did in his, but I savored the pain that was so much easier to take than the loss of that note.

A new voice sliced through the fog and Merle shoved me from him. I stumbled back and saw Norma on the outskirts of the driveway, arms crossed as if to hold herself together, her face twisted with mortified rage.

"What in God's green earth are you boys doing? In full view of the entire street?" she hissed.

I didn't say a word, but wiped my nose on the sleeve of my shirt. I'd never gone running to her over Merle and Shane before. I wasn't a snitch and never would be. But Shane on the other hand was bursting to tattle.

"Look what he did! Threw rocks at our car! The whole back end needs a new paint job now."

Norma Salinger's eyes widened at the damage, then narrowed in with laser focus on me in that look we all knew so well: The Death Glare. "Is this true?"

"They burnt up his note!" Garrett said from beside me. "The one he had since the fire house? From when he was a little kid? They burnt it up for no reason!"

Shane and Merle glared at their little brother, silently promising vengeance.

"Garrett, hush," I said.

For once, even Norma was stunned at her sons' cruelty. "Did you?" she demanded with a crack in the foundation of her normally stony voice. Both older boys quailed under her stare.

Was this the time? Is this when Norma stands up for me and puts an end to Shane's sadistic hatred?

But no. I saw the thoughts behind her eyes sorting themselves out to align with her flesh and blood children without seeming cruel to me.

"We don't poke around in people's private belongings like thieves in the night," she said to my adopted brothers, her voice frosty. Then she turned to me. "And we don't vandalize what isn't ours. None of you did right here. Now get to school. You're late. I'll decide how you're all going to make up for what you did when you get home. Now, get."

We went our separate ways, Shane shooting dirty looks at both me and Garrett, outraged that he'd gotten in trouble. God, what a fucking joke. Norma would give him and Merle some easy chore, while I'd have to pay for the damage to the truck. Or work on the paint job myself at the shop.

Only little Garrett escaped punishment, at least from Norma. I always dropped him off at the Williamsburg Elementary, and as soon as we were on the road, I told him, "Look, you gotta stop standing up for me. It's going to get you in trouble with Shane."

"I know," he said, wiping his nose. "But it's not fair. They're so mean to you."

"I can handle it. But you're too young. You're going to get hurt."

"Aren't you supposed to stand up for what's right? That's what Ms. Johnston is teaching us at school. And what Shane did wasn't right."

I glanced at him. The smoldering concoction of rage and grief in me mellowed to see tears welling in Garrett's eyes. "No, it's not. You keep standing up for me and they're going to turn on you."

Garrett sniffed again, this time defiantly. His little chin was thrust forward, his eyes on the road. "I can handle it."

I recalled the murderous look in Shane's eye when Garrett defended me. *No, you can't.* The burning letter cut me to the core and left a gaping wound I knew wouldn't close any time soon. But more important than that was keeping Garrett safe. No matter what.

I drove in silence, hardening my heart and steeling my courage. I pulled into the roundabout of Williamsburg Elementary as my little brother— the only brother who felt like flesh and blood—hauled his oversize backpack onto his lap. He reached for the truck's door handle but stopped before opening.

"You should leave," he said, looking up at me through his tousled mop of blond hair. "You should get far away from them."

"I'm planning on it," I snapped, and faced forward, my voice as stony as I could make it. "Go. Get out. You'll be late."

He frowned at my cold words. "I'll miss you, Evan. If you go, I'll miss you, but I think it's best. So they can't hurt you anymore."

I clutched the steering wheel in both hands until my knuckles turned white under the red rawness from my fight with Merle. "Get. Out."

I could feel Garrett's hurt wafting over me and nearly broke.

"Why are you being mean to me?" he cried, his voice trembling. "Evan…?"

I couldn't do it. But I had to do it. To protect him. It was safer if he hated me too.

The car behind us honked. I reached across Garrett and threw open his door, then faced forward again, not looking at him. "Get out of the goddamn truck."

Garrett wrangled his backpack and climbed out of the truck's cab. He stood for a moment, staring at me, challenging me. I muttered a curse and reached across to shut the door, but he was quicker. Garrett slammed it shut, his face full of hurt and anger, then turned and stomped toward his school.

The look in his eye hurt almost as bad as the pain of my burnt note.

Good, I thought, watching him storm away. *Better for him.*

I didn't have the luxury of wondering if it was better for me.

CHAPTER

8

JO

That morning, I noticed the jocks were being extra shitty to Evan. I had perfect vantage from my locker, which was on the same bank as Shane Salinger's. I watched the scrawny little asshole mutter something to Jared, Merle, and the others as Evan walked by, his head down, shoulders hunched, hands jammed in the front pockets of his jeans.

"But Merle took care of it," I heard Shane say, louder.

Merle Salinger made a fist in one hand and slammed it into the palm of his other meaningfully.

Jared's eyes widened and he laughed. "Had a little campfire in your driveway this morning, eh, Freakshow?" he called.

Evan ignored him, but I saw him level a blue-eyed glare at Shane that could have frozen all of hell's nine circles. Shane recoiled, fumbling his cane a little, then eased up as Evan continued on.

I was supposed to meet Jared at recess but I ditched him. Blew him off at lunch too. In Western Civ, he shot me a questioning look. I turned away, showing him the wall of hair over my face, which put Evan in my direct line of sight. His head was bowed, eyes down, shoulders hunched looking as if he wanted to dive into his book. I saw a smear of dried blood under his nose. The knuckles on the hand closest to me looked red and swollen. He'd been in a

Who? Probably that meatloaf of a brother, Merle. Or maybe one of the other jocks. Maybe Jared. Jared tried to get my attention again and I gave him the finger. His eyes widened then he shook his head, disappointed, but his lips curled in warning. I knew the rumors would begin immediately. Slut. Whore. Cocktease.

I heaved a sigh. Breakups can be so messy.

I spent the rest of the class wishing Evan would look my way, just once. But it was clear he was having a monumentally awful day. He wouldn't look at me, or anywhere but down for that matter. It was as if last night hadn't happened.

Can you blame him? You were a total bitch.

I looked down at my desk, hiding behind my hair, hiding behind excuses. Evan scared me last night in the worst possible way. I thought he was trying to drown himself. Still, I felt kind of guilty for going nuclear on him. He got enough of that shit everywhere else without me piling on.

Toward the end of class, I noticed Evan was hiding a book under some papers and reading while Mr. Albertine droned about the birthplace of Democracy.

"Hey," I whispered, going for friendly. I probably looked like Wednesday Addams attempting a smile, like in that movie.

Evan glanced at me for a second, his eyes dull and heavy. He nodded once in greeting and went back to his book.

"What are you reading?"

He kept his head down, eyes on the page, as he moved the paper enough to show me the book was *The Count of Monte Cristo.*

"Missed that one. Any good?"

"Yes," he whispered, still not looking at me.

"What's it about?"

"A prison break."

I didn't have to dig too deep to find the subtext. Evan already told me he wanted out of Planerville. Whatever had happened to him today didn't do much to change his mind.

I wanted to ask him about his bloody nose and why his brothers were such assholes to him. I wanted to hear it straight from him, not via the high school grapevine. I wanted, I realized, to know him more, and that wasn't like me. I didn't reach out.

The bell rang and Evan gathered his stuff with lightning alacrity and left without a word or a look back.

That night, I lay in bed with my journal on my stomach, tapping a ballpoint against my lip while Ms. P's love poem assignment clanged around my head.

A love poem.

Me.

She'd have better results asking a mortician to write about the birth of a baby. Love was the wrong end of my expertise spectrum. Death, loss, loneliness—those were my forte. Love was something that belonged in my grayed-out past. Like someone I used to know well, but lost touch with over time. I can't remember their face anymore, or their voice, or what it meant to share the same space.

I started to write a few lines along that thread but it was too depressing. Ms. P didn't want a blackened, rotting version of love. She wanted the real deal.

Summer school was starting to sound inevitable.

I dithered and scratched, crossing out more words than I kept and finally tore the paper out of my journal and chucked it in the wastebasket. My brain wasn't focused on the task anyway. It was thinking about Evan Salinger.

What was he doing right now? Was he getting more grief from his brothers? Or maybe he was at the pool, trying to see how long he could hold his breath. I chewed my lip, wondering if it would be a bad idea to go to Funtown. Why the hell shouldn't I? I could go wherever the hell I wanted. Free country and all that.

What if he goes there to escape? What if that's his only goddamn sanctuary?

I chewed my lip some more.

I'd been in survival mode for the last six years. My mom left me alone, every girl for herself. I didn't give or receive favors unless they were of the meaningless sexual variety. But it wouldn't kill me to go to Funtown and offer to time Evan while he held his breath…

Hold your breath
I will mark the minutes
And guard your peace…

I blinked at the words I'd written.
Good god, what kind of weird shit is that?

I tossed myself back on my bed, thinking I'd try for a full night's sleep for once.

I stared at the ceiling.

I stared at my cell phone. Nearly nine o'clock, it said, and in perfectly good working order. Not cracked. My boots weren't ruined. But I'd been a bitch to Evan, and I hated having that over my head.

I got up and put on some old jeans, and sandals I wouldn't be caught dead wearing at school, and headed out.

I biked to Funtown through a stifling, sticky night. The cicadas were deafening, their constant chirp winding around a town gone to sleep already. Yellow light burned in the windows of only a few houses. No one was on the street. No cars drove past in either direction. A living ghost town.

The water park was deserted, same as last time. Evan was in the pool, same as last time. He rested his arms on the cement of the deep end, his chin propped on his forearms. He looked exhausted. Defeated. As if he'd swum a hundred laps though the water around him was still.

My sandals slapped the pavement, announcing my trespassing. Evan came here to escape, I told myself. I was an unwelcome intruder. I should go back and leave him alone. But I didn't. He looked up without lifting his head— just his blue eyes that looked dimmer somehow.

"Hey," I said.

"Hi, Jo."

What was it about my name in his voice? He was always saying my name. Even in my dreams. I don't think I'd ever said his out loud.

"I don't want to bother you," I said.

"You're not bothering me."

"I'll go if you want to be alone."

He murmured something against his arms.

"What?" I said.

"Nothing," he said. He went under, came back up and pushed the hair back from his face. "Why did you come here?"

I sat down on one of the loungers nearest the deep end. "I have my phone. It has a timer. I thought maybe I could time you. You know…holding your breath?"

"Is this really how you want to spend your Wednesday night?" he asked. He shook his head, silently answering his own question. "You should go. If someone sees you here, you'll never hear the end of it."

"Like I give a shit what people think of me." Evan looked me up and down, his gaze coming to rest on my long hair that covered my scar like a shield. I crossed my arms. "Do you want me to time you or not?"

"No, thank you, Jo," he said quietly. "Not tonight."

I got up, gathered my bag. "You want to be alone. I get it. I shouldn't have come. Sorry."

"No, I'm sorry. I'm just not good company right now."

"Bad day?"

"You could say that."

I sat back down. "What happened? I mean…if you want to talk about it."

"Nothing that doesn't happen every other day." A thought occurred to him; darkening his face and erasing his smile. He ground his thumb into the cement on the edge of the pool. "But this time he went too far."

"Who did?"

A beat of silence. "Have you ever lost something precious to you? I don't mean a person or an emotional loss. I mean like an object."

I thought of my stuffed blue whale. I'd carried it with me everywhere when I was a kid. I couldn't even remember why it was so important. Just a comfort thing, I guess. Somewhere in the chaos of my mother dying and Jasper going to jail, I lost it.

"Yeah," I answered. "But gone is gone, right? What can you do?"

Evan nodded. "I keep telling myself that. It's not helping."

"What did you lose?"

"You really want to know?"

I started to bite off a smart-alecky remark that I wouldn't have asked otherwise, but Evan seemed like he was genuinely curious that I wanted to talk to him. And that sucked. Loneliness taken to a whole new level.

"Yeah," I said. "I want to know."

He looked ready to spill it, and then shook his head. "It's my brothers. My *adopted* brothers, which they don't let me fucking forget. They know how to dig in so deep and push the right buttons until I lose my shit."

"They both need a good ass-kicking." I said with a smirk. "Just my casual observation."

Evan smiled wanly, and pushed off from the wall to tread water. "It'll be better after graduation. When I get away from here."

"You're leaving?"

"The second the ceremony's over."

"Oh." I brushed a dead leaf off the lounger. "Cool."

"What about you?"

"I don't know. I turn eighteen in a few weeks. I think Gerry is going to cut me loose

"Gerry?"

"My mother's cousin. My guardian."

"He'd do that? Just kick you out?"

"Yeah. He stepped up for six years but now he's done."

Evan's brows furrowed. "What will you do?"

I shrugged. "I've saved up some money. I'll be fine. Get a job. Get a place, I guess." I coughed. "I'll be fine."

A short silence fell, waiting.

"What about you?" I asked. "Where will you go? You mentioned the Grand Canyon the other night."

"The Grand Canyon, definitely," Evan said. His arms moved to keep him afloat. "Lake Powell that's near there. I want a cabin around lake. I figure I could work at some local mechanic shop. I don't want to do that forever, but it's a start until I get my EMT training done."

"You want to be an EMT?"

"A firefighter. I want to be a firefighter. You have to have EMT training."

"Really?"

"Yeah."

"Dangerous work, isn't it? Putting out raging infernos, hauling people out of burning buildings?" I quirked a smile. "Rescuing cats out of trees."

Evan burst out with a short laugh, and I swear to God, I felt it in my chest.

In my heart.

"All that stuff," he said. "I like to help people."

"I could see you being a firefighter."

"Yeah?"

God, could I. I pictured Evan's tall frame garbed in the heavy bulk a firefighter's uniform. You had to be strong just to wear it. The fantasy bloomed: Evan's handsome face covered in soot and sweat as raging fire burned behind him. He carried a small child and placed her in the arms of her grateful mother…

What is wrong with me?

Evan Salinger had infiltrated my brain. I was trying to keep him out and he kept seeping in.

"What about you?" he asked. "You said you'd get a job but what about your poetry?"

My eyebrows shot up. "How did you know I wrote poetry?"

"I sacrificed a lamb on the altar of Ba'al and a vision came to me." He laughed at my slack-jawed expression. "I read that 'zine? *Mo Vay Goo?* The one with the grainy Xerox of Moby Dick on the cover?"

"Oh. Right."

His laughter died. "I get it. I know what they say about me."

It was on the tip of my tongue to ask him about his stint at Woodside, his breakdown in class, about how he thought he knew things from dreaming them. And I could see he was bracing himself for it.

Don't do that to him, I thought. Evan had been ground up in the rumor mill long enough. No more Freakshow talk. I decided to talk to *him*.

"You read *Mo Vay Goo?*" I asked. "I thought people filed it in the circular bin six nanoseconds after Marnie handed it out."

Evan moved to the pool's edge again. "I usually read it, though I haven't been all that impressed until your introduction issue. Your poem was good."

"Thanks."

"*Really* good," he said. "Is that what you want to do? Be a poet? I mean, as a career?"

"Not a lot of money in poetry. *Any* money, really."

"Teaching?"

I shrugged. "I don't know. I'm not big on standing in front of people and talking. Besides, to become a teacher I'd have to go to college. Gerry moved us around so much, my grades are shit. I can't get a scholarship and I'm not too keen on spending the rest of my life in debt up to my eyeballs. I'll probably get some restaurant job and write on the side." I glanced down at my hands. "I know that's not very ambitious…"

Evan rested his chin on his forearms, watching me. "I'd like to read more of your poetry someday. If you don't mind, I mean."

"You would?"

"I would."

I imagined Evan reading my collection. The poems I wrote in the darkest part of the night with ghosts whispering in my ear. "They're not exactly light reading."

"Are they about your scar?" he asked quietly.

"Some. They say to write what you know."

Evan nodded and I could hear the unasked question.

"Car accident," I said automatically. "When I was thirteen. Killed my mother and my uncle, and I…got cut. On a window. I mean… Anyway that's how I got the scar."

I looked away. I'd lied those words a hundred times and the words always rolled right off my tongue. But with Evan, it felt wrong. Like I was insulting his intelligence.

"It must've been hard to lose family like that," he said.

And hell if I nearly told him he was only half right, and my uncle wasn't anyone to be mourned. I wanted to spill my goddamn guts to Evan, and tell him the truth about my scar. He was putting crack after crack in the seal I tried to keep so airtight. I kept my mouth shut.

After a short silence, Evan said, "Where is your dad?"

"He died in Afghanistan when I was two."

"Damn. I'm sorry, Jo." He shook his head, his expression pained. It wasn't pity—I can smell pity from a mile away and it smells like dog shit. Evan's tone sounded like regret. Like he'd arrived at the scene of a disaster but it was too late to help.

"Yeah, well, what can you do?" I leaned my elbows on my knees. "So…What about your family?"

"Not much to say there." He smiled wryly. "Why? What have you heard?"

I smirked. "Plenty. Rumor-mongers can suck it."

"Yes, they can," he agreed, and his smiled turned genuine. The air between us warmed and I sort of wished I'd brought a bathing suit to swim in.

"What about your real parents?" I asked. "Do they know where you are? Do you know who they are?"

He shook his head, and the heaviness in his eyes I'd seen when I first arrived returned. "No. They left me at a fire station in Halston when I was three. I got bounced around to a bunch of foster homes until the Salingers took me in three years ago."

Another vision bloomed in my mind, and this one hurt—all thorns. A little blond boy, wandering alone into the driveway of a firehouse. Crying and confused and maybe calling for his mama…

I'd like to be a firefighter.

I flinched and pretended to be swiping away a mosquito. "Have the Salingers officially adopted you?"

"Yeah, but it doesn't seem much different from foster kid limbo. I mean, I have their name now, but I feel like a guest in the house. A guest who's overstayed his welcome." He pushed off from the wall again, to the middle of the deep end. "Jesus, that sounds pathetic, doesn't it?"

I shrugged. "I get the picture."

"I think they plan to cut me loose at the end of the year, too. Except Harris needs me. He'll probably kick me out of his house and then offer me a job right after."

"Can he do that?"

He shrugged. "I turned eighteen last month. He's got no legal reason to keep me. I don't think he was onboard with the whole adoption in the first place. Norma's idea. But Shane is too sick and Merle too stupid to handle the business, so I'm useful to him."

"But you won't stay in Iowa," I said.

"No. I'm leaving no matter what."

No matter what. My brain unhelpfully offered up some math: twenty-two days left until graduation.

I inwardly scoffed. *So what? He's leaving, good for him. You're going to have your own problems to deal with in twenty-two days. What do you care what Evan Salinger does or doesn't do? So what if he leaves and you never see him again?*

Yeah, so fucking what?

I kicked at a dead leaf too close to my lounger and looked up through my hair to see Evan still treading water, still watching me.

"What?" I said.

"The thing I told you earlier, about what I'd lost?"

"Yeah?"

"I was talking about…a remnant. A scrap of paper that was left with me at the fire station. It was pinned to my shirt. A note with my mother's handwriting, I think." He nodded to himself. "No, I know it was her writing."

"What did it say?" I asked, my hard voice broken down to a whisper.

"*Take care of him, please. Please.* It's the only thing I had from my real family. It doesn't sound like much. Just a scrap of paper. But it was everything to *me*."

"And it's lost?"

"Shane burnt it up. This morning."

I felt like I'd been punched in the gut, and the air around me felt fifteen degrees colder. "He *burned* it?

"Yeah," Evan said dully. "He sure fucking did."

"*Why?*"

"Because he's an evil, bitter little shit," Evan said, his voice rising. "I let my guard down for one fucking second…" He shook his head. "But it's gone and done and there's nothing I can do about it."

"I'm so sorry, Evan," I said quietly.

He nodded and moved back to the edge of the pool, resting his forearms on the cement. "She wrote 'please' twice. She did. My mother…she cared about me. To write two pleases? It has to mean she cared, doesn't it?"

"Yeah, it does," I said, blinking hard.

"Two pleases," he said.

"It means something. It really does."

He nodded and mustered a smile, pulled himself back together with a few breaths. His pain was miles deep. I could feel it, and instead of making me uncomfortable or embarrassed, I wanted to drop kick it far away. At that moment, I'd have done anything to make it go away. But I couldn't. I had no words and no time machine to go back and stop his awful brother.

I could only change the subject.

"So what's with the breath holding?"

He smiled gratefully. "It's just something I've always needed to do. It's like training."

"Olympic breath-holding? Is that a thing?"

His smile widened. "I'm not trying for a world record. I just like to do it. I need to do it."

"You were under for four minutes last night. What's your goal?"

"Four minutes is pretty good. Pete Colat held his breath for nineteen minutes. David Blaine held it seventeen on live television. If they can do it that long, I figure I can probably reach seven or eight minutes. Maybe more."

"Why?"

"I don't know. Maybe it's part of my craziness."

"I don't think you're crazy."

He smiled a little. "That's a first."

I smiled back and another silence fell. This one felt like it was going to stick around and get awkward. It was telling me to quit while I was ahead.

"I'd better get back," I said, and gathered my bag and phone. "You sure you don't want me to time you before I go?"

"Nah," Evan said, not quite looking at me. He cleared his throat. "But maybe...tomorrow night?"

A fluttery feeling rippled through my stomach, almost making me drop my phone. *He wants to see me again.* "Sure," I said, shrugging, all casual-like. "I can do that."

A full smile broke out over Evan's face and it was the most beautiful damn thing I'd seen in a long time. It was genuine. Unguarded. The flutter in my stomach spread to my chest.

"Cool," he said. "I'll see you then?"

"Yeah," I said, rising. The strap of my bag hooked on the chair arm as I was trying to shoulder it. It yanked off my arm and smacked on the cement. *Fuck.* "Cool. See you." I snatched up my bag and walked out of the pool area without looking back.

And I felt it.

Evan's eyes following me

A warm chill skimmed over my skin. Shivers of heat danced up my bare arms and the hairs on the back of my neck stood on end.

What in the ever-loving hell...?

I don't know what prompted me to turn around. Maybe wanting more of that feeling. Maybe because I had something I needed to say. Or something he needed to hear. And if I didn't say it, I'd feel even worse about being a bitch to him the night before.

I took a few steps back toward the pool. "It sucks that Shane burned your note. It was a fucking shitty thing to do."

"Yeah," Evan said, craning forward without moving a muscle.

It's too personal. Don't do it. You'll make it worse.

I silenced the thought and swallowed hard.

"But the words your mom wrote… They're real. You'll always know she wrote them and she had a reason for putting in those two pleases. Shane can't erase them. He can't erase the *intention.* Your mom wanted you to be taken care of. You'll always have that."

Evan didn't move or say a word. In the dimness, I could hardly see his face. But I knew I'd done the right thing even before I heard him say gruffly, "Thank you."

"Yeah, sure. No problem."

"Goodnight, Jo."

"Goodnight." I smiled under my hair and turned to go. "Evan."

CHAPTER 9

JO

The following morning began with rumors. Jared couldn't do the dirty work firsthand, lest he give away to his girlfriend what he and I had been doing for the week. He outsourced the job to his buddy Matt King.

Matt had no compunction in telling anyone who would listen the things I did to him behind the bleachers. Jared gave him a few truthful details to make the story believable and the tiny school ate it up. By lunchtime, it was everywhere.

Worse, someone spilled the beans I'd given two different reasons for my scar. Now everyone was calling me Joker. I heard it whispered as I walked down the halls and one kid jumped in my face to demand, "Why so serious?"

Marnie and Adam didn't quite know what to make of me when I sat down with my lunch tray at the *Mo Vay Goo* table.

"Is it true?" Marnie asked straight away. "You and Matt King?"

Adam shivered. "Ugh. He's such a beefcake. You couldn't pick someone with a little more personality?"

"I wouldn't touch Matt King with a ten-foot pole," I said.

"Really?" Marnie regarded me intently. "Given the specific details I heard, you were quite intimate with his pole."

I rolled my eyes. "Hilarious. I didn't touch him."

"Then why the rumors? Every time I turn around, someone else is regaling your exploits behind the bleachers."

"They're assholes. You need another explanation?"

"Okay, they're assholes. But why you?"

The million-dollar question. Why me? Why had I done this to myself? Or more to the point, why did I suddenly care? In the past, I took the slutty reputation and wore it with a twisted kind of pride. My terms, my call. The *Pretty Woman* code. I say who, I say when, I say how much. But this time around it was *too* much. I wished I'd never touched Jared Piltcher and not just because the whole school heard about it.

Because Evan is going to hear about it.

I looked up to see Marnie and Adam waiting for an answer.

"I'm new. I've got no reputation beyond what they decide to make for me. Easy pickings. The scar is just icing on their cake."

Marnie nodded. "Makes sense. Matt is going around saying he felt sorry for you." She wagged her fingers over her cheek. "You know what I mean."

"Yeah, I know what you mean. This isn't my first rodeo."

"It's horseshit anyway," she declared. "It's totally okay for random guys to screw around with random girls. It makes the guy a god but the girl gets called a slut."

"Sounds like a good editorial for our next edition," Adam mused.

This got Marnie all excited, and the two of them began chattering away about the last issue of *Mo Vay Goo* before the end of school.

My thoughts drifted away to Evan. They were tethered to him with some kind of invisible string. No matter how hard I tried to think of other things or distract myself, I always came back to last night, our talk, and how he wanted to see me again.

Rumors of me slutting it up with Matt King might change Evan's mind.

The gods of attendance were smiling on me: Evan wasn't at school that day. I didn't see him anywhere and his desk beside mine in Western Civ was empty. I was relieved as hell while hoping he wasn't sick, because then I wouldn't see him at the pool that night.

For our date.

I had a date with Evan Salinger. It was as far a cry from dinner and a movie as you could get. I had no reason to think of it as a date, but I did.

I sure as hell did.

As I biked home, I realized I was in danger of becoming one of those girls who gets all flustered about a boy. Part of me recoiled at the thought and part of me reached for it. Wasn't it what *normal* girls did? They met a guy, they liked him, they wanted to hang out. No big whoop.

I could admit I liked Evan. A little. But it didn't mean I was going to be stupid enough to get attached. Everything and everyone I had ever been attached to had vanished or died. Evan was going to vanish too.

He's skipping town in three weeks.

With that thought shouting loudest in my head, I almost didn't go to the pool that night. Then changed my mind back again, like ping-pong. Not showing would mean I couldn't control myself. Screw that. I wasn't some weak, lovesick airhead. I was the school slut, right? Not only would I go to the pool, maybe I'd fuck Evan sometime before he left town. A little going away present...

I sank down on the edge of my bed, suddenly on the verge of tears.

What the hell is wrong with me?

I huffed deep breaths, pressing the air inside, pushing the emotions down with the rest of the sewage. When nine o'clock rolled around, I put a bathing suit on under my clothes and headed to the pool.

My stupid heart fluttered like mad to see Evan already there.

Waiting for me.

He was treading water in the deep end, wearing boxers and a plain white t-shirt that clung to his skin. I wondered why he bothered with a shirt, but I was too relieved to see him there to ask.

"I didn't see you at class today," I said, keeping my tone ultra-casual.

"Harris needed me at the shop," Evan said.

He wasn't keeping it casual. He was smiling like a fiend, watching me, staring at me. Wrapping me in his attention with a soft heat as I set my bag down on the lounger. "I didn't know if you'd come back."

"I said I would, didn't I?" I twitched a smile to show it was my version of teasing and pulled out my cell phone. "You ready? Got the timer all set up."

"Not really. I liked talking to you yesterday."

"Me too." I set the phone down. "Later?"

"Maybe."

A silence. I needed to stop being a chickenshit and just swim, but taking off my clothes in front of Evan made my stomach twist in nervous knots.

Some school slut I was.

"It's really hot out," Evan said. "You want to swim?"

I tucked a lock of hair behind my right ear. "I was thinking about it. I brought my suit."

Evan beamed. *Beamed.* "Come on in."

"It's not too cold?"

"They keep it heated. It's perfect."

"Can't argue with perfect." I heaved a breath. "Turn."

"What?"

"I'm not doing a striptease for you. Turn around."

He obliged and I stripped off my jeans and t-shirt.

My suit was a black one-piece with a vintage style. The material skimmed my hips. The straps of the heart-shaped bodice were wide instead of stringy. I was a little too thin for it—it was a suit made for a gal with hips and boobs. I thought it was pretty, but I couldn't let Evan watch me parade around in it, not when he seemed fully-clothed by comparison.

I quickly took the steps in the shallow end and submerged myself to my neck. The cool water did feel perfect against the night's stifling heat. Keeping my hair anchored over my left cheek, I swam with my head above water toward the deep end. I stopped and stood where the cement under my feet slanted down.

Right on the edge.

"So," I said into the silence. "Come here often?"

Evan laughed. "Yeah, I do, actually. Pretty much every night."

"Why? No air conditioning at Chez Salinger?"

He grinned in a way that made me want to keep making stupid jokes all night.

"Yeah, we have it. I just like being here. It's peaceful. And when I'm under, holding my breath, it's peaceful *and* quiet, and I can just…be."

"Like meditation?" I asked.

"Something like that. It helps to hold my breath for a long time if I'm kind of…detached from my body. If I were sitting under there, counting the seconds, I don't think I'd get very far." He waved his hands, making little ripples in the water. "Anyway. I'm sure there are far more *normal* things we could talk about."

I smirked. "Normal is overrated."

"I keep telling myself that," he said with a dry smile. "Doesn't take."

"Yeah, me too."

We exchanged looks, a commiseration; the girl with the scar and the boy with the freaky rep, and something shifted between us. An unspoken understanding that drew me closer to him without having moved an inch.

"So what *normal* stuff shall we talk about?" I asked. "Our favorite colors? Favorite food? Political affiliations?"

"How about…What's your movie?"

"*Raising Arizona,*" I said automatically.

Evan broke out in a surprised laugh. "Oh man, that's a classic!" His slightly southern twang morphed into a full-blown drawl. *"Son, you got a panty on your head."*

I busted out laughing. "That entire movie is one big quote-fest."

"Agree," Evan said. "Favorite band?"

"All-time or current?"

"Both."

"Current favorite would be Cage the Elephant. All-time fave is Tori Amos."

"Why?"

"Because she's honest and poetic, and she makes inhaling a breath to sing so beautiful, like it's part of the song."

"Yeah?"

"Yeah. You should give her a listen sometime."

Evan smiled. "Maybe I will."

Another little silence came and went; taking with it more of the awkwardness that exists between two people getting to know each other, until one moment it's entirely vanished.

"So...you." I said. "Favorite band?"

"I like old school stuff."

"Like New Order or...MC Hammer?"

He laughed. Damn, I liked hearing him laugh.

"No, I mean like *old*, old-school. Like from the 1940's and '50's. Otis Redding, or Roy Orbison...Ever heard of the Robins?"

"Can't say that I have."

"I should play them for you sometime. 'Smokey Joe's Café'? A classic."

"Why do you dig so far back to find music that you like?"

"Old music like that..." He shrugged. "I don't know. It just seems really honest. And simple. Not simple, like elementary, but simple like...pure. I like simple."

"Me too." I skimmed my fingers over the surface of the water, pushing dead leaves that floated on the surface away from me. "I like *uncomplicated*. Security, stability. I like those things too." I blink and look around. "Sorry, what was I saying? Don't mind me and my random word associations."

"I don't mind. Security and stability are good. The Salingers are always harping on that. To keep the business strong, and the money coming in to stay secure."

"You don't agree?"

"I don't care about money. That's not my idea of security." Evan made a face. "I'm sure that sounds arrogant or ungrateful coming from a foster kid who was lucky enough to be adopted. I am grateful for that kind of security. For the roof over my head and the food on table. But it's not enough of what counts."

"What counts?" I asked softly.

"How you feel when you're there. Home. It's not the same word as house, is it? Not even close."

I nodded, my fingertips dancing over the water. "I know what you mean. My guardian—a cousin of my mother's—he's a trucker. Switches companies a lot to get the longest hauls. That's why I transferred to Wilson so late. We move constantly. Every six months or so, at least. And he rents houses or apartments, but they're not a home to settle down in, you know?"

"I think I do," Evan said.

I don't know why I kept talking; I felt like I hadn't said so many words in a row out loud in ages. If ever. But I did, and I didn't worry about it. Evan listened intently, and I thought maybe it had been a long time since someone had spoken to him more than a short string of words in a really long time too.

"We came from Missouri before Iowa," I told Evan. "In the suburbs of Kansas City. We had an apartment, not a house. And it sucked."

"Yeah?"

"Yeah. I mean, not because it was small or anything—which it was. But because...Okay, so my bedroom overlooked the parking area, right? And every so often a car would pull up at night, like dropping someone off. And they'd just idle their car in the parking lot, lights on, talking loudly with whomever lived in our building, and it just fucking irritated the hell out of me. They weren't even being vulgar or playing loud music, they were just idling their car and talking for the whole complex to hear. And every time it happened, I would feel so...*unstable*. Like, this was supposed to be *my* home, right? And the parking lot was sort of *my* driveway, and these people would just *hang out* there. And I didn't know them and they didn't know me but there they were, at my home, and there was nothing I could do about it."

I scowled, and slashed at the water.

"I know that probably sounds totally insane," I continued, "but I hated that apartment. If I think about what my ideal life might be, it's not having a big house all gated up or anything. I don't want that. I don't need a lot of money or *stuff*. I just want a little place, somewhere near a beautiful mountain or forest or lake that I can wake up to every morning and look at it while I write. My place. My home, and I wouldn't have to leave it six months after I settled in. I don't need much. A little life, you know?"

"Yeah, I know."

I looked up sharply to see Evan watching me with his eyes that could be described as the color of ice, but that always looked to me like the sky on a cloudless, hot summer day. That gaze...it just wrapped around me, like my reverie, meshing and blending with it, until I was almost there, in my own place with a view of something beautiful in the window, and strong arms holding me...

I blinked and surged back in the water. I'd just unloaded some deep, secret of my heart to an almost total stranger. I remembered how I'd first thought Evan would be the one willing to spill his guts to anyone who would listen. Turned out that was me.

But I was right about him being a good listener. He didn't judge or question, or even add his own commentary. He just let me put it out there, and it was okay, and he was already moving on to something else. My embarrassment floated away like so many dead leaves.

"So, Jo," he said. "Is that short for Joanna?"

"Josephine. After Jo March from *Little Women*. It was my mother's favorite book. If you haven't read it, Jo was the writer in the family."

"So your mom knew you were going to become a poet early on," Evan said, grinning. "Before you were born, even."

I smiled. "Doubtful. I think she liked that Jo was the strongest sister. Mentally strong. Jo didn't fall into the arms of the first guy who liked her, like my mother did. Mama was young and she fell hard, but she didn't get the happy ending she envisioned. I think she admired Jo March, who knew her own mind and found true love in the guy who least looked the part."

Evan stretched his arms out, skimmed his hands over the water. "Your mom sounds like a wise lady."

"Not really. She moved me and her around a lot when I was a kid, on a whim almost, chasing some dead-end job or another. She was sweet and fun, but I don't think anyone would call her wise. We lived with my dad's family when I was older and she needed help, and none of them took her seriously." I cut the water with my hand. "She wasn't mentally strong herself."

Evan shrugged. "Who is?"

I smiled in gratitude. "No one I know," I said and splashed water at him.

He laughed. "Do you want to talk about her?" he asked after a moment.

"I've done a shit-ton of talking already, don't you think?"

"No, I like listening to you. If you want to talk about your mom, you can. I know I would if I could remember mine."

"You don't remember her at all?"

Evan smiled but it didn't touch his eyes. "Nope. I've tried. But it seems like my life began at the firehouse."

"I can't quite remember my mom, either. Not really. Or, I *can* remember her, but all those years feel grayed out to me. Like I can't quite reach them."

"What do you mean?"

I moved to the edge of the pool and folded my arms on the cement. Evan did the same, a few feet away, and we rested our heads on our arms, looking at each other.

"This one time, when I was a kid, my mother took me to Tybee Island. We had the best time. I know we did. But I can't recall how it felt. I know it was sunny but I don't remember feeling warm. I know I laughed but I don't remember feeling happy." I glanced sideways at him. "Weird, right?"

"I don't think so," Evan said. "Coping mechanism, maybe, for her death."

"Coping," I said, looking away.

I hadn't told him the truth about my mother, or my scar. I felt like I should—or could—but the words stuck in my throat. It was all so ugly and terrible, and I wanted Evan to keep thinking of me as a girl who'd been in a tragic car accident. Not one who'd cut up her own face to stop her uncle from touching her in the middle of the night. I swallowed the words down.

"Yeah, coping. We all have our tricks for it."

"And here I am," Evan said, indicating the pool with his head.

A silence descended. I pulled myself from my own memories to look at Evan. This close to him, I could see so much. His white T-shirt was threadbare. Through the thin, wet fabric I could see the planes of his chest and the cut of his abs. I could even see the greenish tinge of an old bruise on his right pec.

I moved closer along the edge, until I was right beside him. He didn't move but let me look at him. Watched me take in the dark purples and blues of fresher bruises on his back and arms.

My heart thudded in an unfamiliar cadence. It had been a long time since I'd been afraid for someone beside myself.

"Who does this to you, Evan? Your brothers? Or your dad?"

God, tell me it's not his dad...

"Brothers," Evan replied. "Merle, specifically. We fight a lot."

"Why?" I raised my hand, poised it over a particularly dark splotch on his right shoulder blade.

"He's not bright. He does whatever Shane tells him to."

"But why does Shane tell him to do this?" I gently touched the bruise beneath his shirt, covering it completely with the flat of my hand. The skin on his arms broke out in gooseflesh.

"To remind me I'm not blood," he said, looking straight ahead. "And that I'm different."

I removed my hand. The bruise beneath was still there. "That's no reason."

Evan didn't reply. The air between us seemed to tighten, grow a little colder. "Why are you being nice to me?" he asked in a low voice.

I blinked, my defenses going up at once. "What do you mean? Because—"

He turned on me and I pulled back from the intensity in his gaze. "I'm fucking serious, Jo. Why are you here? Why are you hanging out with the town freak at a waterpark in the middle of the night? Tell me the truth, please. Please."

Two pleases.

My jaw worked soundlessly as my brain shuffled through a half-dozen bullshit answers. I had nothing. No words. Instead, I brought my hand up and moved the hair from the left side of my face.

The air felt cold against my damp skin. My left eye, so used to having only a curtain of hair to look at, was suddenly free. It looked at Evan. The suspicion melted off his face; I'd already forgiven him for it anyway. No one was kind to him; I'd have been suspicious too. But mostly I just watched him take what I was offering, my breath held tight in my chest.

He smiled at me.

His eyes roamed over my scarred face. I didn't sense a shred of revulsion or disgust or even curiosity. Evan Salinger smiled at my messed up face as if it were a gift he wasn't expecting.

"This," I whispered. "How you're looking at me right now. This is why I'm here. I thought...if you saw me, you wouldn't care that I'm ugly." I swallowed hard. "You might not think I was ruined."

Evan's smile melted into a pained expression, his brows furrowed. He moved closer to me, facing me. "You're not ruined," he said softly. "I already saw your scar. When you dove into the pool to save me. When you came out of the water with me, your hair was back and I saw it."

"I didn't save you," I said, hardly able to breathe and he moved even closer, into my space. I felt the heat of his body across the water that separated us, and felt myself pulled toward it.

"You did, Jo. It might not seem like it, but you did. And God, you are not ugly."

His hand rose up out of the water and I watched it move to my face. I didn't stop him. His fingertips touched my cheek and his thumb traced the line of my scar from under my eye down to my jaw.

"You're the most beautiful girl I've ever seen."

It was too much. No one looked at me like this. No one told me I was beautiful. And no boy had ever moved to kiss me like Evan did. His face slowly coming toward mine, his eyes gentle, the warmth of his attention like a roaring fire over me.

He covered my mouth with his and inhaled a little while I exhaled. A little sigh that turned to a soft moan as his mouth opened and mine opened with him, letting him in. I let go. The shields guarding my heart lowered. Evan wasn't taking, he was giving. His kiss gave me those impossible things I'd desperately wanted all my life: tenderness, consideration, reverence.

I took everything in his kiss, turned it around and gave it all back to him. Willingly. Never once wondering what it would cost me later. No price to be paid, only this moment with this boy. The beauty of time and him and his sweet kiss.

I let go.

He caught me and held me up. My arms went around his bruised and beaten body, and I held him up too. Together, we stood upright and unwavering. I was strong in Evan's arms. And I never wanted it to end. Ever.

My mouth couldn't get enough of his sweet, clean taste and the scratch of his stubble on my cheek. The scent of his skin in my nose that carried little particles of his life to me: the pool, the auto shop and his own goodness. We kissed forever, the earth ceased rotating to give us more time.

Evan didn't try to push me past kissing. His hands never stopped moving but they kept to my back or tangled in my hair. They caressed my face and neck while his mouth explored mine. His gentle sweetness broke me down.

It was too much.

I broke our kiss and held him tightly around the neck, buried my face against his warm skin, my body trembling against his. It wasn't safe to let anyone in this close. I fought to find something to say, to dismiss or joke away the kiss before he could.

He kept holding me.

"This doesn't happen to girls like me," I whispered against his neck. "Do you know what I mean?"

God, I hoped so. I couldn't explain it and didn't want to try. I was beyond words. And because it was Evan, I didn't need them.

"I know," he murmured against my neck. "It doesn't happen to guys like me, either. Believe me." He held me tighter. "No one touches me."

No one touches me.

It wasn't self-pity. Just a simple fact. The pain and cruelty of his life was buried so deep in him, only faint echoes rose up anymore. I held him tighter.

"You're shivering," he said after a moment.

"I know, but I'm not cold."

He pulled away, smiling gently. "Come on. I'll walk you home."

He took my hand as we stepped out of the pool, letting go only so we could dry off. I pulled jeans and shirt over my damp suit, the material soaking up pool water and sticking to my skin. The heat had relented a bit: the air carried a slight chill to it for the first time in weeks.

"Next time, I'll remember a towel," I said.

Evan took up his shirt—a blue and black plaid flannel—from the lounger and hung it around my shoulders. It left him in only a wife-beater and I could see the gooseflesh broken out over the muscles of his arms and shoulders.

"Won't you be cold?" I said.

He only shrugged and smiled. The smile stayed on me, and instead of feeling self-conscious, I let myself bask in it.

We looked quite the pair of wet rats walking home, Evan pushing my bike for me. My hair dripped water in our wake, leaving a trail back to the pool. The one place I could live as myself, not the actress I felt everywhere else. We walked slowly, reluctant to return to the real world that felt more like a stage.

On the sidewalk outside my house, Evan dropped the kickstand on my bike and shoved both of his in the front pockets of his jeans. "Listen, Jo, tomorrow... At school..."

"What happens tomorrow?"

"I don't know. More of the usual horrible shit, I suppose. And I think...it would be better if you..." His words trailed away and his gaze drifted to the ground.

I crossed my arms. "If I what?"

Evan looked at me and I swear I could feel the weight of his pain rest on me. Only for an instant, then he took it back. "I just think it'll be better if you pretend you don't know me."

The words punched me in the gut. My arms dropped to my sides.

Evan went on in his flat, matter-of-fact voice. "I don't want you to feel like you have to—"

"Shut up," I said.

He blinked.

"Don't say that again." I softened my voice. "Don't say anything like that ever again. Not to me."

I put my arms around his neck and kissed him long and hard, stealing his breath to keep for my own. When I stepped away, the smile on his face was dazed.

"See you tomorrow," I said, taking my bike down the walk to my front door. "Okay?"

"Okay." I could barely see him in the light of the streetlamp, but I heard the smile, coloring his words. "Good night, Jo."

I went to bed that night and for the first time in my teenage life, I fell asleep like a normal girl: not remembering tearing skin or bathtub suicides, but thinking dreamily of her first kiss with a boy she liked.

If there was never anything more between Evan and I, if the ground swallowed him up or if Gerry moved us the next day, at least I had those minutes in my bed when I felt nothing was wrong with me. When I felt beautiful and important.

I drifted between awake and asleep.

Floating.

Not on air, but on water.

CHAPTER 10

JO

And the next morning, it was back to good ol' rock bottom.

"Hey, it's Jo-Jo-Joker, the Ho-Ho-Whore."

Laughter followed me down the hall. I walked faster, head down, stomach roiling. Not at the stupid insult or the snake hiss of whispers behind me, but because I had been so careless. So stupid.

Evan's going to hear and I hadn't warned him last night.

I was at my locker during first break, switching out my calculus book for chemistry, when I heard a scuffle further down the hallway. Sounds of swearing and scuffs. A fight and I knew without looking who it was.

Too late, Jo-Jo-Joker…

I wanted to turn and run. Instead, I hurried to where a small crowd was starting to gather around Evan and Matt King. Evan had Matt pressed up against a bank of lockers and his normally unreadable face was twisted with rage. Matt was nearly a head taller than Evan but looked ready to piss his pants.

"Shut your ugly mouth." Evan's voice was a snarl I'd never heard before. He looked like he was barely keeping himself in check.

"Get the fuck off me." Matt's voice was choked from Evan's forearm shoved under his chin. His eyes darted around the hall, looking for help from his posse. "Jared," he managed to call out.

I looked to see Jared Piltcher rounding the corner with girlfriend, Laney, his arm slung over her shoulders. He stopped in his tracks, eyes widening at the situation. Then he strode into the crush of bodies, shoving his way through. His hand grabbed for Evan's shoulder. Evan shoved him off without taking his eyes from Matt.

"You're done, asshole," Evan said "You're fucking done talking about her. You got it?"

Jared had a fistful of Evan's shirt, yanking hard. "Get off him, freak."

Evan's head turned back. His eyes were murderous. Then the rage melted out of his expression, and a peculiar look came over his face. His forearm fell away from Matt's throat and he turned all the way to face Jared. The noise level in the hall dropped, except for Matt coughing as he staggered away.

I held my breath as Evan and Jared stared each other down.

"It was you," Evan said, carving each word out of the air.

Jared took a miniscule step back, his face pale. I would've laughed if I weren't so nauseous.

Laney Jacobson had come to stand next to Jared. His eyes flicked to her, then back to Evan. He hitched the strap of his backpack higher on his shoulder. "What the hell are you talking about?"

Evan's eyes found me, standing at the edge of the crowd.

I read an apology there, for dragging this stuff out into the hallway for the whole school to see.

Evan took a step back. "Forget it. Never mind."

"Oh, no you don't." Now Jared moved after him, his hands balling into fists. "I want to know what you're getting at, Freakshow."

I saw the ire rise up in Evan's face again and the clench of his jaw against it. He glanced at me, his expression a mix of pleading forgiveness and heated anger.

"Forget it, Piltcher," he said, and turned to go.

Jared gave him two steps. Then let his backpack slide off his shoulder as he lunged toward Evan. He seized the collar of Evan's shirt and spun him around, the other fist swinging. Evan side-stepped the blow and slugged a left hook into Jared's face.

The sound of fist on flesh is like nothing else. The tense hush in the hallway made the blow even louder, like the thwack of a basketball on a gym floor. Then everyone seemed to yell at once and surged like a mob, tightening the circle around the fight. Laney's shriek rose above it all as she knelt by Jared, who had sunk to the floor. He brushed her off, spitting out a mouthful of blood and a tooth.

"You're dead." Jared spat another wad of blood as he looked up at Evan. "You're done, Freakshow. I will fucking *end* you."

The crowd stared, bristling with anticipation. Evan shook his head with a disgusted exhale. He pushed through the crowd, heading for the exit doors. A clanking rattle as he shoved one open and stepped into the rectangle of blinding light outside. Then he was gone.

The bell rang, shattering the air. Everyone jumped in their shoes and began to clear out, murmuring commentary and playing the action back.

Head down, I hugged the wall until I reached the exit doors. The heat outside was like a blanket thrown over me and my eyes screwed up against the sun. I could just make out Evan striding past the bleachers, heading across the football field.

"Hey! Evan, wait!" I hurried to catch up with his long strides, but he kept going. "*Hey!*"

He stopped, shoulders slumped in defeat, waiting for me. I caught up to him, glared with my one visible eye.

He glared right back. "Why?" he demanded. "Just…why, Jo?"

I recoiled. "Okay, fine. Yes, I should have warned you last night…"

He jabbed a finger toward the school. "You hear the shit they were saying about you?"

"So what?" I fired back. "I expected it. I didn't expect you to make it a million times worse by picking a fight with Matt King."

"You're right. Because I picked a fight with the wrong fucking guy." He scrubbed his hand over his face, his knuckles bloody and swollen. "It was Jared, right? Why him?"

"What the hell business is it of yours?" I said, crossing my arms. "Or anyone's? And how the hell did you know it was Jared and not Matt?"

"Jo…"

"Why are you even *asking* me about Jared?" I said, clutching the sides of my shirt. "Why don't you ask *him* why he whores himself out to strange girls?"

"I don't give a shit about Jared," Evan cried. "It's not about the fucking politics of it, Jo. You're not a slut and I'm not going to let anyone say you are. Secondly, it *hurts* to hear you were with another guy, okay? Especially when that guy has been one of the biggest assholes to me for three fucking years, never letting me live down my time at Woodside." Evan's eyes darkened as he looked harder at me. "Is that why you picked him? Jared of all fucking guys?"

I rocked back on my heels. "Are you serious? I picked Jared because he was *there*. That's it. There's no conspiracy. You haven't told me about the time you were at Woodside, and you know what? I haven't *asked*. Did you notice that? I didn't ask because I was *trying* to give you space about it. Or the benefit of the doubt. Because I don't give a shit about what the rumors say."

Evan ground his teeth, thinking; I could see the muscles in his jaw twitch.

My instinct was to snap back, to walk away. But I moved a step closer instead.

"And I should have told you about Jared, but it all happened before you and I. And he wasn't there last night. He wasn't there, Evan. It was just you and me. For the first time, the old pain…that wasn't there either."

A short silence and then Evan relented. "Yeah, okay, Jo."

"I fucked up with Jared," I said, my arms crossed. I kicked at a clump grass. "I'm sorry that I didn't tell you."

Evan sighed. "You didn't fuck up. I'm not pissed at you. Maybe I should be, but I'm not. It's none of my business, like you said. But what they say about you, that's my business. It's my business now. I know you can handle yourself, Jo, but that doesn't stop me from wanting to take care of you."

I turned my head away to hide the sudden sting of tears in my eyes. "That's just the future firefighter in you talking."

"Hey, come here."

Evan drew me to him, wrapped his arms around me. My eyes fell closed with relief, as we held each other in the center of the football field, with the early morning sun blazing down on us. And then I felt Evan tense a little, a shadow falling over us.

"Who else wasn't there, Jo?" Evan asked quietly. "The old pain. The other person who hurt you."

I looked up to see him staring at me with the question in his eyes, and the vulnerability that he asked it. He somehow knew about my ghosts. I fought for something to say but the truth was sitting like bile on my lips, waiting for me to spit it out. And he knew.

I drew back to look up at him. The eyes staring back me were vulnerable, yet certain.

He knew. And instead of freaking me out, it felt a little bit like relief.

"I'm scared, Evan," I said. "I'm scared to let it out."

"I know, sweetness. I'm scared too. About telling you my stuff. I'm afraid you'll think I'm crazy like the rest. And that scares me more than anything."

Evan brushed the hair from my scar, and trailed his fingers over it softly. He kissed my cheek, my tears. "Let's be different, Jo. I need us to be honest. I don't want to hide anything from you. Not one damn thing. My whole fucking life is *not* talking about the things that feel right to me. Things as natural to me as taking a breath."

I turned my face up. I lifted my chin and let the light and warmth of day shine on my scar. "It wasn't a car accident."

His smile was sad. "I know, Jo. I want to hear your story. And I want to tell you mine. Tell you about Woodside and why they sent me there." His fingers ran through my hair and caressed my cheek. "Let's do something really fucking crazy and trust each other."

I laughed a small sob. "Okay."

"Mr. Salinger?" A man's voice was calling. "A word? And Miss Clark? You're late for class."

We looked around. Assistant Principal Wallace stood outside the school's exit doors, sunlight glinting off both his glasses and his bald head.

Evan took my hand. "Come somewhere with me."

I blinked and glanced at Wallace. "We'll get in trouble. You're already in trouble."

"Come with me. There's something I want to show you."

Wallace called our names again, his voice echoing off brick.

Fuck it.

I squeezed Evan's hand tight. "Let's go."

CHAPTER 11

JO

We ran to the parking lot, heading for Evan's tomato-red Chevy truck. It looked like a clunker, with a scratched up paint job and one dented fender. But the interior was immaculate, the old leather free of holes and clean, the dash polished and gleaming. Evan took good care of this baby.

The inside smelled of him—engine grease, little bit of chlorine, the scent of his skin and clothing. As it drew over me, like another seatbelt, I felt safe. Even safer when he slid behind the wheel and started the engine. A little tingle shivered along my skin. Something about sitting in a guy's truck and watching him drive with masculine expertise was such a turn-on.

The color rose up high in my face and I turned to the window to hide it. Evan drove east for twenty minutes, past fields and fields of corn. An ocean of green stalks stretching past forever. We turned north along the Mississippi River, where it borders Wisconsin. A thick forest of rich, deeper green replaced the cornfields.

A sign came up on my side: *Effigy Mounds National Monument*.

"Are we going there?" I asked. "Burial mounds?"

"Yeah. Have you ever been?"

"Never. What is it, a cemetery?"

"Sort of. It's old. Older than this country. Before Planerville built the water park I'd come here sometimes. It's peaceful. I think you might like it."

He parked in front of squat, brown visitor center and we went inside. It was library-quiet, only soft footsteps and the hushed voices of a few other tourists. Native American artifacts behind glass hung on the walls. In the center of the main room was a table with a huge 3-D map of the park, hiking trails marked in different colors.

I pointed at a strange chain through the model trees, rudimentary outlines of animals. Bears and birds mostly.

"Those are the burial mounds," Evan said. "They can be up to forty feet wide in some places."

"Who made them?"

"The First Nation tribes, from Iowa, Wisconsin, and Ohio. Hundreds of years ago."

Visitors weren't allowed to climb atop the mounds, but the hiking trails would take you right alongside the ancient graves. We left the visitors' center and picked a path at random, heading into the cool woods.

Evan was right about the peacefulness of this place. The air between the trees felt thick and rich with history and time and legend.

We crested a hill and came out overlooking one of the mounds. Flattened at the top and overgrown with grass, we could just make out it was in the shape of a bear.

"I see why you like coming here," I told Evan. "So peaceful."

"Yes. But it's not the only reason."

His low voice carried through the trees as we walked around the base of the mound. He held my hand, but kept his eyes up on the rise of land.

"In my junior year, we studied the First Nations in my American history class," he said. "I loved it. Best thing I ever learned in school. We learned about the Ojibwe tribe, their beliefs and traditions and about these mounds. It just…made sense. Everything I read, everything I learned…It made a part of *me* make sense."

"You think your parents are Native American?" I asked, taking in his very Caucasian blond hair and blue eyes.

"I don't know. I don't think I'll ever know." His fingers wove tighter with mine. "I'm okay with it. I just want to be okay with the rest of what I am. Be at peace with what I do know."

We walked along the trail and sat down on a fallen log, back-to-back to prop us up. Evan told me about his stint at the Woodside Institution. He told me everything, and I felt his trust as if it were something tangible. Something delicate and precious that he set in my hand.

"I was fifteen years old, and the ink on my adoption papers had hardly dried. I'd been a Salinger for about a month. And this one morning, I woke up feeling like I was in tune with my new family. I could feel this…*hum* running through the house, like a power line had gone down outside. I thought maybe I was so happy to have been adopted that my imagination was working overtime. But it felt good. Natural. And then I thought maybe it wasn't just me. Maybe everyone else could feel it too. All of us, sitting there, in each other's space and feeling…everything."

I could hear in Evan's voice how much he wished that had been true, and my heart ached a little already, because I knew it wasn't.

"What happened?" I asked, my fingers tightening around his.

"The good feeling didn't last, but the feeling of being in tune with everyone got stronger at school. I was in algebra class. With Becky Ulridge. She was this girl I had a crush on, and she turned to smile over her shoulder at me. And that's when it happened. A shooter, right at that moment, walked into a factory in Jefferson County. The employee break room. And he had an automatic weapon and he opened fire."

"How did you know that?" I asked.

"I dreamed it," he said slowly, and I could feel his back tense against mine, waiting to hear how I'd react.

I'd heard the rumors of course, but hearing it from him… A rumor could be brushed off as fiction. Here was Evan asking me to believe it was real. I froze for a moment, unsure what to do or think. But I'd already vowed I wasn't going to be like everyone else who never gave Evan the time of day. I could keep that promise at least and hear him out.

I let out a slow breath. "Go on."

I felt Evan's relief, could practically see him smile a little. He gave my hand a grateful squeeze.

"The shooter in Jefferson fired the first time and I let out a scream. Right there in algebra class. My body jerked and I sent papers flying off my desk. My textbook hit the kid in front of me. Whatever was happening in that factory... I was feeling. Seeing and hearing it. Living it. I fell out of my chair. Like I'd taken a bullet.

"Nobody knew what to do, not even the teacher. Everyone was staring while I begged and cried out for it to stop. Jesus, someone make it stop. Becky was staring, too, but she came a little closer. I took one look at her and...I knew."

"Knew what?" I asked, my voice small.

"Her dad was in the factory," Evan said miserably. "He was in the break room."

I sucked in a breath, my heart pounding. "Jesus, Evan..."

"The exact instant I looked at Becky's eyes, I knew he was there. I kept telling her how sorry I was..."

"You...saw it all happen?"

"Yeah," he said heavily. "It brought me to my fucking knees. A breakdown, I guess. Not the kind you usually hear about, not a nervous collapse. I broke down because I felt all the horror and pain in that factory. I'd dreamt it the night before, but couldn't remember it all until that morning. Then it all came back."

I didn't know what to say. I knew I was supposed to be skeptical, that I should chalk up the shooting and his breakdown to a coincidence. A crazy coincidence, and nothing more.

But it wasn't, was it?

"What next?" I asked, my voice small and breathy. "What happened next?"

"I just lost it. They hauled me away in front of the whole school, kicking and screaming and crying."

"To Woodside."

"Yes. I was there three weeks. The first week I spent trying to convince them I wasn't lying, that I wasn't crazy. That I'd had dreams like this before but it didn't mean I was a mental case or dangerous. The second week I spent trying to take it all back. Everyone thought I was suffering some huge break with reality. No one believed what I was telling them. The third week I spent admitting they were right. Yes, I made it all up. Yes, I'd been depressed lately but I was fine now. You're absolutely right—being adopted had triggered some kind of breakdown over my abandonment. Anything and everything so they'd let me out."

"And they did."

"Yeah, but the damage was done. I went back to school and the whispers were deafening. My reputation, which wasn't all that hot to begin with thanks to Shane, was destroyed. They called me Nostradamus, and asked me to read their palms or pick lottery numbers. They called me Freakshow and a nutjob and a loon. And Shane told them I'd had ECT, and said I'd heard voices that told me the future. Just piling it on, and they still do, until I'm about ready to crack. It's been a fucking nightmare that I can't wake up from."

"And what about Becky?" I asked in a small voice. "Where was she when you got out?"

"She was gone," he said, his words dropping like stones between us.

"What do you mean?" *This is it. This is where the truth lives...*

"She moved out of Planerville."

"Because...?"

"Because her dad died in the shooting. Shot in the head. Just like I'd seen in my dream."

"Oh Christ..."

"There was nothing I could do about it. I couldn't help her dad, or anyone else at that factory. I couldn't stop it. I told you the kids ragged on me about predicting the future...lottery tickets and all that shit, but it doesn't work like that. No premonitions. Whatever these dreams are, they come back to me in the moment, not before. I don't wake up with them. They hover just out of sight, until the time comes for me to remember."

Evan shifted on the log so he could look at me. "But that doesn't keep me from feeling that there is some purpose to what I can do. I just can't see it yet. But I'm tired of feeling like it's unnatural or wrong or that it makes me a freak. I told the doctors at Woodside the truth, Jo. It's in my dreams. Or from my dreams. I don't know how or why. I've moved beyond hows and whys. I just want to be." He held my face in his hands, his eyes begging me silently. "Can I, Jo? With you? Or is it too much?"

"It's not too much," I whispered. "I'm here, Evan. I'm not going anywhere."

He pulled me to him then, and held me for a long time, breathing deeply, like one long sigh of relief.

"But I'm scared," he whispered into my hair. "I'm scared it's ruined my future. I'm scared I'll never be free of what happened here. That it will dog me forever."

"Do you still have those dreams?" I asked quietly.

"Not often," he said, pulling away to look at me. "When I do, I've learned to keep them to myself. Until now." His eyes held mine, unblinking. "Now I just dream about you."

"About my scar."

"Yes."

"I told you it wasn't a car accident and you said that you already knew. You had a dream?"

"Yes, Jo. I knew. Like a flash of something once forgotten and now remembered."

"Once forgotten and now remembered," I repeated.

I touched my fingers to my scar and it seemed I really felt the texture of it, the little interruption of smooth skin. All the lies of how it got there began to loosen their grip and fall away. The truth I'd buried for so long, unspoken and unacknowledged—even in my poetry—cried out to be heard. He'd told me his truth, and now it was my turn. I leaned in to him and he put his arms around me at once.

"I did it. I did this to myself."

"I know. Tell me why."

"To make him stop."

The circle of his arms flinched, then settled. I rose and fell against his chest as he pulled in a deep breath and let it out. "Your uncle."

"He called me his pretty girl. *Who's my pretty girl?* I wanted to puke when I heard it. It meant that later that night he'd come…"

Evan held me tighter as my breath hitched.

"I didn't want to be his pretty girl anymore. I thought if I made myself ugly, if I stopped being pretty he would stop. So I took a screw…" I gripped Evan's hands hard.

"I'm here," he said. "I'm right here."

"I took a screw and carved a path down my cheek. The skin tore open and the blood came out. The pain was like nothing I'd ever known but mostly I felt *relieved*, Evan. Because whatever he wanted from me came pouring out too and it was the end. I wasn't his pretty girl anymore. It was over."

"Was it?" Over my head he sniffed and whispered, "God, please say yes."

"I went to bed that night, bleeding all over my pillow and nightgown. I waited for him to come and see. I was ready. I had it all planned out. He'd come in and see what I did. How I'd cut him out of me. He'd say, 'My pretty girl is gone forever.' He'd leave, close the door behind him and never come back. Ever. And I could go to sleep. I was so tired. So fucking exhausted. Finally, I could have one night to sleep without fear."

Evan's grip on my hands was just short of painful. But I wanted it. I needed the solidity of him.

"What happened?" he asked.

"I fell asleep. I don't know how. I was in so much pain. Maybe the shock... Anyway, I woke up and I had a burning fever and my mother was screaming. She came in to wake me, saw the blood and the gash, and she screamed and screamed. She thought someone had broken into the house and attacked me. God, I wish that were true, because the truth destroyed her..."

"You told her," Evan said.

"I told her everything. Jasper tried to deny it, but even the family members who thought my mother was crazy took one look at my ripped-up face and knew I wasn't lying. Who would do something like that to themselves? And my mother... She couldn't take it. She cried and cried, shut up in her dark bedroom for days crying..."

The light's off, Josie. Go away and let Mama be...

I shuddered. "It was too much for her. She couldn't handle the guilt of what happened to me, and so she... She killed herself."

I sobbed. Great wracking sobs for saying those words out loud for the first time in years. "She killed herself, Evan, but... but wasn't that my fault?"

"No."

"I drove her to—"

"It wasn't your fault, Jo," Evan said fiercely. "None of it. None of it was your fault. Not what Jasper did. Not your mother. Nothing."

"But isn't that why she's gone? Even the good memories of her are gone. Grayed out and so far away. Because I did that? Isn't that why?"

"*No*, Jo. That's not why."

"I just want her back. Even one little piece of her, one happy memory…"

I cried hard from my chest and throat. Evan held me. His heartbeat steady and strong, his breath even and deep. The crying lurched to an end. I sank further into the circle of his arms, drained.

"What happened to your uncle?" he asked finally, wiping my tears with the cuff of his shirt.

"He's gone. He died in jail waiting for a hearing. Asshole croaked of a heart attack before he could feel the weight of any justice and that sucks. But he's gone. I never have to worry about him getting out parole." I sniffed. "I don't care about him anyway. I just want her back. My mother. I could have survived Jasper, I *did* survive Jasper."

Evan held me tighter, not offering empty words. Only his presence, which was more valuable to me than anything. But for how long? He knew the whole truth about what my uncle had done to me. The shame of it made me tremble.

"Do you…" I swallowed, tried again. "Do you still want to be with me?"

Evan's dark eyes looked down, irises colored by my story. His jaw muscle twitched, and it took him a moment to answer.

"Shut up," he said, his voice gruff. "Don't ever say that again."

I half-laughed, half sobbed as his hands came up to brush the hair from my face. "Evan…"

"You are the bravest girl I've ever met." He kissed my forehead, pressing his lips to my skin. Then his mouth whispered down my cheek and kissed the scar. "And beautiful."

I closed my eyes as he kissed the rest of my face: my other cheek, my chin, the tip my nose. And finally my lips. His mouth soft on mine, with no intention except sweetness.

We kissed and held each other, together in that place where ancient tribes came to lay down their dead and release their ghosts. A private communion between two lost souls. Two ghosts who thought they were too broken to be of worth to anybody, now reborn. Alive and at peace as the sun sank behind the trees, rimming them in fire.

CHAPTER 12

JO

The house was empty that night. Gerry was on his long haul and wouldn't be back for another week. I sat at my desk in my dark bedroom. The window was open and except for chirping insects and the occasional truck trundling by on the highway, all was quiet.

In the dark, I wrapped Evan's blue and black plaid flannel around myself tighter and my fingers contemplated a blank piece of paper on the desk.

I tapped my pen to my lips. They were still warm and swollen from Evan's voracious goodnight kisses. I sucked on the lower one, still tasting him. My body could feel his hands. My eyes remembered him looking at me one last time before he went away down my front walk.

I put the collar of his shirt to my nose. I inhaled deeply, eyes closed. Words—the right words, the most perfect words—bloomed in my mind. My thoughts put down roots, reached stems and leaves out and up. The patch of dry dirt in my soul, dead and barren for years, now a garden.

The light's flipped on, Josie!

I clicked on the reading lamp, inhaled Evan's scent again, then put my pen to paper.

I wrote it all down.

CHAPTER 13

JO

"Ready?" I said.

"Not yet."

Evan took in short breaths, one after another, then let them all out. He did this several times and the smartass in me itched to make a joke. But Evan's eyes closed and his face grew so still, I doubted he would've heard me. It looked like meditation.

Then he dropped under the water.

I hit the "go" button on my cell phone and watched the seconds take off and add up. I tapped my feet, then gnawed my lower lip. One minute, two minutes, three...

With a spraying arc of water, Evan surfaced.

"Three minutes, forty-eight seconds," I said.

"Damn." Evan swam to the edge and rested his arms on the cement, breathing heavily. "That sucked."

"Sucked? I've never seen anyone in my life hold their breath almost four minutes."

"I was *over* four minutes the other night," he said. "Go again?"

"I don't know. It's freaking me out. Like I'm sitting here watching you drown."

"Maybe later?"

"We'll see."

I put my cell phone away and stripped down to my bathing suit, letting Evan watch me this time. I was in the water and in his arms moments later.

He smiled his beautiful smile, the one that made me feel like a gift that fell in his lap.

"Hi, Jo."

"Hi, Evan," I said and then we were kissing.

We kissed forever. I'd never known anything so goddamn good. Evan's mouth, his lips, his *tongue*... I'd never wanted a boy so badly. All my meaningless hookups were about control. Me calling the shots, deciding when, who, where and how much.

With Evan, I gave it all up. It was only about him and me.

We kissed and let our hands roam, the force of his desire pushing me backward through the water until I had nowhere left to go. I fall back in the shallow waters of the pool steps and he was over me. Grinding his hips against mine, kissing my neck, his stubble chafing the delicate skin beneath my ear. I pressed my hips up, feeling his erection through the loose material of his boxers. My hand reached down to stroke him. His hardness settled thick and long in my palm and I gave a moan.

Holy god...

"Jo," he said, groaning. His hand gripped my hip and held me tight to him. "God, I don't want to stop… But we should stop."

"You don't have to. I want this."

He kissed me again, long and slow and deep, but the urgency in his body waned. He moved to sit beside me on the stairs, holding my hand and running his fingers along my palm as we caught our breath.

"Why?" I asked. "What's wrong?"

"Nothing's wrong. It's not you, Jo. You're perfect. And I want you so bad I can hardly control myself."

"You don't have to control yourself." I leaned in to drag my lips along his neck. "I want to, Evan. I do."

"I do too. But I want it to be perfect. The first time should be perfect." He looked at me intently. "My first time, anyway."

"Oh," I said, comprehension dawning. "You've never…?"

His smile didn't quite touch his eyes. "One of the many perks of being the town mental case."

"Oh," I said again, turning to face forward. I didn't know what to say or do. Seconds slipped by as I tried to comprehend the enormity of what he'd told me.

"Is it a turnoff?" he asked, and I didn't miss the vulnerable edge in his voice. It snapped me out of my surprise.

"No, *no.* God, no. I'm sorry, I'm just a little bit overwhelmed."

"Because I'm a virgin?"

"*No,*" I insisted. "It's not that you are…but that you'd want to *not* be. With me."

Evan laughed with palpable relief, and took my face in his hands. "You're amazing, Jo. And beautiful and smart and sexy." He bent to kiss me, his mouth so warm and sweet on mine. "I want to spend the night with you. All night with you. And make it perfect."

"All right," I said, trying not to sound overeager. "When is this night of unbridled physical perfection going to happen?"

Evan didn't laugh, but kissed my jaw, my chin, my lips one last time, before resting his arms on either side of my thighs on the stairs, his legs floating out behind him.

"Well… I was thinking we could spend the night together after prom."

I stared down at him, not sure I'd heard right. "*Prom?*"

"Yeah. You know, the big dance in the gym, with a crappy DJ—?"

"I know what prom is, thank you," I said with a small laugh that faded quickly. "I just…hadn't thought of it."

The truth was I'd never been asked to a dance. I changed schools too often to secure a date. Or so I told myself as I spent the night of every Homecoming or Winter Formal alone, watching a bad horror movie.

Evan was looking up at me, his expression amused, but hopeful too.

He's probably never been to a dance, either.

A mini-fantasy played out in my mind: walking into the gym with Evan on my arm. He'd be in a suit or tux. Devastatingly handsome. All the girls would be kicking themselves that they never paid him any serious attention. Only laughed or whispered behind his back. They'd see exactly what they were missing when a slow song came on. It was the scarred-up new girl who got to press her body against his. They'd gape with regret to see how he looked at me. As if the rest of the world could blow up around him and he'd never notice, because all he saw was me.

I blinked to dissolve the reverie, tried to laugh it off. But a silly little thrill had sucked all the snark right out of me.

"You're serious?" I said. "I mean… I don't know. Should we?"

Evan grinned. "We should. We totally should. It's our senior year. Last chance."

I bit my lip. "I'm not one for dressing up…Do you really want to?"

"*Yes*, Jo." His smiled turned softer, his eyes warmer. "I want to." He took one of my hands, pressed the back of it to his lips. "Josephine Clark, will you go to prom with me?"

I looked down at him, no bullshit, no hiding behind a joke or a laugh. "I'd love to go to prom with you."

His smile was ridiculously adorable as he pulled me off the stairs and brought my hands up around this neck. "I knew you were going to say that." His hands skimmed up and down my back. "Ask me how.'

"It came to you in a dream," I said, laughing. "What am I thinking right now?"

Evan bent to kiss my shoulder, his teeth grazing my skin. "You're thinking prom is a long four days away."

"Mmmhmmm," I murmured. I slipped my arms down, around his waist, pulled him closer.

"And that's a long time to wait," he breathed, kissing my throat, his tongue flickering to taste my skin.

"Right so far," I breathed back.

Evan brushed his lips against my ear and whispered, "And now you're thinking…"

"Yes…"

"You want me to go down on you until you come so hard you're screaming."

The words made a breathless flush of heat surge through me. My mouth fell open against his cheek. "Am I?"

"Aren't you?" His breath was hot on my neck as he pressed me against the wall of the pool. His body gliding up then settling tight to mine.

"Josephine." He laid a kiss on my collarbone. "I want to make you feel so good."

I nodded, my voice lost in a rush of desire. Fierce. Strong. Stronger than I'd ever thought possible. Just the idea of his mouth between my thighs sent shivers skimming over my skin, down to my breasts and into my stomach. My nipples hardened, straining through the thin fabric of my suit.

Evan saw it happen and a gruff sound of want escaped his throat. His mouth trailed with a harder intent, biting kisses along my neck. Below the water, his hands brushed my waist then took hold of my hips. A little cry came out of my mouth as he lifted me out of the water to sit on the lip of the pool. I looked down at those clear blue eyes, soft and electric. His pulse trembled in the soft hollow under his jaw, but his voice was calm and low.

"I won't do anything you don't want me to," he said.

"I know you won't. I trust you. But you...really want to?"

Evan nodded. "More than anything."

Yeah, that about sums it up.

"All right. I've never done it before. I'm nervous as hell. Kiss me again."

Evan moved between my legs. My calves dragged through the water and hugged his sides. He craned up for a kiss, licking his lips. A flush of wet heat between my thighs as his hand cupped my jaw. His thumb on my chin, pressing down to open my mouth wide. Wider.

He hovered there, dangling on the moment, his breath warm and soft in my mouth. I'd never wanted a kiss so bad in my life. I leaned toward him and he brushed his lips over mine. Just a brush, nothing more, wanting me to want him.

Another heartbeat, another breath, then I couldn't take it anymore. My legs wrapped tight around Evan's waist, cinched hard like a knot. I pulled him to me, his mouth to mine. He gave me his tongue and I nearly came right then and there.

With my mouth held open, Evan kissed me in a way that I'd never known people could kiss. His tongue... God, it swept through my mouth, demanding and deep. He captured my lower lip in his teeth and sucked hard. Within moments, I found myself wanting to push his head between my legs and beg for his kiss there.

"Evan," I said, breathing hard against his lips. "Please."

His hands came up to cup my small breasts. They fit perfectly in his palms. He rolled the ball of his thumbs over my nipples, pressed up hard and wanting inside my suit. His fingers ran along the straps then peeled them down, his eyes eating up what he found beneath.

His head leaned and he laid a kiss over my heart. Then his mouth found one breast, sucking and nipping at the naked nipple.

Oh my God...

I pulled in air between my teeth at the sudden tingling thrill skimming over my skin. He moved his mouth to the other breast, licking and sucking until little sounds of want were spilling out of me. Nothing I could do to silence them. I didn't even try.

Evan released my nipple from his teeth and gave my mouth a last, lingering kiss before he drew away, his hands working my suit down my hips. I lifted enough so he could peel it all the way off. Then I watched him take me in. His stare unabashed as it took in my naked body.

Under his gaze, I waited for my old friends, shame and disgust, to come find me.

They didn't show. Only this glorious, eager need and only Evan so willing to satisfy it.

He parted my legs wider, slowly. He moved in, his head dipped. His mouth...

The pleasure was literally shocking. With the first flick of his tongue, I shuddered as if an electric current were ripping through me. My back arched, my hips pressed up into his mouth, his lips, his *tongue*. Wanting more, nothing but more. Evan groaned, the vibration of his voice adding another strata of sensation. He built me up, layer upon layer, raising me up toward some unknowable peak.

Without breaking his kiss, Evan wreathed his neck with my legs. I braced my hands on the pavement behind me, let my head fall back and gave myself up to him. My hips were undulating now, bucking against the hands that held me steady. He never broke contact but sucked and licked and kissed until I felt myself start to shatter.

I sat up, my hands threaded tight in his hair as he made me come on his tongue. Come on his mouth that didn't stop its perfect, skillful movements.

He only slowed, gently, gradually, until one last shuddering, pulsing shard ripped through me and then faded to a thrumming ache of pleasure.

"Oh God," I whispered, breathing hard, unclenching my fingers. "Oh my God, Evan…"

"Goddamn, you taste so good," he groaned. Shoulders heaving, he rested his forehead against my stomach, spent, as if I were the one who'd turned *him* inside out.

"The things you say…" I whispered. "Jesus, Evan, how did you learn to do that?"

He shook his head, his breath uneven, his face flushed and smiling wide. He moved away from the wall to run his hands up and down my thighs. "I just did what I thought you'd like. Did you like it?"

"You know I did. Mind reader."

Evan hauled me off the edge with a splash, and wrapped his arms around me. I could feel his erection straining against his boxers.

"Pay no attention to that," he said, laughing sheepishly. "Comes with the territory."

"Yeah, well… Do you want me to take care of it? I mean, it's only fair. I owe you—"

"No." His smile faded. "I didn't do it so I could get something in exchange. You don't *owe* me anything. That's not how this works."

"How what works?" I asked in a small voice.

"Us."

"This is us?" I felt shy, unsure and completely exposed. Even more than when he had his face between my legs.

"Yes, Jo," Evan said. "This is us."

I felt something break open in me. I wanted to cry. I laughed instead and threw my arms around his neck, driving us both under the water. I kissed him, tasted both myself and his own sweetness on my lips before the chlorine water washed it away.

CHAPTER 14

JO

The hallways were lined with colorful streamers. Posters with balloons pinned to every corner screamed the date and time of *Island Dreams,* Wilson High's senior prom.

The prom committee had set up a folding table and a lockbox to sell tickets between classes. June Taylor, president of the prom committee and Annie Jackson, captain of the cheerleading team, chatted and laughed at the table, exchanging cash for "passports to island paradise."

"Looks like a Party City threw up in here," I muttered. I looked up at Evan beside me. "You ready?"

"I'm afraid when the big night comes they'll dump a bucket of pig's blood on me."

"If they do, I'll burn this place to the ground."

Evan laughed, thinking I was kidding, but I wasn't. I took his hand and laced my fingers with his, gave it a squeeze. "Let's do this."

Annie and June gaped as we walked up to the table hand-in-hand.

"Two passports to paradise," Evan said with a chuckle at the silly theme. He glanced down at me with a suggestive look and muttered under his breath. "They got the paradise part right."

I groaned and rolled my eyes as a flush crept up my neck.

"Um…sure." Annie took out a certificate and I watched with smug satisfaction as she wrote out *Evan Salinger and Josephine Clark.* She handed it over, staring at Evan. Instead of walking hunched over, bracing himself for derision, he now carried himself at full height. His confidence was gorgeous. And those prom committee girls knew it.

June unabashedly gawked at my boyfriend. "Seventy-five dollars, please."

My smug smile collapsed. I watched Evan pull out his beat-up old wallet and hand over the money. Money he'd need after graduation, so he could escape Planerville. He paid for the tickets with a grin and wink but I suddenly felt sick.

"I should pay you for my half," I said when we turned away from the table, leaving June and Annie to whisper behind our backs.

Evan frowned. "Why? I got this."

"No, I know. It just…seems like a lot."

The last thing I wanted to do was make him self-conscious about something he was obviously proud to do. I vowed I'd make it up some other way.

Because he needs that money. Because he's leaving. Evan is leaving…

The bell rang and Evan kissed my cheek. "You're worth it. Every penny and more."

After second bell, Marnie and Adam cornered me around my locker.

I glanced at them sideways. "Something on your mind?"

"You could say that." Marnie crossed her arms. "You and Evan Salinger."

Adam chimed in. "June Taylor is blabbing to everyone how you guys bought prom tickets this morning. *Prom tickets.* Since when are you and Evan this much of a thing?"

"Since none of your business," I said a little more sharply than I'd intended. "And I've got a great idea for an editorial for the next *Mo Vay Goo*: the hypocrisy of the lower social strata of high school. You can call it

'Punching Down.'"

"Yeah, okay girl, we get it," Adam said. "We were bitches about associating with Evan. But we've come in peace and with like, a million questions."

I couldn't help but smile. "Sorry, I don't kiss and tell. No matter what Matt King might say."

Marnie's kohl-lined eyes widened. "Oh my god, did you kiss Evan Salinger? What's it like? Was it totally weird?"

"Seriously? That's a ridiculous question and you know it," I said. But just to stick it to them a little harder, I added, "He's an amazing kisser. I get wet just thinking about it."

That did it. They gaped like doors with busted hinges.

"Are you guys like boyfriend and girlfriend now?" Marnie asked.

I started to say hell yes, when it hit me again. Evan was leaving town after graduation. Were we really boyfriend and girlfriend? After all the incredible moments we'd shared, and the talks we'd had, and the *us* that he'd been so insistent on...

I'd bared my soul to him. We couldn't be a fling. It was impossible. But he hadn't said a word about what would happen next.

Marnie and Adam were waiting for an answer. I shrugged it off. "We're just hanging out. Whatever. It's no big deal. I gotta get to class. See you guys later."

I practically ran away. I told myself to chill, all the while a voice in my head helpfully pointed out, again and again: *only ten days left.*

Ten days. And because the old walls and thick armor had only been down for a little while, it was easy for me to resurrect and retreat behind them.

The entire time I was at the strip mall after school, my rational mind told me I was being stupid. But my subconscious-self warned I had to be careful or I was going to be smashed to pieces.

At the sporting goods store and I spent $85 of *my* saved up money on a waterproof watch with a timer function. I waited with mounting anxiety until nine o'clock rolled around, then I threw my purchase in my bag and rode to the pool.

The pool area looked empty and for a horrible moment I thought Evan wasn't there. But no, he sat on a lounger totally dry. He scrambled to his feet when he saw me, a beautiful, open smile broke out over his face.

"Hi, Jo."

I took the watch out of my bag and put it in his hands.

"What's this?"

"What's it look like?" I said, crossing my arms. "It's a waterproof watch. So you can time yourself underwater."

He turned the box over in his hand, and tried to hand it back to me. "Jo, I can't take this. It's too much."

"Exactly," I said. "And the seventy-five bucks you paid for the prom tickets is too much. Not to mention a tux and dinner or whatever." I sniffed and flapped my hand at the box. "You need a watch. So take it. And we're even."

"Even?" Evan said quietly. "Jo, what are you doing?"

"I'm being a bitch. What do you think I'm doing? It's the only thing I know how to do. I know we're supposed to be honest with each other, but if you tell me you're still leaving after graduation, then it's a little *too much* honesty. So don't say it, okay?" My voice started to crack and tears flooded my eyes. "Take the watch, but don't say anything. Not a damn word."

Evan set the watch down on a lounger, a tiny smile playing over his lips. "Can I say something *now*?"

"No," I sniffed. "And don't get cute with me. I'm scared shitless."

He moved to put his hands on my elbows and he wasn't smiling anymore. "Me too. Because I want to be with you all the time. Every fucking minute. When we're apart, all I do is think about you and the *next* time we're going to be together. Do you do that too? You think about me when were apart, Jo?"

I nodded, unable to look at him. "Yes. I can't stop and it's so scary."

He moved closer, and I could feel his body humming with tension.

"So let's not. Let's not be apart. Let's keep going after graduation."

Now I raised my teary eyes to look at him. "To the Grand Canyon?"

"Yeah. Let's go."

"Really? You mean it? You have to fucking mean it, Evan, because I can't take it if you don't."

"I can't take it if you say no," he said. "I'll stay with you. Or go wherever you want." He pulled me to him, his arms wrapping around me. "I don't want to stop feeling like this."

"Neither do I."

His mouth found mine and we kissed. We laughed through the kiss and then I cried through it. Tears streaming down my cheeks until he kissed them away. We lay down on a lounger, him on his back and me curled up beside him. We kissed more, talked and made plans while the stars wheeled above us.

"You really want that with me?" I asked.

Evan grinned. "It's the only way I'm going to keep that watch."

I laughed and felt a tidal wave of joy drowning me as Evan raised both hands and brushed the long, dark locks from my scarred face. I held still, letting him see me.

"You're so beautiful," he whispered, and kissed me long and hard and deep. I sighed into his mouth, leaned into his body, fell into him. I wasn't beautiful, but it was nice to hear.

"I know you don't believe me," Evan said, his words echoing my thoughts with uncanny precision. "But you don't have to believe it for it to be true."

His fingertips moved soft and warm across the lightning crack that marred my cheek. "The Grand Canyon was carved by a river. It sliced through the rock, revealing layer upon layer of beauty. Beauty that couldn't be seen until the earth was cut open. One little sliver of water…"

"Evan…"

"One little sliver." He traced the ragged seam down to my chin. "The majesty of the Canyon is that depth. All that beauty lay buried for years until the river cut it open. Then all was revealed."

I felt tears sting my eyes and pressed my cheek into his hand. "Don't," I whispered.

Evan snuggled me closer. He didn't force it. Years of feeling ugly couldn't be erased with a few poetic similes, but now we had time. We had all the time in the world, and I knew someday I would believe him.

Evan walked me to the front door of my house like the gentleman he was. I was less than ladylike. I wanted to drag him inside and spend the night celebrating our future.

"Wait here." I ran up to my room to grab his blue-and-black plaid flannel shirt, still in my possession. Back on the porch, I handed it over.

"My shirt. I forgot you had it."

"It's *my* shirt. You need to go home tonight and sleep in it. I made the mistake of washing it and now it doesn't smell like you anymore."

He turned the shirt over and over in his hand, laughing and shaking his head.

"And I want it back first thing in the morning. You read me?"

"Yeah I read you." Evan pulled me in for a deep kiss that left me weak.

When he'd gone, leaving me with the taste of him on my lips and the feeling of safety and security wrapped around me, I went up to my room. I sat at the desk and finished the poem for Ms. P.

It turned out perfectly. It was going to be an A+. Thanks to Evan, I knew what love was. This time it wasn't grayed out and faded like an old memory. It was fresh and new.

And I stupidly thought I would feel this way forever.

Chapter 15

EVAN

For once the breakfast table scraping didn't bother me. My thoughts were too full of Josephine to let anything bother me.

Merle and Shane talked about prom. They both had managed to secure dates. One of the older jocks had a cousin he hooked up with Merle. Shane asked mousy Kristi Taylor to go with him. She was a shy little thing, desperate for attention. More desperate than Shane. I guessed going to prom together was more of an alliance than anything romantic, but it didn't stop me from feeling sorry for her. Then again, maybe Shane was a different guy around other people. Maybe he only showed me his bad side.

It was a generous thought, but I was in a generous mood because of Jo. Jo Clark was going to prom with me. Then I was going to make love to her and after graduation, she was coming with me to the Grand Canyon. We were going home.

So much goodness in my life. I was almost afraid to think about it. This joy was a piece of blown glass—handling it too roughly meant it could shatter. I tried to concentrate on my food, but it was hard to eat when I couldn't stop smiling.

"You'll need to go to the department store and pick out tuxedos," Norma was saying to my brothers. She turned to me. "And you, Evan? Are you attending the dance?"

"Yeah, I am."

The whole table froze. Even the rustling behind Harris's newspaper stopped. I could tell he was listening from behind the baseball scores and classifieds.

Shane shattered the silence with a barrage of questions. "You *are*? With who? That girl? With the scar?"

"*Yes*," I said, meeting his gaze, daring him to say more. He shut up, but I saw malicious thoughts in his eyes as he pondered this new development. I turned to Norma. "Her name's Jo and we've been seeing each other for a few weeks now…"

"Jo-Jo-Joker," Merle said and chuffed laughter.

My hand gripped the edge of the table. "Don't call her that."

Norma paid them no mind. "Is that so?" She spooned brown sugar over her oatmeal. Harris coughed behind his paper. "I haven't heard of a Jo before. Is she new?"

"She's the school slut," Shane offered.

"Watch it," I said, knocking over my empty juice glass. "Don't fucking say that again."

Shane's mouth gaped and Garrett snickered. "You said a bad word." My little brother's smile beamed across the table. Apparently he forgot he was mad at me for being cold to him these last few weeks.

Shane looked at Norma for back-up but she only pursed her lips and murmured, "Language, please."

I righted my juice glass. I'd banked too much happiness to let Shane get to me as badly as he usually did. "She's my girlfriend so watch your smart mouth."

Girlfriend was a balloon of joy rising up from chest. In a nanosecond I went from scowling at Shane to smiling like an idiot.

"She's my girlfriend," I said, taking the word out for another spin. Amazing the second time, too.

Shane snorted. "Some girlfriend. Has a scar up half her face."

"So?" I snapped.

Shane curled a lip. "You couldn't do better than the slut with the scarred-up face?" He elbowed Merle who was busy shoveling in his oatmeal and spilling glops down the front of his shirt.

I ground my teeth, fighting for calm, then Norma's voice cut across the breakfast table like a knife.

"Go and get yourself a tuxedo too, Evan."

Another tableau of frozen faces around the table, including mine this time. Norma arched an eyebrow, spreading butter on toast as she spoke. "Today after school. I'll give you my credit card and you take it to the department store in Halston."

I gaped, then glanced at Harris. "I'm supposed to work at the shop."

Norma dabbed her mouth with a napkin. "I'll not have any one of you look shabby on a night such as this. What color is this *Jo's* dress?"

It took me a moment, but I found my voice. "I don't know. She wants to surprise me."

"Then go with a black tux. And her corsage should be white. It will match nicely with any color."

I could only stare, a strange warmth in my chest I hadn't felt in years, if ever. "All right," I said faintly.

I was conscious of Shane's attention on me, watching me through narrowed eyes. The miserable shit. The more happiness I showed, the more he'd work to take it away from me or turn it rotten. I vowed nothing would ruin prom night. None of Shane's petty evil would touch Jo.

I shot him a warning look as I said to Norma, "Thank you."

Norma sniffed. "Dishes, boys."

Which meant breakfast was over. As we all cleared our plates, I felt the daggers of Shane's gaze in my back.

"Well, look who gets to the go the ball," he sneered at the kitchen sink. "Our own Cinderella. Only instead of a princess waiting for you, you have a scarred up slut—"

I choked off Shane's words simply by towering over him, cornering him against the cabinets. "You want to say that again?" I asked, deadly casual. "Go ahead, Shane. Say it again."

"Or you'll what?" Shane said, staring at me through wide eyes. "You'll break my face like you did Jared? You don't think that's not going to bite you in the ass, Freakshow? His parents are pissed. They're going to *sue,* you know. They'll press charges."

"Let them," I said,

Merle slipped in between us. He pushed me back and looked about ready to clock me but Shane waved him off. He straightened his shirt over his bony, caved-in chest, and laughed darkly.

"Go ahead, Freakshow. Enjoy your little prom fantasy with Matt King's leftovers while you can."

He shuffled off, leaning heavily on his cane, Merle following behind like he was put on this earth to do nothing but be Shane's muscle. Garrett appeared at my heels.

"Hey, Evan," he said in a small voice. "I'm happy you're going to the big dance."

I should've told him to mind his own business. To protect him. But he was staring at me, his little face open and sweet, and I knelt down and hugged him.

"Thanks, buddy, I'm sorry I've been such an ass to you lately. I just want you to be safe."

He laughed at 'ass.' "Safe from what?"

"Shane. And Merle. I don't want them pissed at you for being nice to me."

He looked at me like I was crazy. "You're my brother. Of course, I'm going to be nice to you."

He patted me on top of my head and skipped out of the pantry. Shane's dirty words about Jo faded out, and I sort of felt like skipping too. Or flying.

Or floating on water.

CHAPTER 16

JO

Prom Night arrived and I was a nervous wreck. I laid out my dress on the bed and stared at it, my fingernail tapping my front teeth. I bought it at a department store at the mall in Halston, not from a thrift store like I had planned. It cost me $150, which is way more than I was comfortable spending out of my travel fund.

Our travel fund, I amended silently, and had to clap a hand over my mouth to hold back a sob. Or maybe it was uncontrollable laughter bubbling up. For the first time since my mother died, I felt I was moving toward something instead of being hurdled into a black unknown.

Evan.

God, how had he happened to me?

I studied the dress and let go of worrying about how much it cost. I wanted to be beautiful for him.

I showered. Shaved everywhere. I even put perfumed lotion all over my skin, making me smell like lilacs. I had new black lace panties and matching bra, bought on sale at Victoria's Secret. I hesitated after I put them on, looking at my reflection. Black made my pale skin more pale, but the underwear set was the sexiest thing I owned. I wanted to be that for him too. I trailed my fingers between my breasts, touching the edge of the black lace. I hoped Evan liked it, but if he didn't…

Then he can tear it off me.

My eyes fell shut as both the thought and its visual shot through me, leaving me weak. I inhaled sharply.

"Focus, Josephine. Focus."

I braided my hair loosely and pulled it over my left shoulder, letting a few tendrils curl down to conceal the scar. I put on more makeup than I usually did, but with more finesse than the raccoon look I had going most days. I made it lighter and prettier, trying to bring out the green in my eyes. A little blush for color, a little lip gloss Evan would kiss off immediately.

I could not stop smiling.

Finally, I slipped on the dress, struggling to pull up the zipper tab myself. The dress was black and slinky without being witchy or slutty. The skirt fell to my ankles in lacy waves and the bodice had black lace embellishment at the neckline. It didn't look too much like a prom dress, but it looked right for me. I studied myself in the mirror when I had everything put together, and I liked what I saw.

Gerry was still gone. I had no one to take pictures, no parents waiting for me at the bottom of the stairs. Then I remembered they would take pictures at the school, probably with us in front of some sort of cheesy, palm tree backdrop. But at least we'd have souvenirs. Souvenirs were also cheesy and yet, I loved it. I couldn't wait for Evan to drive up. We had dinner reservations at a restaurant in Halston. Then the dance. And then back here…

I turned my attention to my bedroom, my stomach fluttering at what was going to transpire here tonight. I'd dug up as many candles as I could find around the house and purchased one of the scented kind during my shopping spree. I arranged them around the bed and on the bedside table. I'd gotten some guy to buy me a bottle of wine outside a liquor store, but Gerry had luckily left a few beers in the fridge. I'd give them to Evan in case he didn't want to drink wine. He was a guy after all.

Everything was set. I knew in the deepest part of me that it was going to be everything I'd ever hoped. We'd come back here tonight. The zipper on the back of my dress, which had been such a struggle to pull up—in Evan's fingers it would glide down in one smooth motion. We'd make the night perfect for our first time. He was a virgin, but so was I. I decided I was. Nothing came before tonight. No one mattered before Evan.

Taking a deep breath, I smoothed my dress and went downstairs. I left my defensive bullshit behind. I couldn't wait to see him and I let myself be giddy about it. I let myself be happy.

Evan was going to pick me up at six. I glanced at the clock. Quarter till. I sat in the living room to wait, flicking on the TV. The news said a storm was set to hit tonight. A big one. As the clock rolled over to 6:00, I rolled my lip, tasting the gloss.

I waited.

At 6:10, I thought about texting Evan, then changed my mind. Ten minutes wasn't a big deal.

At 6:20, we were in danger of losing the reservation Evan made for us in Halston. I sent him a text and tried to infuse each keystroke with as much casualness as I possibly could.

On your way?

No answer.

At 6:30, I texted him again.

Are you okay? Where are you?

No answer.

I called him and it went straight to voicemail.

At 6:45, the fear he really wasn't coming took root and refused to let go.

I should've known, I told myself, feeling it all unravel around me. *I shouldn't have let him in. I should've been more careful. I'm such a fucking idiot.*

But another more insidious truth wound its way between my paranoia and defensiveness. It seeped into the cracks of my walls and broke them apart. Evan wasn't standing me up. He wouldn't do that. He would *never* do that. Something was wrong. Very wrong.

I called him again. Getting no answer, I threw my phone into a little clutch purse and headed out. I hiked up my dress around my knees so I could mount my bicycle and tore off down the street. A fierce wind ripped at my elegant braid and made my eyes water. The sky was yellow and gray, with fat rain clouds rolling in. My heart was thundering in my chest, the fear fueling my furious pedaling, racing ahead of the storm.

A block from the Salinger's house, I saw the red-and-blue lights of the police car and the brighter blood-red lights of the ambulance. I coasted up to the front of the house just as the first light raindrops began to fall.

Chaos.

Or maybe just my panicked vision watching my night with Evan fall apart around me. They were putting a little boy onto a stretcher and his face was covered with blood. A heavyset lady—Mrs. Salinger—was holding the boy's hand and crying inconsolably. Merle and Shane Salinger were standing off to the side, both wide-eyed, their faces filled with panic. I got the impression from them immediately: two people who had started a small campfire and then watched helplessly as it roared into a giant inferno.

Evan was nowhere to be seen.

But I knew where he was. I wheeled my bike around hoping no one had seen me. Faintly over my shoulder, I heard the word "Funtown" and Norma Salinger's hard-edged voice saying Evan swam at night.

Now it was a matter of time. I had to get to Evan first. Race the storm, get to him first. That's all that mattered.

CHAPTER 17

EVAN

An Hour Earlier

I studied myself in the hall bathroom mirror. Norma had spared no expense, allowing me to rent a fine black tuxedo, white dress shirt, black cummerbund and bowtie. No less expensive or classy as Shane's or Merle's.

When I went downstairs at five to six, Norma was snapping pictures of my brothers. They had a limo waiting out front to take them to pick up their dates. Norma fussed over them, smoothing down their lapels and straightening their bowties. Shane looked like an overdressed scarecrow and Merle's bulk strained the shoulder seams of his tuxedo jacket. I kept my mouth shut, my mood too good to waste on ill will. I had Josephine waiting for me. I had tonight with her. I'd have *all night* with her.

I gave myself a shake and ducked into the hallway to wait until the hot flash of lust and desire that ripped through me subsided.

When Norma saw me, she gave a small gasp. Her hand flew up toward her chest, rested a moment against her heart. Then she cleared her throat and her hand dropped, straightening her skirt. She smiled as she approached me and reached to smooth my lapels, the same way she had for my brothers. The small, maternal gesture made my heart full. She smelled like the pot-roast she was cooking for tomorrow night. Her hard, dark eyes were softer as she looked at me.

"You look quite nice," she said softly.

"Thanks, Ma." I never called her that. That night I felt like I could.

"Yes. Well." Norma was intent on brushing invisible lint from my suit. "Have you a corsage for Josephine?"

"Oh shit. I forgot."

"You said a bad word," Garrett said. I smiled down at him, ruffled his hair.

Norma went to the kitchen, and came back with a plastic container. Inside was a corsage made of three small white flowers on a bed of delicate green.

"I don't believe in ruining the girl's dress with pins on the bodice," Norma said stiffly, putting the box in my hand. "This goes on her wrist. Do you see?"

"Yes," I said, my voice threatening to close on me. "I see."

"Go on, then. Don't keep her waiting. All of you." She waved her hand. "Have fun. Don't stay out too late and don't get into trouble. And watch the weather. See that you don't get rained on."

All this time, Merle and Shane had been staring in slack-jawed dismay at the exchange between their mother and me. Now they headed for the front door. I made to follow them, then stopped and went back to Norma.

I was a good head taller than she was, but her bearing had always made her seem like a giant. We'd all spent our childhood—Garrett too—waiting for her precious affection, like baby birds waiting to be fed by a stingy mother. What she did for me tonight was almost unprecedented. I put my hands on her shoulders and bent to kiss her cheek.

"Thanks, Ma," I said softly. "For everything."

A wavering smile flickered over her lips. She waved me away. "You're going to be late."

I was already late. I was supposed to get Jo at six o'clock. I pulled out my phone to text her saying I was on my way. Garrett skipped at my heels behind me.

Outside, the sky was a strange yellow color with fingers of dark clouds clawing across it. A sleek black limo was parked at the curb so I was surprised to see and Shane and Merle standing by my truck.

I stopped halfway through my text as a black, ugly feeling took root in my gut.

"You want something?" I said warily.

A sick smile stretched over Shane's face, looking as proper there as on a corpse. "I don't want to fight anymore. I feel awful for what I did to your note. You remember your note?"

"I remember," I said, the old pain flaring and then fading. "Forget it."

"I wish I could," Shane said. "I just feel so *burnt* up about it. It was the only tie you had to your real family. The people who abandoned and dumped you at the fire station."

I breathed carefully, one hand clenched around my cell phone, the other around the plastic box with Jo's corsage. The cover bent under the pressure. "Leave it alone, Shane."

"No, really. I feel terrible for burning up that note. Especially since it was the only thing you had to remind you that you're not, and never will be, a genuine part of *this* family."

My vision was turning a hazy red. Garrett was at my heels like a little puppy, asking what was going on in a high, piping voice. For his sake, and for Jo's, I fought for calm.

"But good news!" Shane declared. "I found *another* note! It was the strangest thing. I was looking around the house for a gift to make up for the horrible thing I did, and what do you know? I found this!" Shane held out a crumpled piece of paper folded in half. "Go on, take it. It's yours."

Garrett frowned. "What is it?"

Shane ignored him. "Go on," he said to me. "Take it."

I stared, riveted.

No. Don't fucking do it. It's a lie and you know it.

I broke my gaze away and tried to move past them, rolling my eyes. Merle put his hand on my chest and shoved me back. "Take it," he said.

Shane wagged the paper. "It's a miracle I found another one. I mean, what are the odds?"

"Impossible," I answered, my heart a sledgehammer. I fought to calm my breath. "Look Shane, let's be cool for one night, okay? Go to the prom. Have a good time. I'll see y—"

"That's exactly what I want. For you to have best night. Which is why I'm giving this to you now."

Merle eyed me darkly. Things would get ugly quick if I didn't play along. Plus, I was already late for Jo. I held out my hand to Shane even though every instinct told me not to. Shane's eyes widened in a kind of nervous anticipation and once I had the note, he inched a step closer to Merle.

"Evan, don't," Garret whimpered.

I opened the paper with trembling hands. The words were written in a boy's messy scrawl. *Please take the freak off our hands. PLEASE.*

"What is it?" Garrett asked, his voice sounding tiny and distant.

"Uh oh." Shane pouted. "Turns out the note wasn't too good after all. I may have forgotten to mention that part. Turns out, your real parents thought you were just as strange and freakish as we do. And did you notice, there? Two *pleases*."

My vision fogged up red as a horrific glut of pain and rage coiled around my chest, flooding me with the burning fire. I fought not to implode. I sucked in deep breaths, the note in my hand crumpled in a tight fist.

It's bullshit. Shrug it off. For Jo. Don't ruin this for Jo.

I chucked the note at Shane's dress shoes. It took every bit of willpower to keep from breaking him in half. I headed toward my truck. I couldn't drive, not yet, but I could sit in the cab alone and pull my shit together. I felt dizzy, my vision still blurred and my blood on fire.

"What? That's it?" Shane cried with mounting fury. "Don't you fucking walk away from me!"

His cane snaked out and hit me in the shins, tripping me up. I fell flat, yanking the cane out of Shane's weak hands. First my chin scraped on the gravelly drive, then my chest, scuffing my white dress shirt with dust and oil. The corsage fell out of my hand and landed a foot away.

"Isn't that fucking precious," Shane said, his voice shaky. "But a *white* flower for that slut you're taking to the dance? Seems inappropriate if you ask me."

I watched as Merle's foot came down on the plastic box, crushing it easily, destroying the delicate flower beneath. Garrett, somewhere behind me, gave a little cry.

"There you go," Shane said, as Merle lifted his boot. "Dirty and used.

That's more like her, I think—"

I flew off the ground as if propelled by a jet engine. Shane's sentence died as my hands circled his throat. He let out a howl as I swung him around and slammed him against the side of my truck. He was lighter than air and his head smacked against the cab with a satisfying *thunk.*

"Shut the fuck up!" I screamed. "Just shut your goddamn mouth, you miserable piece of shit!" I squeezed my hands and Shane clawed feebly at them, his eyes bulging. "You talk about her like that again and I'll kill you. Do you hear me? I will fucking *kill* you!"

Shane couldn't speak, and I saw his fear-stricken eyes dart to something behind me. A split second later, heavy hands clamped down on my shoulders. Merle wrenched me from Shane and hurled me to the ground. My back scraped against the pavement and my head hit down hard. But the pain felt distant. Even the fire burning in my gut was muted.

No more! No more! No more!

The thought echoed in my head. No more fighting. End it tonight. The bullying, the unthinking hatred—I'd had enough.

No more.

But Jo was waiting. She was more important than this. I had to get to her. It wasn't too late. I could salvage the night.

I started to get to my feet and Merle's foot planted in my chest, shoving me back. I grabbed his leg and twisted it, rolling to my feet at same time. He was right there ready with a left hook to my cheek. Pain exploded all up the side of my face but I ducked his second blow and drove my fist into his gut. It felt like hitting a slab of meat. I followed it up with another. He grunted and staggered backwards, and the battle hit a short lull, like the quiet in the eye of the storm.

"No more," I told Shane.

His eyes were wild as he pointed at me with a bony finger. "I hate you," he said, his voice shaking and tears welling in his bulging eyes.

"Why? Why, you fucking bastard?" I cried, the fake note and Jo's ruined corsage lying at my feet. "Why don't you just leave me alone?"

"That's what I want to ask *you* every morning of my life," Shane cried. "I wake up wanting to ask why the hell you're here. Why don't you just go? You don't belong here and you never have!"

"I'm leaving. After graduation you'll never see me again."

"No." Behind me, Garrett gave a little cry.

Shane turned his wild eyes to him. "You shut up! You always loved him more than us. Always."

"Leave him alone." I moved to stand between Garret and Shane. Merle stood near, rocking from side to side, itching for more fight.

"No, *you* leave. Leave all of us alone." Shane was working himself up into a fury. "You don't deserve the business. You don't deserve any of what we've given you. That tuxedo and the flower and Ma looking at you like you're not some freak when you are. You fucking *are*."

The red haze was back in my eyes. My stomach burned as if I'd swallowed acid. My phone chirped a text—probably Jo asking me where I was, worried I was standing her up. I sucked in breath after deep breath.

"I'm leaving," I said again. "A few more days..."

"Go now," Shane screamed. "I don't want to see your face ever again. Go now and take that scarred up slut with—"

Like a lit match on gasoline I blew. The years of pent-up anger and pain burst free and I fought for Jo. Fought for the love of this girl who'd seen past the lies and rumors surrounding me. The *truth*. Jo learned the truth about me and still she stayed.

I flew at Shane again, only this time Merle was ready for me. Like the linebacker he was, he tackled me to the ground. I went down hard and his hands went for my throat, choking me as he slammed the back of my head against the pavement.

Shane circled us like a caged beast, shrieking and inciting Merle to greater violence. Garrett threw himself at Merle's back and began pummeling him with his little fists until Shane hooked the little boy about the throat with his recovered cane and yanked him off.

I saw Garrett fall to the ground, coughing and crying. Rage filled me again, a second dose of gasoline to the fire. Merle's hands squeezed harder and I fought for my life. Starbursts in my vision. My lungs screaming for air. The crushing grip at my throat. I pummeled Merle's face, punched and writhed in more and more frantic attempts to gain freedom. Over and over, my feet kicked the empty air...

Until the air wasn't empty.

My foot struck something hard. Somewhere between the red haze and my choking gasps, I felt flesh give and bones crunch. And then a sound I would never forget. A little yelp, like a wounded dog. From somewhere behind Merle's great bulk, I heard Garrett strike the ground.

Everything stopped. Silence. Merle's hands on my throat loosened as he turned to look behind him. I hauled myself out from under him, to my hands and knees, sucking in great gulps of air.

Garrett lay on his back in the driveway. Blood streamed from his crushed nose to coat his mouth and chin and throat. His eyes were partially open and rolled back in his head, eyelids fluttering. His little body twitched as if a current of electricity were running through it. Horror like I had never known in my entire life doused the fiery rage, making me numb. Beyond numb. Icy cold with dread.

"Garrett…" I crawled toward him.

Shane turned to me. "You did this. You did this to him!" He looked behind me. "It's Evan's fault, Ma. Evan's fault!"

Norma pushed past us and stopped cold at the sight of Garrett. The streetlights came on, now Garrett lay in a pool of yellow light, blood still flowing maroon on his face. So much blood. Too much.

"My boy…" Norma knelt beside Garrett, her hands shaking as they moved to touch him and then pulling back. "What is this…?"

"It was Evan," Shane cried. "He freaked out. He had one of his fits and just went berserk. He attacked all of us: me, Merle and even Garrett!"

I shook my head, staggering back on watery legs. I wanted to go to Garrett, to put him back together. Put the blood back in his nose… Oh, Christ, his nose…

"You did this!" Shane shrieked. Neighbors were emerging from their houses; in my peripheral, I could see dark shapes coming out on porches and walking down driveways.

"You're a freak," Shane cried. "You're a crazy nutjob." He spun to Norma. "And I warned you! I warned you but you never listened."

"Someone call 9-1-1! *Now!*" Norma's command cut through Shane's rant and tore the night air into ribbons. She cradled Garrett's trembling little body to her, his blood staining her dress, his body hitching in a way that scared me to the marrow of my bones.

"Someone call an ambulance!" called a voice from the crowd.

"Did you hear what he did?"

"He attacked that little boy."

Everything was closing in. I was in a whirlpool. A black hole sucking everything in: all the pain and fear, the shocked expressions, Garrett's limp and bloody body, everyone and everything. All of Planerville falling toward me. I staggered backward under the impossible weight.

Garrett. I wanted to fall at his feet and wait for the sirens. Wait for the rough, grabbing hands to haul me to my feet. The dark of a car that would take me away and I'd never see Jo again…

The night's plans were blown apart and scattered like ashes of the dead. A different future from the one I sought with her was ordering itself around me. I had to find Jo and tell her to not be afraid. To hold on and wait for me. Wait for us.

I had to tell her goodbye.

"Garrett. I'm so sorry," I whispered.

Then I ran.

CHAPTER 18

JO

I pedaled as fast as I could to the pool, but police cars were already parked at Funtown's front gates. Blue-and-red lights flashed and sirens in the distance told me more cops were on the way. I circled to the park's northeast corner, tossed my bike to the ground and scaled the fence. Climbing over, my dress snagged and tore on the chain link. Another piece of what should have been a perfect night ripping away.

The sky looked bruised, darkening into green-blue. The wind howled. The storm the forecasters said was coming had arrived. The rain that had been a soft patter was becoming heavier.

Evan stood at the pool's edge, his back to me, looking down into the water. In the park's lights I could see his tuxedo was scuffed and blood matted at the back of his neck.

"Evan!" I screamed against the howling winds, running to his side. He turned slowly, and I gasped to see his face, his beautiful face, swollen and bloody.

For a moment, his eyes looked through me, as if he didn't recognize me. Then filled with tears. In his hand was the crushed and dirty remains of a white flower.

"I'm so sorry," he whispered. "I did this. I ruined everything and you… God, you look so beautiful."

"Evan, what happened?" I felt panic welling up in me, yet Evan seemed so calm. Defeated. I clutched his arms. "What happened? Tell me what's going on. I saw an ambulance at your house, they said—"

"Garrett. I hurt him bad. It was an accident but it was still my fault." Evan's gaze flicked over my shoulder and then back to me. He took my face in his hands, holding me gently as the wind howled. "I have to go now."

My heart cracked in two. The clang of gates and a thunder of footsteps behind me.

"Jo, I have to go with them. But I'll find you. I promise. I'll find you and I will come back to you."

I shook my head, not understanding. Not wanting to understand or even hear. Then the police surrounded us. Evan was wrenched away from me and pushed to the ground. One cop pressing his knee between his shoulder blades as he handcuffed Evan's hands behind him.

They were taking him away. The truth slapped my face and I screamed, "Leave him alone!"

I flew at the two officers leading Evan away. Rough hands grabbed my arms and hauled me back. It was pouring now, falling in thick sheets.

As he was marched away, Evan looked back over his shoulder at me. Through his grief-stricken expression, he smiled. So sad, so full of love, and so full of what might have been.

Then he was gone

Police surrounded me, barking questions until they realized I was just a bystander. His prom date. His hysterical girlfriend.

"Evan would never have hurt him on purpose! It was all a mistake! A lie! Please..."

But they weren't listening. They were hearing me but not listening.

"For years," I cried, tears streaming, "they bullied him. I can testify…I saw his bruises…I can tell you the truth."

They just smiled pityingly at me. One cop offered me a blanket. Another offered a ride home. I stared, no more words left. I walked home, my bike forgotten. The rain kept coming down. The wind tore at my ruined dress and pulled the last weaves of my braid apart. Lightning screamed across the sky.

Yes! I screamed back.

The storm raged for me, shattering the sky and weeping for Evan.

I stumbled into my house, sodden and shivering, and went up to my room. On my desk lay the love poem I'd been assigned by Ms. P, ready to be turned in.

My eyes scanned the page and found a line at random.

He touches me and I think
This is what hope feels like

Rainwater dripped from my hair onto the page, blurring the blue ink. I took the poem and tore it in half. Then again. Again. I ripped it to shreds and then brushed the scraps away. I drew out a new sheet of paper and began to write.

In the days following Evan's arrest I fought as hard as I could for him. I made statements, spoke to Evan's public defender. But it was too late, and I was too weak.

The prosecution had the records from Woodside. They had the testimony of Evan's brothers. They had the grief of a mother who saw nothing but her son's broken face, and nothing from the little boy who hadn't woken up to say what happened.

Harris Salinger claimed Evan had been cold and distant to Garrett over the last few weeks, uncharacteristically so. Shane spoke in great detail about Evan trying to choke him. Him, a frail, disabled boy, all the while screaming threats, "I will fucking kill you!" And then Jared Piltcher's family filed their own lawsuit for assault.

It piled on top of Evan, accusation after accusation, and I could do nothing to stop it.

Evan waited out his trial in county jail. While he was in custody, they wouldn't let me see him or call him. I walked the halls of the high school like a ghost. I talked to no one and no one talked to me. Not even Marnie or Adam.

Whispers followed me down the corridors, sounding soft and unthreatening, but cutting me to the bone.

Planerville was less discreet. They talked themselves hoarse, gossiping about the situation. They breathed a collective sigh relief when the verdict came back and Evan was sentenced to five years at the minimum security North Central Correctional Facility. A sentence that forever ruined his chances of becoming a firefighter. Destroyed his dreams, and ground them to dust. I didn't even get to say goodbye.

I turned in the final version of my love poem to Ms. Politano.

I waited until the class had cleared out, then went up to her desk. My hair hung around my face in unwashed strands. I'd been wearing Evan's blue and black plaid shirt every day and every night. The cuffs were grimy at my wrists as I laid a crumpled and tear-stained piece of paper on Ms. P's desk.

"Jo," she said, her voice heavy with grief. "I've been wanting to talk to you about Evan. I just wanted to say——"

"Here," I said sliding the paper closer to her. "This is my assignment. So I can graduate."

She took the paper and I watched her eyes skim the uneven pen scratchings that crawled down the page like an erratic waterfall.

"It's a mess," I said dully. "It has no form or structure. But it's the truth. That has to count for something, doesn't it?"

She drew it to her slowly, her eyes never leaving mine. "Yes, it does, Josephine."

I nodded, willing myself not to break, hugging myself tight. But the tears broke free anyway. A scrape of the chair legs and then Ms. P was holding me. I clung to her, great wracking sobs tearing me in two.

I cried and cried, not coming close to the end of my tears. I pulled myself out of Ms. P's embrace, and walked out of her room without another word, down the hallway out of the school.

Nothing was left for me in Planerville, or in all of Iowa, now that Evan was lost to me. He and I had been on the verge of something beautiful.

Something extraordinary. And then it was all ripped away with a violence that shattered me so that I hardly recognized myself, even years later. I lost Evan and lost myself. Faded away like a photo left in the sun too long.

They say all who wander are not lost. But some of us are. We're really fucking lost, wandering until our feet bleed, and it feels like we'll never find our way home again.

I Never Told You

You can fill a book with everything I never said
Or the lines of a poem
Or an empty pool
Or an empty bedroom,
the candles all blown out

I never told you
how the reflection of myself in your eyes
Was the only mirror I could bear to look at
Or how I fought every day
To transfuse the girl I saw there with the girl I am
I tried to breathe in the words you made me:
beautiful
good
brave
I tried to be them for you even though
they were weighted with impossibility

I never told you
how I always feared the rough edges of myself were too sharp for you
And how I fought every day to blunt them
To bring down the walls
To let you in

without cutting you because I could never bear to hurt you
like the others did
Every day
a fierce pride roared in me
I was so lucky to know the truth
I was the beneficiary of your radiance
I basked in it and felt special
And if not for the pain of your solitude
I would have been content to be the only one

I never told you
How your touch made me feel like laughing and crying and singing
all at once
How your hand passing over my skin where atrocities
Had not yet sloughed off,
Skin cells remembering the worst touches,
Was like a tide washing over the ruddy sand
And leaving it whole and smooth
You made my skin forget
Gave me new memories
New sensations that didn't drag the shadows from the past
In your arms I could start again,
Start over.
There is no greater gift in all the world
Than you
to the wreckage
that is me…

I never told you
How I longed to kiss away your every bruise
until there was no evidence
No ghosts of your own suffering
To put your pieces back together
Seal the cracks
Vanish them like they never were

And never, ever
Leave a scar

I never told you
I would take your pain if I could
I would drink it down
And take my comfort
In making you ache a little less
For a little while
Did I?
I'll never know because I never told you
that I loved you

I love you
I love you
I love you

It's too late to say it now
The time has passed for words
How pathetic and small and weak
On the phone
Or on a piece of paper
Starving
Without the force of my own vitality
My voice
My breath
My blood singing in my veins for you
To give them power
They are lost

I love you
It's too late but I love you
And I'm sorry
I never told you.

PART II:
NIGHT TRAVELER

All the things one has forgotten scream for help in dreams. **~Elias Canetti**

EVAN

I dream of a river and I am carried along its currents. No boat or raft. I'm submerged to my chest in cold, dark water as the river cuts through a deep valley or canyon. I see huge, looming walls of rock. In my peripheral are people, places and moments in time. They skim across the rock and vanish when I look at them directly. I can only catch a glimpse. A few scraps.

The blue whale.

The rusted clown.

The melting spire.

Memories.

Hers, not mine. She's carried along with me and she's been cleaved in two, one half of her bright and vibrant, the other half gray and dying. I carry her with me in a current of her memories. We journey together. We run. Men from her broken and violent life chase her and I have to protect her. To pull her out of this deep ravine and carry her somewhere safe.

As the light of dawn begins to spill into the canyon, I'm sucked under by a riptide. It's a cold, bony hand dragging me under. I kick for the surface, but the pull is too strong.

I hover somewhere between the shallows and the deep, my lungs stretched to bursting…

I wake up gasping for breath in deep, greedy gulps. Shivering so badly my cot creaks. My skin is pale as bone, broken out in gooseflesh, as if I had been swimming in freezing cold water. The dream skims just beyond my consciousness and I can only grab onto a few shreds. I remember almost nothing but the words that fall out of my mouth.

"North," I say aloud, still trying to catch my breath, my teeth chattering. "The center."

I don't know what that means except that Jo needs me. She's in danger. Or in pain.

She's slipping away, fading to gray, and I have to find her before it's too late.

CHAPTER 19

JO

Dolores, Louisiana
Four years later

It was a slow day. By two p.m.. Lee's Place was all but empty. Only a few stragglers at the counter hunched over their coffee and greasy hash browns. I finished up my side work and went to the back room to take off my apron and count up the day's tips.

Twenty-seven dollars.

I sighed. "Shit."

Patty appeared at the door to the back room, staring me down with stony gray eyes, as if my shift weren't over and I was cutting out early. I always likened Patty Stevenson to Medusa, with a head full of suspicious snakes watching everything and everyone around her.

"Where you going?" she said.

None of your goddamn business, that's where.

I forced a smile as I looked up at my boyfriend's mother, not quite meeting her eye for fear of being turned to stone. "I've got errands. Some grocery shopping for dinner tonight. Nothing exciting. You're still coming over, right?"

She made a scratchy noise in the back of her throat and patted the coiled platinum curls of her hair. My overactive imagination heard snakes hissing. She glanced at my loose ponytail with the strands I pulled free to help conceal my scar. Her eyes narrowed at the cut that split my lower lip, still dark with congealing blood.

"You take better care of Lee, you hear?" she said, jutting her chin. "If you didn't rile him up like you do, he wouldn't take a hand to you, and you wouldn't have to show up to work looking like this. I can't have my employees looking like trash."

"I know, Patty."

She sniffed again. "I'll see you at your place for dinner. Don't forget Lee likes his fried chicken nice n' crisp."

As if I'd forget. The last time I made Lee fried chicken, he raged it was 'undercooked mush.' I barely managed to dodge the skillet of scalding oil he threw at me, then spent the better part of the night scrubbing it off the kitchen wall.

Patty left me alone and I recounted my tips. I did a few mental calculations and stuffed twenty bucks into my wallet and put the remaining seven in the pocket of my jeans. Seven dollars, plus another fifteen I'd stashed earlier wasn't worth a drive out to Del's. But if Patty—along with a bunch of Lee's asshole friends—was coming over for dinner tonight, I'd need the mental reinforcements of Del's friendship to get me through it.

I headed out through the kitchen, offering a goodbye to the guys.

"Goodnight, boys."

"Night, beautiful," called Hector at the grill.

"Take care, JoJo," said Jeremiah from the dishwasher.

I took their cheerful smiles and tucked them in my pocket next to the seven dollars.

Outside, the thick humidity of a Louisiana July smothered my face like a hot towel. I trudged to my car, noting Patty's Avalon parked in the next slot. An Avalon was an old lady car if ever there was one, but I'd gladly take it over my shitty Ford Malibu. I'd bought it three years ago. Ugly purple, with no air conditioning and pushing 150K in mileage. It was the only ride I could afford.

You'd think after being through so much together, I'd have a certain fondness for the old junker. But it had served as my home on more than one occasion. Sitting in its shabby interior rehashed too many fear-stricken nights: trying to get comfortable to sleep in the cramped backseat, or watching shadows move around outside, peering in, knocking on the glass and trying the locked doors.

I swore I shivered every time I sat behind the wheel.

I headed out on 20 West towards Choudrant, coasting on an almost empty stretch of highway for twenty minutes. Nothing on either side but tall trees, vibrant in the summer heat. Green heat, I called it. Summers here turned Louisiana into a rainforest. I'd started a poem about it when I first got here, a year ago. But then the sweet guy I'd been dating and with whom I'd just agreed to move in with, turned out to be a sociopathic, gasoline-breathing monster. Suddenly a poem about plant life seemed pretty fucking stupid.

I'd written poems throughout my short tenure as a homeless person, but the first time Lee Stevenson hit me I stopped. Like a valve shut off or dammed up with grime. I hadn't written one since.

I turned into a shabby strip mall with a gas station and mini-mart. Rising high over the little pit stop, a tired red neon flashed *The Rio* over and over, its light dim in the late sunshine of the day.

Balding tires spitting gravel, I pulled my shitty little car into the almost empty lot behind the Rio. The bar wasn't too much cooler than outside, but the neon lights were brilliant and bright: rainbows and more rainbows, and the salacious little ditty of a cartoon figure kneeling in front of a standing cartoon figure; the kneeling figure's head blinking off and on suggestively. I loved it. The color and the light, and the safe feeling I got when I was here.

A few regulars hunched over their drinks at the bar. They'd watched my arrival with a combination of suspicion and fear. It seemed pretty late in the history of mankind for these guys to still have to worry about anyone discovering them here. I always wondered why Dellison Jones (aka Del del'Rio) would choose to open shop along an empty stretch of lonely highway instead of in a bustling metropolis.

"It's an oasis, honey," Del said. "Not every gay man got the time or money to be hauling ass to New Orleans any time he wants some company."

I thought that was pretty damn brave. The Rio was *my* oasis, now. A safe place.

I found Del behind the bar in full regalia. Platinum bouffant wig and huge gold hoops dangling from her ears. Her sparkling jumpsuit was pure 70's disco, her makeup over-the-top and flawless. She could've given RuPaul a run for her money had she set down roots anywhere but this dead-end stretch of nothing.

Del was polishing glasses and lip-syncing Gloria Gaynor's "I Will Survive" in between chatting with customers. She let out an enthusiastic cry when she saw me pull a stool up to the bar.

"Well, look at you!" she crowed, her teeth brilliant white against dusky skin. "Ain't you a sight for sore eyes? How you been, sugar?" She started to lean over the bar, arms outstretched for a hug, but stopped short when she saw the bloody rent on my lip. "Oh, I know exactly how you been." Her smile vanished and her eyes flared anger. "Asshole been tweaking again?"

"Yeah," I muttered. "He got a hold of some shit from a new dealer and trying to make his own on the side. It's been nothing but laughs this past week."

It felt weird—in a good way—to be honest with Del. To talk so openly about Lee and in a normal tone of voice. Being with Del was like taking off a heavy, suffocating suit of armor. Her other customers had nothing to fear from me. I came in peace, looking for the same thing they did: sanctuary.

Del examined her manicure. "I don't suppose you here on your way out of town for good, then?"

I tilted my head, giving her a dry look. "Do I look stupid to you? Desperate, weak, and sad, sure, but—"

"Oh, hush your face. You ain't none of those."

"That's debatable. Anyway, I'm just here to make a deposit into my Bank of Del savings account."

"Naturally," Del said with a wry smile at the twenty-two dollars I slid across the bar. She made a clucking sound with her tongue behind her teeth and shook her head.

"I know, I know, it's shit," I said. "But if I take more, Lee will notice. You know how it is."

Del tapped an acrylic against her lip where the cut was on mine. "Yeah, I know how it is, baby." She pulled out a small ledger book from under the cash register and flipped to the back where she kept my savings separate from *The Rio's* accounting.

"Today's deposit brings you to $433. Not bad for three months."

"But not nearly enough." I ran both hands through my hair, my elbows on the bar. "God. Four hundred bucks. Pathetic."

Del put her warm hand over my scrawny pale one. "You're doing good by bringing this money here, honey. And I've had a good month, myself…"

"No, Del," I said sharply, snatching my hand away.

"*Yes*, sugar," Del returned. "I got a little extra and it's going straight into the Josephine Clark escape fund. Every damn penny."

"Dammit, Del, we've been through this. I can't let you do that."

"No one *lets* me do nothing, sugar-pie." Her serious expression softened into a smile. "I do what I want, which is why this glorious establishment is still standing."

I didn't smile back. It wasn't just a matter of pride, or the fact I knew Del was barely scraping by. Her disco balls and glittering costume jewelry sparkled from afar, but up close, it was all cheap plastic. She needed every dollar she had for herself. Her helping me felt like someone giving up their hard-earned money to bail a loser out of jail. I shouldn't have been in the jail in the first place, never mind let someone else pay for that colossal mistake.

"Don't do it, Del," I said, my voice cutting through Gloria Gaynor's girl power anthem. "I have to do this on my own. If I don't, I can't live with myself."

"Pride goeth before a fall." She planted her hands on her hips, smile vanishing again. "And how do I live with myself if that fool beats you to death? How will you be able to work and make money to walk out of here on your own two legs if that meth-head breaks your bones?"

"I'll protect myself. I don't want you to put one damn dollar into that fund, Del, I mean it. Don't do that to me. Just… keep being my friend. Okay?"

She looked as if she wanted protest some more, then her lips rolled together to press back the words.

"Mmm," she said, and I didn't miss that she hadn't agreed. "You do what you got to do. But you do it fast, you hear? Or else Del is going to be taking her fabulous ass to down to your neck of the woods to crack some skulls and you know how I'd hate to mess with my manicure."

I mustered a smile even as the thought of Del being face-to-face with Lee made me sick to my stomach.

Del had offered to let me live with her when she had first learned about my predicament, but I'd said no. I'd tried to escape from Lee once before, early on. I'd had no money, no belongings of any kind. I had been in such state of fear and pain that I even left my car and hitchhiked west. I'd made it as far as the woman's shelter in Calhoun when Lee found me.

Of course, I'd made it easy for him. I was standing right in front of the shelter, smoking a cigarette like a goddamn, naive idiot. I'll never forget the icy sliver of fear down my spine when I saw Lee's car pull up to the curb. He didn't have to say a word. He only rolled down the window and beckoned me over. The look on his face and the deadly cold in his eyes spoke volumes.

See? they said. *I warned you. I will never let you go.*

On the drive back to his house, Lee wondered aloud if Del hadn't put the idea in my head to run off on him. Maybe he and some buddies should drive out to The Rio and "Run that fag outta town with a gallon of gas and a match."

The threat killed any notion I might have had for shacking up with Del. I had gotten myself into this quicksand and I had to pull myself out. Not drag others down with me.

Maybe Del was right and I was too full of pride. I was barely hanging on. Lee sapped the strength I needed to put one foot in front of the other every day. The shame of it weighed me down, kept me from reaching out.

Except at night, when I'm alone and Lee is sleeping. Then I reach for Evan.

I tossed down the shot of whisky Del set before me. As if mental telegrams to a high school boyfriend were ever going to get me anywhere.

Del's velvety voice pulled me from my thoughts. "All I know is you got to have something to look forward to. All the time. It gives you hope. Gives you something to wake up for in the morning." She leaned over the bar. "It just so happens I made the acquaintance of a guy who does fake IDs. One hundred percent legit. Does social security, drivers' licenses... Hell, he can even get you a passport." She fluttered her fake lashes at me. "Know anyone who might need a passport?"

Not to the Grand Canyon, I wanted to say. But even thinking of it was too painful. Like prodding an old bruise that would never go away.

"No passport," I said, turning over this new development. "But if he's as legit as you say, he's bound to be expensive."

Del sighed. "That he is. But he can get you everything you need to disappear, sugar, so that no one will be able to find you. New identity, new name, new everything."

A twinge of pain settled into my chest. *Then Evan won't be able to find me...*

"How much?" I asked.

"Five hundred."

"Shit, Del, I don't even have that now."

"That's why you got to let me help you." She silenced me with a look before I could protest. "I know you feel ashamed but you gotta knock that nonsense off before you get really hurt. You let me match what you bring me. My cut will go to this guy to get you a new life, okay?"

"Del…"

"You do this for *me*," Del said, her voice dropping to a lower, masculine range as emotion filled her eyes. "Else one day it's going to be weeks gone by and you haven't come in here, and then what am I going to do? Or I read an obit in the paper and it's for my girl, who I didn't do nothing for but hold the money she never did use."

I dug my thumbnail into an old groove on the bar. "I hate where I am. What I am. But if I leave him, I'll be homeless again. I will not be homeless again. I will *not*." God, just the idea sent a shiver of dread down my spine.

Del's large, manicured hand covered mine. "I get that, baby, I do. But feeling low… That's on *him*. You just gotta do the best you can and keep yourself safe. Just like I gotta do the best I can, which means I match your money—and whatever bit I can spare—to get you outta here. Okay? Enough is enough."

"Enough is enough," I agreed, not looking up. If I met her eyes, I'd lose it. I hid behind my hair until I had my emotions back in check. I huffed a sigh and wiped the heel of my hand over my eyes. "I gotta get back."

"Can't stay for one more drink?" she asked gently. "It's disco night, and this dancing queen is about to bring down the house."

I managed a smile. "Not tonight."

She sighed. "Well, it's good to see you, baby." She reached over for a hug and I held on to her hard, unwilling to let go.

"You take care now," she whispered in my ear. "And keep looking forward. Never back. Straight through the fog and into the bright sunshine, okay?"

I forced myself to let her go and turned away, clearing my throat. "I'll see you again next week."

"God willing, sugar," Dell replied somberly. "God willing…"

I drove back to Dolores, along the lonely stretch of two-lane road. Overgrown fields of green weeds stretched out, unbroken but for some ramshackle house, sagging on its whitewashed clapboard, or rusted aluminum siding.

I let my thoughts stretch to the horizon, wondering where I would go once I had $500 saved. A new identity, a new life.

A new name. And then Evan will never find you.

Keep looking forward, Del had said. Not back toward the past, where Evan was slowly sinking into the same grayed-out limbo of memories where my mother lived. I caught a glimpse of my reflection in the side mirror: my sallow skin, jutting cheekbones, sunken eyes and split lip. If Evan saw me now, he'd be disgusted with what I'd become.

He wouldn't, the voice of hope whispered.

I punched the gas and my little car groaned in protest.

Fine, then I'll be disgusted enough for both of us.

As the sun started to set on my right hand side, Dolores's minimarts and fast food joints appeared on the horizon like a cluster of warts. I hurried to the grocery store, where I spent the remainder of my tip money on two packs of chicken leg quarters and a bucket of Crisco. Then I drove to the house I shared with Lee—a small, two-story in chipped paint that seemed to be sagging toward its neighbor.

Lee's house. Not mine.

Nothing resembling a home, just a roof over my head. And after talking with Del, I was starting to rethink how much value this roof had.

You need to disappear, sugar… New identity, new name, new everything.

But then the months I'd spent homeless came back to me in a flood. Months broken down to days, days broken down to minutes, because you never knew what would happen from one to the next. The danger was both constant and unpredictable. Lee's violence was unpredictable too, but at least I knew from what general direction the danger was coming from.

My determination, fired up by Del, began to waver.

The front door of our house opened and ten-year-old Andre Wright from three doors down staggered onto the porch. His eyes were glazed and his face wore a sloppy smile. I slammed the driver's side door and ran up to him.

"What are you doing, Andre?"

"Just visitin'," he slurred around the dopey grin.

I bit back a vile curse. "Did Lee give you that shit?"

"I came for Mama, but Lee…he gave me a free sample." Andre staggered past me, giggling. "I feel like I'm floating…"

"Goddammit." I stormed up to the house. The front door and screen were both hanging open from Andre's departure. I went in and let them both shut behind me.

I found Lee in the kitchen. On the table he'd spread out a bunch of bowls, a Bunsen burner and various household chemicals that belonged under the kitchen sink. His laptop was wedged between the mess. As I walked by, I saw the browser window open to an underground forum where people discussed tips on how best to cook meth.

"Why the hell are you getting Andre high?" I demanded.

"He's a customer."

"He's *ten*."

Lee chuckled, his hands flying over the table, twitching like wounded birds over his makeshift meth lab. He and the gang of assholes he called friends had the brilliant idea to turn themselves into a club of Walter Whites. They'd make a fortune, they declared, *just like on TV*. Morons.

"And now you're cooking?" I said. "Right here at the kitchen table, in broad daylight?"

"Mind your business, Jo," Lee said. I could tell he was coming off a high. His eyes were red-rimmed and glassy. His dark hair fell in a stringy mess over his face and his clothes stank of sweat and gasoline. He was a tall guy but had lost a lot of muscle mass thanks to the drugs.

It was only thing I could thank the drugs for.

He'd been doing too much lately. The highs never lasted anymore, which was why he was out to make his own.

He looked at me then. I could see his thoughts rework themselves into suspicion and accusation. I knew what was coming.

"Hey!" he said, as if I'd just walked in the door. "Where the fuck you been, anyway? Ma said you left the diner at three."

Goddamn Patty. Lee scared her as much as he did me and the only way to protect herself was to use me as a human shield. I couldn't blame her: we all did what we had to survive. In Patty's case, it meant pushing others down to keep her own head above water.

"I was out," I said.

"Who with?"

"No one."

He snorted and pushed himself off his chair to stagger toward me.

I backed up. "I was grocery shopping. Your mother and the guys are coming over to dinner tonight, remember?"

"Don't test me, woman," Lee snarled. "You're a liar. I smell it on you. The lies."

You can't smell lies, asshole.

I held up my bags from the grocery store. "You going to let me cook or not? Food, I mean."

He glowered with watery, hate-filled eyes. I didn't back down.

"You talk to the cops about our little disagreement this morning?" He brushed his thumb over the cut on my lip, making it sting.

I resisted the urge to roll my eyes. The one and only time I'd gone to the station, bleeding and dizzy from a "disagreement" with Lee, I'd been hustled to an officer's home where his wife patched me up and gave me a lecture about how secure Lee was—what with his popular diner—and how lucky I was to have him. She said all this as she held a bag of frozen peas to my swelling eye from where Lee hit me for buying the wrong brand of beer.

That damn diner made Lee a big fish in the little pond of Dolores. He'd known the sheriff up in Claiborne since he was a kid and the local officers were all his drinking buddies. Some of whom were going to come over tonight to participate in their new drug enterprise.

"I didn't talk to the cops," I said. "But if I did, the first thing I would say was that you were getting a ten-year-old fucked up on—"

Lee's backhand struck me across the upper cheek. Pain exploded through my face. My head whipped to the side and the grocery bags dropped from my hands, but I kept my feet.

"That's for backtalk," Lee snarled. His fist came up. "This is for making threats…"

He swung clumsily. I dodged.

"Fuck you!" I cried and shoved him as hard as I could with both hands. It was a gamble: the last of my strength against the last of the drugs slugging through his blood.

I won.

Lee staggered backwards and then fell on his ass. I bolted from the kitchen and dashed upstairs. I slammed the bathroom door and locked it as Lee pounded down the hall like a rabid dog, barking vile threats. I slid down to the floor with my back against and the door, bracing my feet on the toilet to form a barricade. The reverberations shuddered against my back as Lee pounded and kicked and cursed.

I squeezed my eyes shut.

Evan. Where are you? Come back to me. I can't breathe…

The doorbell rang. Patty was here. Or Lee's friends.

"You can't stay in there forever," Lee said, smashing his fist a final time, and then his voice retreated down the stairs. "Come down here and make dinner for our guests like you're supposed to."

I would've preferred to stay in the bathroom forever, but I heard Patty shriek as Lee barked at her about the dinner that I had been supposed to cook. If I didn't come down, she'd be left to deal with that pack of hyenas, alone.

Trapped again.

Trapped by fear, by the streets, by Lee and his swinging fists and his threats.

I thought I was becoming more numb, but instead I felt ready to burst. At some point, I wouldn't care if I shattered into too many pieces to put back together.

But not yet.

I hauled myself off the bathroom floor and went downstairs to cook

dinner. Fried chicken, extra crispy.
Just how Lee liked it.

CHAPTER 20

EVAN

The white house glowed in the falling darkness. The streets were quiet and empty. Still, I crept along the bushes and kept to the shadows until I was under the dining room window. A square of warm yellow light. Through the summer screens, I could hear the sound of cutlery against ceramic, and actually felt a rush of nostalgia. A few muttering voices. I felt like a creep skulking about like this, but I had to know. I had to see it for myself.

Carefully, I peeked through the window. Dinner was just wrapping up. Norma was bustling around the table cleaning plates. Harris was barricaded behind his paper, as usual. Merle was there, looking fatter and more piggish as he shoveled food into his mouth.

Beside him, Shane sat in a wheelchair, pulled up close to the table. His chest under his shirt looked caved in. His hands were bony claws, his face sallow and skeletal. He stared down at his untouched food. The sharp cunning expression I'd remembered had slipped off like an old mask. He was giving up, second by second. If he survived the year, it would be a miracle.

My chest tightened at this picture of decay. For the millionth time in four years, I wished everything had been different between me and Shane.

My eyes moved across the table to my youngest brother, now eleven years old. I searched for signs of health. I wanted perfection. No disability, no disfigurement, no residual effects of the trauma I had inflicted on him four years ago.

I waited and watched as Norma fussed over him more than she ever had when I lived there. Little touches all the Salinger sons craved: hair ruffled, a hand resting on his shoulder. Garrett's sweet smile seemed unchanged. My heart clenched when he jumped out of his chair to carry his plates to the kitchen.

Perfect.

Tears of relief blurred the scene in front of me. I slumped against the wall, sliding down until I hit the ground.

"He's okay," I whispered. "Thank God."

I held onto the comfort. A scrap of food to a starving man. My public defender had told me how bad it'd been for Garrett while I was locked up. I was locked up *because* it had been so bad. A coma for two weeks, reconstructive surgery on his broken nose, cheekbone, then rehab. So much suffering for such a little kid.

Nothing would ever erase the feeling of my foot striking Garrett's face. All my strength had been behind that kick. True, I'd been fighting for my life against Merle's choking grip, but four years locked up in prison seemed fair for causing Garrett so much pain and suffering.

Four years away from Jo.

Jo.

I'm coming, I thought and had every day since I'd busted out of the correctional facility. *I'm coming, Jo, just hold on.*

I crawled around the back of the house to the detached garage and sat beside it, waiting for the hours to pass. My spare key was under a terra-cotta pot by the garden, right where I'd left it four years ago. I held it in my hands, turned it over and over in my fingers as the night grew quieter. I waited there until the lights in the Salinger house went off. Then I waited a little more to be sure.

I rose from my crouch and crept to the side of the house, back to the dining room window. They'd left it open. I detached the screen with a minimal amount of noise, though every sound was amplified when you were breaking the law.

I snuck up to my room that was just as I'd left it; I don't think anyone had stepped foot in here since I was sent up. I knelt under my bed, moved a loose floorboard and pulled out a small lockbox, breathing a sigh of relief it was still there. Inside, was my life savings from when I'd worked at the auto shop. Harris had always paid me under the table for his tax purposes. I had $1,112. Not a fortune, but enough to take Jo away with me.

I snuck back through the house, replaced the screen on the window, and crept back to the garage where my old red Chevy truck was parked. Would it still run? If no one had driven it in four years, the battery would be shot and I'd be screwed. But looking through the window, I saw an empty coffee cup in the holder next to the gearshift and yesterday's newspaper on the passenger seat.

Maybe they used the truck for errands. Maybe they were going to give it to Garrett when he turned sixteen. Another thing I might take away from him, but it couldn't be helped. Jo needed me and I couldn't wait. Already it felt too late.

Fuck it, it was my truck anyway. I'd paid for it with my hard-earned money. The truck was mine.

I unlocked the truck's driver's side door, slid half my ass onto the seat, one foot on the break, the other still on the driveway. I slowly let out the brake and the truck rolled backward. The sound of tires crunching over the gravel was so loud, I was sure the upstairs windows would start lighting up any minute.

But the street stayed dark, as did the Salinger house. When I had the truck down the street a few yards, I jumped in and turned the key. The engine roared to life.

I should've taken off then and there, but I stared back at the big white house that had been my home for six years. The old ache filled my heart for what could've been, what was and what would never be. But urgency filled me as well, a single thought rising up stronger than the nostalgia: Jo needed me.

I said a silent goodbye to Garrett and offered up a prayer—to whoever was listening— that his life would be happy and long. And maybe he would choose to remember only the good parts of our brotherhood.

I drove away and didn't look back. Only forward to Jo.

CHAPTER
21

JO

You could say the business dinner had been a success. Lee and his rowdy buddies were loud with grandiose plans. It was decided his friend Warren Jeffries would use his hookups at the parish office to keep the cops off their backs, and Ron Barlow would run "distribution" through his trucking company. Patty did her best to pretend she was okay with their scheme to bring methadone to the greater Dolores area. I tried to eat a bite here and there, and stay more or less invisible until I could slip upstairs.

Long into the night, I heard Lee pacing around downstairs, holding an intense conversation with himself. I knew he was jonesing for a fix. Practically climbing the walls with need. Then came the unmistakable sounds of him cooking up. Soon the smell of ammonia and rotten eggs drifted upstairs, followed by the angry crash of breaking glass. Telltale signs of a bad batch.

I slept fitfully, afraid he'd burn the house down from under me. At dawn, I crept downstairs. Lee was passed out on the living room couch with an empty bottle of Wild Turkey in his lap.

The kitchen was a fucking disaster, the table littered with beer bottles, chicken bones, and industrial household chemicals. My growling stomach went silent. No point trying to scrounge up breakfast here. The diner was a better bet anyway. I'd let Lee stay unconscious a little longer and hope the booze would drown out the itch for another high.

I arrived at the diner thirty minutes early for my 7 a.m. shift. Patty was already there marrying ketchups, her back to me, though I imagined a few of her Medusa head snakes turning to hiss at me.

"You're early," she said when she saw me. "You take care of my boy? Get him breakfast?"

"He wasn't hungry." I headed for the back room.

Patty followed me. "Why not? He's a man. Men need to eat."

I turned around and stared down her death glare with my own exhausted eyes. "He got high last night after everyone left. Then he drank himself down, passed out on the couch and that's where I left him."

Patty straightened and sniffed, crossing her arms over her bony chest. She hated that she was losing her son to drugs. Her worry was both maternal and practical: legally, the diner belonged to Lee. Before meth took over his life, he ran the cash register and shot the shit with the locals. Now, Patty managed the place, single-handedly, working too many double-shifts for a lady pushing seventy. I took as many as I could, to help save up more money for my escape but Patty still got stuck when Lee didn't show up. She was trapped, the same way I was. Her only coping strategy was to take the frustration out on me.

"You take care of my boy," she snapped. "That's your job. It's only reason you got *this* job. You gotta keep him happy. Do you hear?"

I heard. And saw. The stone-wall gray of her eyes was crumbling with desperation. As Patty flounced out of the back room, I almost felt sorry for her.

The breakfast rush was on. Half a dozen tables were seated; Patty took one half of the small diner; I took the other.

I started at a table in my section where a lone guy had his face in the menu.

"Morning," I said. "Ready to order?"

He set the menu down, looked up at me and smiled. "Hi, Jo."

He smiled a beautiful smile, the one that made me feel as if I were a gift fallen in his lap.

"Hi, Jo," he said, pulling me close.

"Hi, Evan," I said. Then we were kissing...

My order pad fell from my hands. The pen bounced off the table, hit the ground and rolled away.

Evan.

Here. Right here. Right now. Looking at me.

I stared at this mirage, my mouth agape, my exhausted brain trying to work out if he were real or a figment of my desperate imagination.

His face was filled out, more chiseled, yet leaner too. His jawline squared and shadowed with beard growth. His blond hair was longer, pulled back in a short ponytail that curled in on itself at the collar of his denim jacket. Broader shoulders in that jacket. Thicker arms on the table in front of him.

His body had changed, but his eyes were the same shade of sky blue. Beautiful, kind eyes. Not laced with suspicion or contempt. Not glassy and empty from drugs. They looked tired. Full. Like he'd seen more than he'd wanted to in the past four years. I recognized that kind of heaviness. I saw it in my own reflection every morning. I saw it reflected now in Evan's warm, weary gaze.

Evan.

The same beautiful boy I'd known, now transformed into a ruggedly handsome twenty-two year-old man. The same kindness in his eyes and the inherent goodness he radiated. Time-tested and a bit frayed. But still there. A glut of emotion swamped me. Flashes of memory, shards of sensation. Feeling safe, feeling taken care of, feeling *happy*…

Evan Salinger stared at me and I stared down at him. Everything we'd had and everything we'd lost sitting right there in the short distance between us. All I had to do was reach through that cloud of time and memory, touch him and it would all come back…

My hand raised on its own, fingers reaching out to his shoulder.

"Evan," I whispered.

"It's me, Jo," he whispered back.

His hand rose to touch mine. Our fingers reached. Then a gale of laughter erupted from a table in Patty's section. The diner resolved around me. I snatched my hand away and glanced around, the blood racing through my veins.

"What are you doing here?" I said, fighting for breath and calm.

"You called me," Evan said.

"You… I called you?"

"Can you sit? Have a cup of coffee with me?"

I started to slide into the opposite chair and damn if it didn't feel like climbing into a lifeboat as the ship sank from underneath me. But before I touched the seat, I remembered where I was. I peeked over my shoulder. Patty was staring at me with that dagger glare. I was more worried about her wagging tongue.

I picked up my notepad and the pen from the floor, nearly whacking my head on the table as I straightened up. "I can't." I set my pen to paper. "What can I get you?"

Evan's blue eyes had followed mine to Patty and back. He nodded and said, "Eggs up, bacon, coffee."

"Got it." I jotted the order down, my shaking hand turning my normally neat handwriting to chicken scratch.

"Jo…"

"You shouldn't be here," I whispered and hurried away.

I put Evan's ticket in the window, still feeling Patty's eyes on me. I inhaled deeply several times, willing my nerves to stop their twitchy jangle. Excitement, terror, *hope:* I was a fucked-up cocktail of emotions.

I managed to wait on other customers, but I felt a constant pull toward Evan. I wanted to be near him. My eyes sought him out, drinking in the sight of him, unable to believe he wasn't a ghost that would vanish the moment I looked away.

I took his order to his table and set the plate down slowly. My hands fiddled with the ketchup bottle, moved salt and pepper shakers so they'd be in easy reach. Anything to prolong the moment.

"Why are you here?" I whispered.

"I told you—"

"Don't mess with me, Evan. I didn't *call* you. I don't have your number. I don't know where you've been or…" A terrible thought dawned on me. "Wait, you were supposed to serve five years. It's been four. You didn't…?"

"I got out because you needed me," Evan said.

I stared. "You mean, you busted out? How did you find me?"

"This isn't a good place to talk. I see that now. Can we meet somewhere? Somewhere safe?"

"Safe?" I blurted. "There's no such thing in this town."

As if to illustrate my point, Warren and Ron walked in. Both guests at last night's drug-dealing dinner party. They took seats at the counter and Patty came over to serve them. As she poured coffee, her chin jutted in my direction. Warren and Ron turned heads to follow her gaze and give me and Evan a onceover.

Shit. My heart dropped to my stomach and I hurried away to tend to other customers. I forced myself to saunter by the counter and bullshit some small talk with Warren and Ron. Acting calm and steady while my heart hammered in my chest.

I avoided Evan's table until I had to drop off his check. I wanted to tell him it wasn't safe here and he needed to get the hell out of town. To leave and not look back...

"I'm off at four," I muttered out the corner of my mouth.

His sweet smile brightened his face, sucking me backward in time. "Where?"

"Behind Miller's Inn. You know it?"

"I'll find it." Evan pulled out a battered brown leather wallet and laid some bills on the table. "I'll be there, Jo. And I can't wait to see you." He pushed back his chair. He left without a glance back.

"Who was that?" Patty asked the nanosecond he was gone, joining me at his table to watch through the window. Evan walked away, denim jacket in hand.

"Some guy I used to know in high school," I said, sounding as bored as possible. I gathered up Evan's breakfast plates. "Haven't seen him in years. Random."

"Oh yeah?" Patty said, her dark eyes boring into mine with her stony Medusa glare. "He a *good* friend of yours?"

I snorted. "God, no. He just got out of prison, for crying out loud. Back in high school he was the class freak. Spent time in the local mental ward." I pointed a finger at my head and made circles in the air. It felt ugly as hell but I had to protect him.

Patty narrowed her eyes—the snakes zeroing in. "He's awfully good-looking, don't you think? For a loon?"

"Order up!" Hector called from the window.

I crossed to it, Patty on my heels. The smell of grease and ham was making me nauseous.

"A loon, exactly," I said. "Not surprised he ended up in prison. I told him to move on and he is."

I didn't wait for a reply, but headed to my table, hoping I'd satisfied Patty's curiosity. This dude wasn't a threat and I was still loyal to her drug-addicted, woman-beating asshole of a son.

But Evan was here.

He came for me. I called out to him and he heard. He came for me.

I banished the ridiculous thought, along with the hopeful flutter of my stupid heart. He tracked me down the old-fashioned way: The Internet. It was silly to think something supernatural was at work. All that stuff he'd told me in high school about his prophetic dreams seemed distant and muted. Impossible stuff I'd believed because I was so wrapped up in him and desperate to be loved. He could have told me the sky was falling and I'd have believed him.

That's bullshit and you know it, came a thought dressed in Del's voice.

I pushed it away. In any case, it was too dangerous to meet with him. This town was too small. We'd be seen. Word would get back to Patty or worse, some of Lee's asshole friends. If Lee got wind I'd so much as looked at another man, let alone met him behind a condemned hotel, I'd be dead meat.

So would Evan.

But when four o'clock came, I wanted to tear off my apron and nametag and *run* to Miller's Inn. Fear slowed my steps. Fear wanted to turn me around and go home, not keep walking toward Miller's Inn where Evan was waiting.

Evan...

I stopped and sagged against the wall of the corner drug store, slumped under the weight of time. Those days with Evan were a fading dream dimmed by the thousands of days making up four long years. The first week he was gone, I cried myself dry. Then survival demanded every ounce of my waking strength and I hadn't wept since. I wanted to weep now. I felt great gusting howls well up in me, but I pushed them down.

It's too late for me. Too late...

An echo of Evan's words resounded in my mind. *"You're the bravest girl I've ever known..."*

It took every shred of courage I had left to walk to the old inn. I made myself small and invisible. Shoulders hunched, arms crossed, head down.

I walked straight into Evan.

He gripped my shoulders as I rocked back, studying me. I looked up into the blue of his eyes. They were brimming with emotion and longing. So much longing. I felt it like a pull between us, drawing me to him, to fall against him and be held by him again, and make those four years between us vanish.

But he was too good and pure. Even more so when contrasted against Lee. Evan didn't belong here and I didn't belong with him. Not anymore.

"You can't stay," I said. "If they see you, they'll hurt you."

"Who?"

"Lee. And his friends."

"His name is Lee." It wasn't a question.

I watched his gaze take me in, reading the story of the last few years written on my body. My cut lip. A scar above my eye that hadn't been there in high school. The clothes hanging on my bones. I watched as he drew his own conclusions, pain darkening his sky blue eyes to gray.

"We're leaving," he said. "Right now."

"Leaving? Wait...how did you find me?"

"Is that what you really want to ask right now? Get in the truck, Jo. I'm getting you out of here."

I blinked, my throat dry. "You... You want me to drop everything and just skip town with you?"

"Yes."

"Evan, I haven't seen you in four years. I don't know you...You don't know me anymore."

"I know you, Jo," Evan said. "Come with me."

"Where?"

"Somewhere safe."

"Where is *safe?* And I have no money," I said, my voice cracking. "He takes my money. I work. I work so hard and he takes it all. I have nothing on hand. Just a little savings a friend is holding for me."

Evan moved closer to me his voice soft and gentle. "I have the money I saved up to get out of Planerville after graduation. I have it and it's our money now. Come with me, Jo. Or at least tell me what's keeping you here."

"Nothing," I whispered. "I wish I could tell you someone needs me. But nobody needs me."

"I need you."

"I'm scared, Evan. And worn down. I'm so fucking exhausted I can't see straight."

"I know you are, Jo. You have to leave him. Enough. No more."

"But then what? I've been out there before. You don't know what I've been through. I can't do it alone again with nothing…"

"You won't have nothing and you're not alone," Evan said. "You have me. This is *me,* Jo. Remember?"

I staggered back a step, remembering. I could hardly breathe. Evan back in my life again… Like being offered the richest food and the warmest clothes after four years of being hungry and cold.

"I can't force you to come with me," Evan said. "But I can't leave you with him either. I won't. You're going *somewhere* today, Jo. You choose."

This was happening. I was too overwhelmed to fully contemplate it. It was either crack a joke or crack up. I wiped my nose on my sleeve. "So you're my knight in shining armor? Riding into this shit town on a white horse to save me?"

Evan grinned a little. "No horse. How about a beat up old Chevy?"

I started to laugh but it came out sounding more like a sob. "I feel so jumbled up. I don't know what to think."

"You don't have to work everything out right now. Just come with me. Get somewhere safe and quiet. We'll talk more and I'll explain everything. But we have to leave now."

I lifted my eyes to his, felt that warmth of his attention wrap around me. With Evan I had been brave. Beautiful.

"I need to pack," I blurted. "If I'm going with you I need to pack, right? God, this surreal."

"No packing. Let's just go. I'll get you anything you need…"

"No," I said, thinking of my blue and black plaid shirt. His shirt. "There's stuff I need. *My* stuff. I don't have much but I need it. It's all I have."

He nodded reluctantly. "I'll go with you…"

"No. I'll meet you back here in half an hour."

"Jo..."

"He's not home now. He should be at work. It's safe. But no matter what, if I'm going to leave with you, I have to do one part of it on my own. One tiny fucking part, because I couldn't do it before..." I heaved a breath, wiped my eyes, pulled myself together as best I could. "Half an hour."

"Half an hour," Evan agreed, though he had to spit the words from behind a tense jaw.

I started to go then stopped. Slowly, I reached out my hand, fingers trembling, and laid it on his cheek. I felt his warm skin, the scratch of his stubble, and the muscle move under my palm as he sighed at my touch.

"You're here," I whispered. "This is real?"

"I'm right here," he replied, covering my hand with his. "And I'll be waiting."

CHAPTER 22

JO

Lee was home

My stomach lurched, twisted into knots to see his car in the driveway. He was supposed to be at the diner, closing out the day so his mother didn't have to work another double shift. Instead, he was here.

Shit.

The house reeked of chemicals and butane and death. From the door I could see Lee at the kitchen table, cooking up a batch of meth.

I started to sneak upstairs thinking maybe I could snatch a few things, and sneak back out. He'd never know I'd been there.

"Jo?"

His voice, calling from the kitchen, froze me to the spot.

"Hey," I called. "Gotta pee. Bad. Be right down."

I hurried up the stairs, heart pounding. I dug frantically in the bedroom closet for the small duffel bag I kept there. I tossed in a few pairs of underwear, t-shirts, shorts, a pair of cargo pants and Evan's black-and-blue plaid shirt. No fucking way I was leaving the house without it.

Bag packed, a sudden, sharp instinct warned me to put it all back. To keep things just as they were.

No! It's time. Evan's waiting.

I pushed the fear aside and took the bag into the bathroom. I threw a bunch of stuff inside: toothbrush, deodorant, my birth control pills. The fear loosened its hold, replaced by determination. I was doing this.

I headed down the stairs with the intent on just running out the front door and never looking back. I stopped short three from the bottom and gave a little cry.

"Where you goin'?"

My skin broke out in gooseflesh and my heart thudded in cadence to that old fearful beat to see Lee standing in the entry, his eyes red-rimmed and flinty as they darted from the bag in my hand to me and back.

"I'm leaving," I said. I hated how choked with fear my voice sounded. I cleared my throat and said louder, "I'm leaving you, Lee."

I expected rage. My hands clenched the handles of the bag ready to swing. Ready to fight and claw my past him if I had to. Evan was waiting for me. Escape. The time to let the fear run me was over.

Lee just chuckled, his feet danced from side to side, and his fingers twitched.

Then balled into fists.

"Don't test me woman. I'm hungry. Get your ass in there and make me dinner."

I drew myself up. "No. I'm leaving. I mean it. It's over."

"Oh shut up," he drawled, annoyed. "Knock that stupid shit off. You're not going *anywhere*. Nothing is *over*. I'm hungry. Now get in that kitchen and make me some fucking dinner."

I fought for calm; assessed the situation. My way to the front door was blocked, and even if the drugs had sucked away a lot of his bulk, Lee was a lot bigger than me. I couldn't fight my way past him no matter how badly I wanted to.

Plan B. Wait for a chance and run like hell.

I dropped duffel bag on the stairs, pretending to be defeated, and hung my head so that my hair over my face. "Yeah okay," I said dully. "I'm sorry, Lee. I'll make you dinner."

I started to walk past Lee, to hook around to the right towards the kitchen when his hand lunged like a striking snake. He grabbed a fistful of my hair, yanking me to him. His breath smelled like gasoline, and his eyes were watery, hate coursing along their red veins, as he thrust his face into mine. Whatever goodness Lee had when I first met him—and there hadn't been a whole lot—was eaten away.

"You never learn, do you?" he seethed. "You don't leave. You don't even *think* about it. Remember what happened last time?"

"I r-remember it wasn't always like this..." I said, my voice shaking with terror, my breath coming in harsh gasps. "Why do you want me around? Y-you don't even like me anymore. Just let me go."

His face screwed up in confusion. "I don't like you? I'm trying to *help* you, you ungrateful bitch. Do you remember what you were when I met you? A fucking wretch, that's what. You can't make it five minutes on your own without me. The way I see it, you owe me. The very least you can do, Josephine, is make my goddamn dinner."

Lee dragged me by the hair towards the kitchen. I stumbled and nearly fell trying to keep up. Pain burned my scalp and shot down my spine, zinging up over the crown of my head and deep in my neck as he slammed the side of my face against the refrigerator.

"This is where you get my food from."

I let out a cry as he swung me from the refrigerator and jammed my face against the vent hood over the stove.

"And this is where you cook my food." He held me over the dirty pots and pans, and the heavy iron skillet I'd used to make his fried chicken the night before. He gave my head a jerk. "You got that?"

I squeezed my eyes shut, panting through my nose as I tried to hold back the cries. A scream escaped as Lee yanked me to the dirty yellow linoleum floor. His boot buried itself in my gut like a cannonball. I curled up tight as all the air in the world *whooshed* out of me.

Lee's face swam before my vision as he knelt down. "Now look what you made me do, Jo. Look what happens when you try to leave me..."

His hand brushed the hair from my cheek, exposing my scar. "Ungrateful bitch." His hand squeezed. My scalp burned. He raised my head up and slammed it down onto that dingy floor.

The black descended before the pain could find me.

Muffled words and shouts. I listened through a gauzy haze of pain. I tried to open my eyes and but couldn't.

Pacing footsteps. Floorboards creaking. Heavy treads and a crash. Lee was on a rampage.

"It's fucking over…"

That's not Lee's voice. Someone else is here.

My head thundered with pain, drowning even my thoughts. I tried to claw my way to the surface, but slipped back under…

Pain woke me, a dull prodding against my temple. I opened my eyes to a blurred vista of cruddy green carpet strewn with squashed cigarette butts. I moved my gaze up and a flash of pain came like a white beam, lancing through eyes into my brain. When the light faded, I saw a jean-clad leg and a boot. Lee's boot. I blinked and looked again. I was on the living room floor. Lee was lying a foot or two away from me. Lying so still, the carpet stained under his head…

I flinched as gentle hands touched my shoulders.

"Jo?"

I got to my knees, wincing at the agony flared at my neck, while my head kept a dull banging in time to my pulse. My stomach roiled with nausea. The strong hands helped me to stand, but the frantic fear of my fight with Lee awoke and sang in my veins. I pushed the hands away brushed the hair from my eyes.

Evan Salinger. Here in my living room. I struggled to remember what came before.

I was leaving with him. He was waiting for me.

Blood leaked from Evan's nose and split lip. His t-shirt was torn at the shoulder and blood smeared all along the collar. I looked at his hands—

swollen, bloody knuckles—then to Lee on the carpet. The stain under his head pooling now. Red. His head. Jesus Christ, the back of Lee's head was dented in, his dark hair damp with blood.

"Did you do this?" I asked when I'd caught my breath. "You...killed him? Because he's dead, isn't he? Lee's dead?"

Evan stared at me hard for a handful of seconds that seemed like forever.

"Yes," he said finally, and bent to pick up something I hadn't noticed before on the floor—the heavy iron skillet.

Evan took up the pan, twisting the handle in both hands, like he was strangling it. There was a wet, circular splat of blood on the back. I thought I'd be sick.

"I didn't mean to kill him," Evan said, still looking at me, his voice low and calm. "It was an accident. But he was hurting you and it had to stop."

Just that simple. I'd had that same thought a million times a day for the last year: *He's hurting me and it has to stop.* And here comes Evan fucking Salinger, in town for less than five hours, and he'd made it stop. Relief flooded through me, and for three glorious seconds, I reveled in my new freedom. And then reality crashed back in.

"No, no, no," I said, and hurried to the front window, to throw the curtain shut. "You shouldn't have done this. Why did you do this?"

"He was hurting you..."

"Evan!" I cried. "They will *kill* you, Lee's friends. Or prison...They'll lock you up again..."

"We're leaving," Evan said, still so maddeningly calm. "I'm taking you somewhere safe."

I shook my aching head, pacing well away from Lee's body that was so *still*. Not sleeping still, or unconscious still, but dead still.

"There is no place safe," I said, my thoughts a jumbled mess and bursting out of me in fragments. "Not for me...Sure as hell not for you. I might've been able to claim self-defense. I might've...But no. You...you fought with him? You beat the shit out of him and then you killed him. Your goddamn DNA is all over everything..."

"Jo." Evan's voice was like a balm over a raging burn. "I did it. You're not going to go to jail for this." And then a crack in his voice, his jaw twitched and his eyes hardened. "You're not going to pay for this, not after what he's done to you. No. I did this. I'll pay for it. But not yet. Right now, we have to get you out of here."

Get me out of here. Because Lee was dead. *Oh my fucking god Lee was dead.* The enormity of it stole my strength.

I started to sink down. Evan moved to catch me. I tried to hold onto consciousness, but it was like sand through a fist. My fingers clutched Evan's jacket and fell away, boneless. The house, Lee's body and Evan's face blurred together, as if I'd been submerged underwater. Evan's voice grew more and more distant. He was speaking through a wind tunnel. Yelling across river rapids. The roar and rush of blood in my ears.

"Shh, Jo." Evan's voice against my ear. "You're all right."

He got another arm under my knees and lifted me. My head ached as it banged against Evan's shoulder, a thousand hammers pounded from the inside my skull.

The bang of the screen door and the outside humidity wrapped around me. Then I was sitting upright. A car door shut and I smelled clean leather and coffee.

Silence.

I was alone.

"Evan? *Evan!*"

The wail of my voice made my head pound harder. Then he was back, sliding on my left. An engine growled to life beneath me. The house I'd lived in with Lee—pale and drab in the falling night—began to slip away. My eyes fell shut, blinded by a sudden flare of orange in the front windows as a fire caught and roared, and then I went under.

CHAPTER 23

EVAN

In the passenger seat, Jo sat curled away from me, her head leaning on the window and her hair curtaining her face. She'd fallen unconscious as I pulled out of the driveway, and come to a few minutes later. Every few miles, I shook her shoulder to keep her awake, certain she had a concussion.

"Is it over?" she asked, her voice small.

No, I wanted to say, *it's just beginning.* But she meant the nightmare of her time with Lee, and that was most definitely fucking over.

"It's over, Jo."

She didn't say anything else, but I heard the tiniest of sighs and the coiled tension in her seemed to ease. She looked so small. So frail. But she'd always been deceptively strong.

"Stay awake, okay, Jo?" I talked to her nonstop, but she hardly said more than a few words. Now and then her body trembled and I wanted to touch her so badly. My bloody and swollen fists clenched around the steering wheel. Of all the fights I'd been in, the battle with Jo's boyfriend—*husband? fiancé?*—had been the most important of my life.

"Jo, you awake?"

"Where are we going?"

"Shreveport. To a hospital."

"No."

"You're hurt," I said. "I can't take any chances."

"No hospital."

"Jo—"

"*No hospital.*" She shivered and hunched deeper in my jean jacket I'd thrown over her shoulders as we fled. I'd grabbed her bag on the way out, too. Because it had been so important to her to bring it.

"Get me as far away from that shit town as you can," she said.

"You stay awake then. No sleeping."

"No sleeping," she muttered.

I took us due west along Highway 20, straight through Shreveport without stopping. My eyes were getting heavy. The adrenaline rush was tapped out, leaving me drained. We crossed the Texas-Louisiana border around midnight, and I found a roadside motel that looked obscure enough. And cheap. I parked the truck in the front of the office and told Jo to wait while I paid for a room. She nodded from under her hair. I hesitated.

"Jo?"

"I'm awake."

Behind the glass of the tiny front office, a large man in a stained wife-beater was smoking a cigarette and watching the small TV on his desk.

"I need a room for the night," I told him. "Double beds, first floor, but in the back. If you have one available."

He gave me a dry look. "Forty-seven bucks."

I paid cash and returned to my truck. Jo looked like she hadn't moved. I drove around to the back and parked in front of our room. Jo kept her face hidden as I helped her down, her arms wrapped tightly around herself, shoulders hunched.

The motel room was small, plain, and smelled of smoke. Two beds, bathroom, chair, dresser, TV. I wished I had the money to take Jo somewhere nicer. Better. She deserved better.

I led her to the bed furthest from the door, and pulled down the covers. She climbed in slowly and her hair dripped down like black oil as her head met the pillow. I caught a glimpse of the lump on her temple, dashed with dried blood, and I wanted to kill that Lee fucker.

Jo curled into a ball. I pulled the covers up over her thin shoulders and tucked them around her. Her eyes were open, watching me through strands of hair.

"You can sleep a little now, but I have to check on you. Keep waking you up."

She nodded almost imperceptibly and closed her eyes. I think she was asleep in moments.

I wanted to slide into bed next to her, wrap my arms around her and let her know she was going to be all right now. No one was going to hurt her again. No one.

Would she let me?

I didn't know what four years apart had done to her feelings for me. Or if she had any left at all. Mine were as strong as ever. My love was the fuel that had kept me sane in prison. It was the drive to bust out of the correctional facility, to walk off the farm-yard detail and vanish so I could get to her. And I found her caught up in a miserable life, crushed in a giant's hand.

I needed to give her space and wait. Tonight wasn't about anything but making her safe.

I didn't sleep. I spent the night flipping through a few magazines someone had left behind, eating crappy snack food from the vending machine, and occasionally shaking Jo's shoulder. I watched TV—on low volume—for any news about the fire. There was one report out of Dolores: speculation that a home meth lab that had blown up, taking one man with it. So they knew Lee was dead. With any luck, they'd leave it at that, but I doubted it. Forensics was good nowadays. The fact that Lee's skull was smashed in like a hardboiled egg wasn't going to go unnoticed. Nor was Jo's sudden disappearance.

Doesn't matter, I vowed, shutting the TV off. *Nothing touches her. No one hurts her. Never again,*

Next morning, I was hungry as hell but didn't want Jo to wake up alone. When she finally sat up, blinking sleepily, it was nearly 10 a.m.

"Why did you let me sleep so long?"

"I kept checking on you. You don't remember?"

"No." She looked like she was thinking back, trying to grasp at something just out of reach.

"Good, because you needed the rest," I added quickly. "I figure you haven't slept soundly in a long time."

"You can say that again." She leaned back against the headboard, pulling the blanket up to her chin. "Where are we?"

"Terrell, Texas. Just outside Dallas."

She looked to the TV that was dark now. "Any news about us?"

"Yeah. A little."

"What are they saying?"

"They don't know much. A fire. Meth lab explosion. And a man dead."

"A fire," she muttered. "I remember a fire. That was you?"

"Yeah."

She nodded. "Anything about me?"

"Not yet."

"*Yet,*" she said. "Patty...that's Lee's mama. She'll tell the cops that I killed Lee. She'll send them after us."

"Let me worry about that."

She nodded again, winced.

"Your head?"

"Neck. The bastard grabbed my hair..." Her gaze dropped to her hands that plucked the bedcovers, her body bent with grief, shame and a multitude of other pains I couldn't bear.

"He's won't hurt you anymore."

Her lips curled in a wan smile. A long, deep silence stretched between us.

"Are you hungry?" I asked. "You must be."

"I could eat."

"I'll bring you something."

"I want to go out."

"It might be better to lay low."

Jo gingerly tilted her head. "Evan, I feel like I'm dreaming. I need to get out of this bed, out of this motel and go somewhere. Maybe a..."

"Brightly lit space with clearly marked exits?" I finished with a small smile.

She didn't smile back. "Something like that. My life just got rearranged in a heartbeat. I need to eat something and just...sort it all out." She looked at me hard. "And sort you out, too."

"I don't blame you for being confused."

"I don't know what I feel."

"I'll pull the truck around."

"No, I want to walk. I need air."

She folded back the covers and bent to put on her boots. She winced as she reached to lace them up.

"Let me," I said, kneeling to help her.

This close to her, my chest tightened. My hand on the soft skin of her calf as I eased her foot into a boot. She was too skinny, her eyes shadowed, her pale skin bruised…and so fucking beautiful I could hardly breathe.

She said nothing until I was done, then regarded me with a heart-breaking expression. A glut of emotions crossed her face, too many to count or name.

"Thanks, Evan," she whispered.

I would die for you, Jo.

"Any time."

CHAPTER 24

JO

The digital billboard on a bank said it was ninety-five degrees out but I felt chilled to the bone. We found a Denny's within walking distance of the motel. The hostess seated us at a corner table, away from the windows. I studied the menu, my stomach growling over every glossy photo. I snapped it shut, disgusted with myself.

"What's wrong?" Evan asked.

"I'm really hungry. A man is dead and I want to stuff my face. That's sick."

Evan's eyes darkened. "He could've killed you. I thought he had. I thought I was too late."

I didn't know what to say to that so I cleared my throat and took up the menu again. "The irony is that I usually don't have an appetite at all."

"Eat, Jo. Order one of everything if you want." He grinned. He looked happy. I could feel him watching me as I studied the menu, staring as if his eyes couldn't get enough. Maybe I seemed as unreal to him as he did to me.

When our waitress came, I ordered a Grand Slam breakfast, a chocolate shake, toast, coffee and a side of fruit. I ate every last bite of the greasy stuff and felt good. Better than I had in months.

I sat back with my mug of coffee. "All right, now that I've made a pig of myself…"

Evan pushed his own plate aside. "When was the last time you had a decent meal?"

"I don't remember. I cooked a lot for Lee. But like I said, I never had much appetite."

Evan turned his mug around in small circles on the table. "Do you want to talk about him?"

"I have nothing to say. You saw everything there is to know about Lee and me."

He nodded. "Understood."

I sat back in my chair, enveloped in the old warmth of his attention. "How was it? Prison, I mean. Was it…very bad?"

"It's all you've heard and more," he said with a dry smile.

I wasn't in the mood for teasing. "Please tell me."

"Not too bad."

"You're lying."

He looked at me steadily. "You don't want to hear about it, Jo. Like Lee, it's over and done."

"You shouldn't have been in there at all."

"True. I should've been at prom with you."

My heart ached for the way Evan was looking at me. "No, I just meant…"

"I know what you meant. What happened to Garrett was an accident. On the other hand, I shouldn't have fought with Merle in the first place. I let Shane get to me. I hurt Garrett and ruined us. I ruined our future and left you with nothing. I hate that prison took me away from you." He frowned darkly. "It was both the punishment *and* the crime."

My tongue tied in a thousand possible replies. A thousand more emotions and memories converged on me, threatening to swamp me. I had to shove them back to think clearly.

"On the bright side," Evan said into the silence, "Garrett is okay."

"Really? You saw him?"

He nodded. "I went back to Planerville last week. I didn't talk to him or anything. Just did a little commando mission. Peeked through the windows. Garrett looked good." He smiled faintly. "He looked real good."

"I'm so glad. Did you see your other brothers?"

"I saw Shane and Merle. They look like you'd expect them to look. Not good. Dying in their own ways. I didn't talk to them. I was just there to take my truck back."

I frowned. "What do you mean you took it?"

He shrugged. "I needed it. It's my truck."

"That won't matter to them, will it? They'll say you stole it. It won't matter that it's yours because you busted out of prison." I raised my eyes to his. "I still can't believe you did that. Why? For me?"

"Of course," Evan said. "Do you remember what I told you? That last night at Funtown?"

The rain poured down like tears on our faces. He raised a hand to touch my cheek, his eyes full. "I'll always come back to you."

"I remember," I said softly.

Evan leaned over the table, his eyes boring into mine. "No one is going to touch you, Jo. Not the cops, not anyone. I'm going to keep you safe."

"Safe from what? Lee is dead and you're the one in danger."

If we went back and Evan confessed, he'd be locked up for life. And not some minimum security place like North Correctional, either. He'd go away with the murderers and rapists, and it would destroy him. Destroy me, too. I'd wither away knowing he did it to save me from Lee, because I was too cowardly to get away myself.

"I could confess," I said.

Evan shook his head.

"No, listen. From you, it looks like murder. From me, it's self-defense."

He drummed his fingers on the table, thinking. "Are there records of his abuse to you? Police reports?"

I looked away. "No. The local cops always covered for him."

"Hospital records?"

"He put me in the hospital once. A few months ago." I let my hair fall to cover my face, shame burning my cheeks. "I told everyone I fell down the stairs."

Evan's voice grew more gentle. "Any witnesses who could vouch for you?"

I thought of Del. But what was the word of a drag queen against Patty's? Against Warren and Ron's? Against all of Lee's buddies and their wives, some of whom looked just as beat down and scared as I did.

"No," I said.

"Then it's not an option." He leaned back, held up his hands as if the matter were settled. "I won't let you go to jail for it, Jo. I won't."

"And I can't let you get locked up for life either. So what do we do? Run? Become fugitives?" I rubbed my face, wincing as I accidentally touched the lump on my brow. The pain helped me focus. "Where do we go now? Mexico?"

"No, we have to go north."

"North where? Canada?"

"Maybe."

I frowned. "You're not sure?"

"We have to go north, to the center."

I started to ask him what the hell he meant by that, but his eyes were looking past me, distant and searching, and I knew he didn't know himself.

"Wait." I pushed my mug away, sat back in my chair. "Wait, wait, wait. What are you...?" I firmed my voice. "How did you find me, Evan? Tell me the truth."

Evan turned his coffee mug around and around. "I think you know how I found you, Jo."

"The internet, right? One of those people-search sites?"

He shook his head, his eyes now intent on mine.

I went cold all over. "A dream?"

He nodded.

"You had a *dream*? Like the time you knew about my scar? Or the shooting? It was like that?"

"Exactly like that."

"And going north? To the center?"

"Same."

I stared. I could see Evan set his jaw, bracing himself for the disbelief and skepticism that had plagued him his whole life. I'd never wanted to be one of those people. I'd told him I believed him, but those nights in the pool at Funtown seemed so far away.

"God, Evan, I know you believe it's real. I know you do, but…"

I hated the condescending, patronizing words the moment they came out.

I sound exactly like one of those people.

"I do believe it's real," he said tersely. "As real as the moment in algebra class when I saw Becky Ulridge's dad get shot in the head."

I flinched and he sagged back against the bench, shaking his head miserably.

"I'm sorry," he said. "I shouldn't have said that."

"It's just… So much is at stake," I said carefully. "We can't run away and build a life based on a dream or a hunch."

"It's the only way you'll be safe and I'll be free."

"What does that *mean?* What is the center? Is it *a* center? A literal building, like the CDC?"

"I can't see all of it. Right now I just have bits and pieces. The rest will come as we go along."

"How do you know?"

"I just do," he said, a small, unhappy smile on his lips.

I stared a moment more, then hung my head in my hands. "Do we have to go north? What about the Grand Canyon?" *Let's go someplace real,* I thought.

"We can't go there," Evan replied. "That's home, and we can't lead them home."

I sat back, at a loss for words. Lost in a fog of confusion, a push-pull of hope and logic, fantasy and reality.

Evan leaned in. When he spoke, his voice was low, pitched for my ears alone. "Listen to me, Jo. Four years ago, I told you things I'd never told anyone. I trusted you and you believed me. You told me you believed me. Do you know how long I'd waited to hear that from someone? Being with you and being accepted for once in my goddamn life… Because of you, I felt like I finally had a chance at a normal life. *My* version of a normal life. And I carried that feeling through my entire sentence. It was how I survived."

"I know but—"

"So here we are again," he continued. "I'm telling you secrets, telling you weird, personal, fucked-up crazy shit and it feels just as real and right as…taking a deep breath. Going north is something we need to do. For both of us. And no, I can't see the whole thing but I can feel how it's real and important. Life or death. You will be safe and I will be free. And I'm asking you to believe in me again and come with me."

Tears threatened again but I brushed them away. I believed him four years ago. I accepted him. But were those words easy to say because they had no bearing on my life? Because I was in love and willing to overlook anything?

This is the true test. Do you believe him or not? Do you accept him or not? Because if not, cut him free. Right now.

Evan mistook my silence for rejection. He nodded, and sat back, mustering his dignity in the face of my disbelief.

"I get it," he said quietly. "I do. And I'm sorry. I told you because you deserve the truth and I don't want to hide any part of myself from you. But I'll do whatever you say, Jo. Take you wherever you want to go. Back to Dolores, if that's what you want. Tell me where you want to go and I'll take you there."

I looked across the table, to Evan with his handsome face wearing a gentle expression that hoped for everything but demanded nothing.

Where did I want to go? A question with no geographical answer. North, south, the center or the fucking moon… When all the confusion and doubt and shame were swept away, the deepest truth of my heart sang the exact place loud and clear.

I let out a shaky breath. "Take me with you."

CHAPTER 25

JO

Evan paid our bill and we walked back to the motel in the stifling heat. I peered up at him through my hair now and then, stealing little glances. He was more handsome than I remembered. More masculine, strong and rugged. He'd taken off his denim jacket and carried it in one hand. His t-shirt stretched over muscle and bronzed skin, as if he'd spent a lot of time working outdoors. He seemed taller too, or maybe that was from me walking hunched over with crossed arms.

Evan's stride was confident and his eyes alert. He was like a bodyguard escorting me. I started to relax. He didn't need to take me somewhere safe. I felt that way just walking beside him.

You're doing it again, I warned myself. *You jumped at the chance to live with Lee because that felt safe too.*

I grimaced under my curtain of hair. Evan was *nothing* like Lee. To even compare the two of them felt dirty.

By the time we reached the motel, the doubts were creeping in, eating away my certainty. Was this the right thing to do? Or was I being a love-struck idiot, waylaid by the clear blue of Evan's eyes.

I should've slept on it. I should've told Evan I needed more time...

"Second thoughts?" he asked as he unlocked our door. I stared back helplessly and his eyes clouded. "The last thing I want is for you to be afraid of me."

"I'm not," I said, and that was the truth. "But can we just…go. Drive, I mean."

We packed up our two bags. He tossed his in the back and I kept mine on my lap in the cab of the truck. We pulled out of the parking lot and headed south on Highway 34, leaving Terrell behind.

"Why south? I thought you said we had to go north."

"We need to throw them off the scent. We'll go about fifty miles south, as if we're heading for Mexico. Then you need to call someone in Dolores on your cell. They'll triangulate the signal and pinpoint where you're calling from."

"Done a lot of research on this, have you?"

"We watched a lot of CSI in the rec room."

"A show about cops catching criminals?"

"How Not to Get Caught 101," Evan said with a grin.

Something solid and petrified deep inside me began to crack. *It's so easy to be with him.*

"I could call my friend Del," I said, "but I don't want to get her in trouble. I could call Patty, I guess. But what do I say? I left Lee and I'm fleeing to Mexico? Not very subtle."

"It doesn't matter. Just so long as they can get the signal. Give it a half an hour, then call her."

"I should call Patty. Tell her I'm sorry about Lee."

"*I'm* sorry for Lee," Evan said fiercely. "Not you. Never you."

"I don't know about that."

Lee's death hung heavy on me. Even if Evan had done the actual deed and it was an accident, I felt it weighing me down in a way that felt permanent.

"He wasn't all bad to start. The drugs turned him rotten. He may have been a good kid. In any case, he was her son…"

My cell phone rang, and I let out a little cry. I pulled it from my bag like it was a snake.

Evan glanced at it. "Someone you know?"

"I don't know this number, but it's my parish area code. Do I answer?"

"It's what we need right now."

I hit answer. "Hello?"

"Josephine Clark?"

"Who's this?"

"Ms. Clark, my name is Detective Toussaint. I'm with the Ouachita Parish Police Department."

"Yes?" I covered the mouthpiece and mouthed to Evan, "Police."

Evan made a motion with his hand to keep talking.

"Ms. Clark, are you available to meet at the precinct this afternoon? Answer some questions?"

"Not really."

A pause. "Can I ask if you're still within the boundaries of the State of Louisiana?"

"You can ask."

"You sound a little hostile, Ms. Clark. Are you aware that your fiancé, Mr. Lee Stevenson, was found deceased in a house fire yesterday evening?"

"Is that so?"

"You don't sound surprised."

"He was a meth head. And not my fiancé."

"I see," Toussaint said. He sounded young. Overly friendly. "You're not particularly saddened over his passing?"

"He was violent," I said, lowering my voice and turning away from Evan. "If you're any kind of halfway decent detective you would already know that."

"Are you glad he is dead, Ms. Clark?"

"Are those my only two options?" I asked. "Glad or sad? How about conflicted? He beat the hell out of me, Mr. Toussaint. That doesn't mean I want him dead but it also doesn't mean I'm going to shed a tear that he's gone."

"Fair enough," Det. Toussaint said. "I have another question for you, Ms. Clark. Are you acquainted with a man by the name of Evan Salinger?"

"What about him?" I glanced over at Evan, and saw his hands tighten around steering wheel.

"Is he with you now? Are you able to speak freely?"

I said nothing, as the enormity of what was happening struck me. To run from the police; it was a serious fucking thing to do, with dire consequences. There was no going back. If Evan and I went north, we'd be fugitives. If we turned back, we had a shot. Lee's death was an accident. Evan was protecting me. Or I could claim self-defense. We could rely on the system to do the right thing…

I knew what would happen if we turned back. Evan wouldn't let me plead self-defense. He'd confess to Lee's death, and given his history, they'd lock him up forever. It wouldn't matter that it had been an accident, or that Lee had beat the shit out of me that night…They'd take Evan away from me. Again.

"Ms. Clark?" Toussaint's voice in my ear. "Are you still there?"

This is what a second chance looks like. For both of us.

"Ms. Clark?" Detective Toussaint persisted. "Are you aware that—"

"Yes, I'm aware, detective," I said, cutting him off. "I'm very aware of everything. Thanks for calling."

I ended the call, rolled down the window, and chucked the phone out of the truck. In my side mirror, I watched it smash onto the highway behind us and break into a dozen pieces.

A smile spread over Evan's face like a sunrise after a dark night. Then he burst out laughing, a hearty deep bellow that tapered away into a warm, affectionate expression of relief and joy and everything good.

I sat back against my seat and lay my head against the headrest, smiling lazily, feeling more heavy boulders of time and regret crack inside me and fall away.

CHAPTER 26

EVAN

After Jo ditched her cell phone, I hooked the truck back around onto Highway 35 north, which would take us around Dallas. Elation surged through my veins, pressing my foot to the gas. I wanted to get wherever we needed to go as fast as possible.

It was late afternoon when we hit Denton, Texas. I checked us into a small motel towards the center of town and paid cash again.

"We need supplies," I said. "I'll go. You stay here and rest."

"I can go with you."

I shook my head. "Police are sending out APB's with our descriptions right about now. I can put on dark glasses and a hat but you…"

Her fingers touched the scar on her cheek. She nodded, wincing at the pain in her neck. "Can't argue with that." She started to climb into one of the two beds. "Hurry back, okay?"

I hurried. I hated being away from her, leaving her unprotected. I zipped through the local Walmart, tossing whatever I thought she might need into the cart. What did women need to travel? Lotions? Hygiene products? Makeup? It looked like Jo didn't wear makeup anymore. Good. She didn't need it. She was as hauntingly beautiful as I'd remembered—even more now that she was with me. Flesh and blood, not ghost and memory.

At the last minute—and fueled by some serious wishful thinking—I grabbed a box of condoms. Jo didn't have to see them. We might never use them, but if the moment came, I'd be goddamned if I wasn't going to be prepared.

I stopped at a pizza joint near the Walmart, waited while they made me a large pie with everything, then hurried back to the motel.

Jo stirred as I came in, sitting up and sniffing deeply as I set the pizza on the dresser. I dumped out the Walmart bags on the bed. Tampons, deodorant, toothpaste, hairbrush and travel size hair conditioner and shampoo. "Wasn't quite sure what you needed."

Jo rested her chin on her hand, smiling. "This is so obviously a *guy's* shopping trip."

"Did I forget anything? I can go back."

"No, you thought of everything." She picked up a tampon box. "Not many men would brave the feminine hygiene aisle alone."

I grinned. "It's not like anyone would think they're for me."

Her smile slipped. "Thank you for this, Evan, but I still don't have any money. And that still sucks."

"I told you, I have enough. A little over a thousand bucks."

"Is it enough to get us wherever we need to go?"

"I think so."

She nodded, winced, and rubbed her neck. I brought the pizza around and set her up with a few slices. I sat on the other bed and we ate in silence.

"How about the news?" she asked finally. "I'm curious as to how my phone call with the detective went down."

"You sure you want to know?"

"Don't we need to keep tabs on how fucked we are?"

"I just don't want you to worry."

She smiled dryly. "Too late."

I took up the remote and scanned around for a local channel. Within moments I found a report about us.

"That's Patty," Jo said, around a mouthful.

Outside the diner where I'd found Jo working, a reporter was interviewing a thin, older woman with a short perm. In an angry and tearful tirade, Patty called for Jo to be arrested for Lee's murder. Behind her, a half-dozen brutish-looking guys nodded darkly in agreement.

Jo sat back against her headboard, pressing herself back as if being pushed by the images.

The scene changed: locals comforting Patty while the reporter talked over. "What was first deemed an accidental house fire is now being classified as possible arson. Two persons of interest, Josephine Clark and Evan Salinger—an escaped convict—are now suspected of foul play."

Side-by-side pictures flashed on the screen: Jo's senior portrait and my booking shot from North Central Correctional.

The camera cut to a man in a brown police uniform, captioned *Sheriff Griggs, Ouachita Parish.*

"I can't give too many details at this time, but we've gathered enough evidence that indicates Mr. Stevenson's death may not have been accidental. We have issued a warrant for Mr. Salinger's arrest, and we'd very much like to speak with Ms. Clark."

An off-camera voice: "And if Ms. Clark doesn't comply?"

The Sheriff looked grave. "We'd have to start making some serious assumptions about her participation in Mr. Stevenson's passing."

I shut off the TV.

"You were right," Jo said, setting aside her plate. "I didn't need to see that." A tense silence passed, then Jo spoke, so quietly I almost didn't hear her. "It's my fault."

I tossed my slice of pizza back into the box, my appetite vanishing. "What's your fault?"

"This." She gestured at the TV. "Everything. This mess. Lee…" She shook her head and winced. She touched the back of her neck, scrubbed at it, as if she were trying to rub off something dirty left on her skin. "God, this fucking hurts. All of it. It just hurts."

"Can I help?"

She looked at me and I felt the air thicken. I hadn't touched her in four years, and I wanted to. I wanted to so badly I could hardly breathe.

"Thanks," Jo said. She scooted forward on the mattress as I sat behind her.

She was wearing a white tank top and no bra. I stared at the graceful length of her neck and the curve of her shoulder. My pulse jumped and my groin tightened as I took up her silky dark hair and moved it over her shoulder, revealing the smooth skin of her back.

Then I put my hands on her.

I had to close my eyes against the onslaught of physical memories that swamped me. Our first touches, our first kisses. My hands sliding up this same skin that was wet and warm under the water…

I sucked in a breath, forcing my body to settle the hell down. Carefully, I kneaded the tight muscles in Jo's neck, feeling the fragility of her body beneath my hands. She was small and thin. Malnourished. Yet I could feel her strength, too. A soft heat emanating from her skin. A furnace inside that never burned out, no matter how hard life had tried to snuff it.

She needed peace now, and safety. To eat well and sleep long hours. To rebuild and regroup, nurture that strength and use it for herself instead of basic survival.

I wished I could take her someplace safe and permanent but we had to go north. To the center. If we didn't we'd be ruined. I hadn't told Jo that last part; it was a miracle she was putting up with my crazy-sounding story at all. But it was as real to me as my own flesh and bone. The drive to obey the dream—that I could only see in fragments yet—was as natural to me as my own pulse driving the blood through my veins.

My hands gently rubbed at the knots in her neck and shoulders, loosening the tension coiled in her. Jo slumped, her protective walls coming down a bit. They didn't crumble—she'd built them strong. But I heard her sigh, letting me in a little. She leaned into my touch.

"It didn't start out bad with Lee," she said. "He wasn't a prince by any goddamn stretch of the imagination, but he wasn't a monster. Not then. Not until he got into meth." Her breath hitched. "The drugs turned him nasty…"

"It's okay, Jo."

"I'm telling you because I'm not stupid. I don't want you to think I'm stupid."

"You're not stupid."

"I'm weak."

"*No.*"

"I let my body become a receptacle for Lee," she said miserably. "A punching bag, a spittoon. I traded my soul for shelter, a house to live in and food on the table. It was survival, not a life. Not a life…"

A sob bent her down, and her shoulders shuddered under my hands. I wanted to hold her to me so badly, hold her together as she came undone. I kept rubbing her neck and shoulders, waiting for her to let me know what she wanted. What she was ready for.

"I was exhausted and shit-broke and desperate," she said. "But I would never… If I'd have known, he would hit… I'd never…"

She collapsed back against me, turning into my chest. I held her close, tucking her head under my chin and stroking her hair. My heart ached for her and soared for us at the same time.

"You don't have to explain anything to me, Jo. I know. I know how strong you are."

She shook her head, her tears dampening my shirt. "No…"

"*Yes,*" I said, holding her tighter. "You're strong. Even strong people get stuck in in fucking terrible situations."

"A strong person would've left."

"A strong person figures out how to survive. And then you escape or fight your way out. Or you give in. You never gave in."

"And now he's dead," she said. "It's my fault. I know it was an accident but I really fucking wish you didn't have that on your hands or heart. You're too good to have to carry that."

"I can take it," I said. *I have no choice.*

She sat up and looked back at me with red-rimmed eyes. The lump on her temple was green with a purple seam of dried blood. "I'm sorry you got involved in this messed-up situation. But I'm really glad you ended it."

I wished with everything I had, I could take away her pain—all of it, from the scar up to that moment—and keep it so she'd never have to suffer it again.

"It's not over yet, Jo," I said. "Not until I get you somewhere safe. Where none of this—" I gestured at the TV with my chin. "Can touch you."

She didn't say anything. A handful of seconds passed when neither of us moved. I wanted to tilt her face to mine and kiss her. Kiss her all night. But I'd only just found her yesterday. Abused, scared…I wondered when the last time someone was kind to her. Or touched her softly. When was the last time she made love with someone? With Lee? Was he good to her? Or did he abuse her behind the closed bedroom door, too? I wanted to ask but couldn't, and my muscles stiffened with rage at the mere idea. Jo felt it and pulled away.

"I'd like to sleep now," she said, her walls back up. "My neck feels better. Thanks."

"No problem." I rose from her bed so she could climb under the covers. "You should sleep. We'll leave at dawn."

"Sure."

Jo crawled under the covers, and settled her head on the pillow. I covered her shoulders with the stiff, cheap polyester comforter. She closed her eyes, the furrow in her brow smoothed.

I turned out the bedside table lamp and lay down on my bed. It was only nine o'clock, but sleep was dragging at me too. I hadn't realized how wound up I'd been, on the run for weeks, and then trying to convince Jo to come with me. Now that she was here, I felt myself melting into the bed. We had a long way to go, but she was here.

I was at the place where thoughts broke and started to scatter before sleep when her sleepy voice drifted across the space between our beds.

"I feel it getting closer."

"Feel what, Jo?"

"Whatever is going to come and take you away from me."

In the dark, she couldn't see the expression on my face. Maybe she heard how my breath hitched at her words. Maybe she didn't mean what my heart wanted her to mean, that she couldn't stand the idea of being apart from me again. Maybe she meant my imminent arrest. Or maybe her thoughts were breaking apart too, and she didn't quite know what she meant.

But I harbored the hope that some part of what we had four years ago was still alive in her, even if she kept it locked up.

I staved off sleep for another few minutes, waited until her breathing was deep and even, and I was sure she was asleep.

"Good night, Jo," I said softly. And then, a whisper, "I love you."

CHAPTER 27

JO

"Where are we going?" I asked. "I mean, aside from north?"

"Just north," Evan replied. "For now."

The sun had just pulled itself completely over the flat horizon, and there was nothing to see on all sides but miles of flat land, sparsely dotted with greenery. Evan drove the truck on the mostly-empty road, its engine the only sound for a long stretch. The silence felt as heavy as the heat. I started to make a comment about how hot it was already, then bit off a curse instead.

Evan glanced at me. "You okay?"

"I don't want to make small talk with you."

He grinned. "Then don't."

"My catalog of topics is pretty limited, and none of them good."

"What happened after that night I was arrested? Did you graduate? I think you told me you did in your letters."

"Yeah, I did," I said. "It was a minor miracle, given all the shit that went down. But my English teacher had mercy on me, I guess. I wrote a poem and…"

My skin suddenly flushed red, and a strange combo of grief and longing flooded me, remembering "I Never Told You."

I took back my words, and turned my head to the flat vistas around us.

"Yeah? What was the poem about?" Evan asked after a minute.

"Nothing." Jesus, I was too flustered to even lie. "So, uh, do you still hold your breath?"

Smooth, Josephine. Real smooth.

But Evan broke out in a laugh. "Yeah, I do. Not underwater. No pools in prison, but I had lots of time to kill in my cell, to say the least."

"How long?"

"Almost six minutes."

My eyes widened. "No shit?"

"No shit."

"That's…really long."

"It's okay."

I frowned. "How long does it need to be?"

"Eleven minutes," he said, deadly serious, eyes forward.

"That was a rhetorical question."

He shrugged. "That's the actual answer."

I stared at him a minute more, then laughed. "Weirdo."

Evan laughed too, and shook his head. "I missed you, Jo."

My laughter died a swift death, as my heart kicked it into high gear. "I missed you too," I said faintly.

Evan was shaking his head. "No, that's not right. I more than missed you. I felt like a piece of myself broke off and I've been spending the last four years trying to get used to living without it. Like a phantom limb, you hear about. It's gone, but you can still feel it, and feeling it just makes you want it back more and more."

I looked away, shame coloring my skin now. "I'm sorry I didn't stay in touch. I tried…"

"Don't do that, Jo," Evan said, his blue eyes like hard chips of glass. "It's not your fault."

"Isn't it? It just was all so fucked up, how they treated you. And what Shane said to put you away…" I shook my head, my hand balling into fist. "I couldn't do a damn thing. No one would listen to me."

"I know. It's okay."

"Not remotely. But I tried. I really did. But life…just got in the way. It sounds like a pathetic excuse, but it's true."

"What happened?" Evan asked quietly.

"After your sentencing, Gerry told me he wasn't going to cut me loose after all. I was a mess. I guess he felt sorry for me, or was worried about me."

"I remember that from your letters," Evan said. "I was so glad to hear you weren't on your own."

"For a glorious six months. But then Gerry died. Pulmonary embolism. Too much sitting and too much trucker food. After that, I…struggled." I fixed my gaze on the flat horizon, plucked a thread on the hem of my t-shirt. "I was homeless for a while, living out of my car. This was in Arkansas, now."

"You were *homeless*?"

"That's why my letters stopped. I didn't have an address. Or if I did, it didn't last. I wound up heading south, met Lee, and the rest, as they say, is history." I smirked. "Or a true crime story. One of the two."

"Jesus, I'm sorry, Jo."

"For what?" I asked bitterly. "I made a mess of my life, and it was already fucked up to begin with."

"I wasn't there for you. I should have been there for you."

"I should have been there for you. We were…torn apart."

He looked about to reply, but stopped short, his eyes narrowing at a sign coming up: *Exit 51 77N toward Turner Falls Area.*

And below that, *Davis, Oklahoma, pop. 2743*

We'd crossed into Oklahoma, steady on the 35N, but now Evan took that exit, heading east.

"Where are we going?" I asked.

"Uh, Davis," Evan replied after a minute. "Are you hungry? Let's get some breakfast."

"Sure," I said slowly.

It was true, I could eat, but that's not why Evan had veered off the 35. Whatever inner compass guided him had changed our course. I was sure of it.

We stopped at the Boomerang Diner. I ordered the Big Ham Country

Breakfast: eggs, hash browns, biscuits and gravy, a side of fruit and coffee. And I ate the whole damn thing. Apparently, being a fugitive from the law did wonders for the appetite. Food tasted good again. Diner coffee tasted as a million times better than the swill at Lee and Patty's diner. Even the pale, unripe honeydew tasted amazing.

I stopped eating long enough to glance at Evan across from me. He was devouring the same breakfast with the same voracity as me. He caught me staring and we laughed when I made oinking noises.

"Am I that bad?" he laughed.

"No worse than me," I said. "I think I swallowed my fork."

He laughed harder and nearly choked on his bacon.

It's all coming back, isn't it? Him and me?

He told me a story about prison, how one of our favorite movies, *Raising Arizona,* was a cellblock cult favorite and the movie was shown, by request, every Saturday night in the rec room.

"The most quotable movie in the history of cinema, next to *The Princess Bride,*" I declared.

Evan put on a drawling, affected southern accent. "We ate crawdad. And when there was no crawdad to be found, we ate sand."

I picked up the cue. "You ate what?"

"We ate sand."

"You ate *sand?*"

Laughing after a huge breakfast made my insides ache in the best way, like they hadn't in years. I was full of food and joy. My eyes were full of Evan.

This is a dream. It's too good to be real.

Then a pair of policeman sidled up to the breakfast bar, their shiny badges and weapons strapped to their waists, reminding me it was all too real. Talking and laughing with the waitress, they didn't appear to be scoping the place. Evan met my eye and reached for his wallet. He dropped some cash on the table and we slipped out of the diner casually, but quickly. In his truck, I shut the passenger door and locked it, my pulse a little jumpy from the cops, but the good feeling hadn't left me.

We stopped at a local country store to buy lunch for the road. On impulse, I threw in a red-and-white checkered picnic blanket. Evan drove us north along a quiet stretch of highway bordered by shrubbery and trees. The land was green with summer. The sky pure blue and empty of clouds. It felt like Evan and I were the last two people on earth.

I stole glances at him: his large hand as he searched for an Oldies station on the radio and the way his arm muscle stretched the sleeve of his t-shirt. His presence filled the cab of the truck. He exhaled a sigh and I breathed it in. I smelled his skin, warm and clean and familiar.

We drove north for another hour and a half, then Evan turned off the main highway toward Catoosa.

"Are we stopping?" I asked as he paid the toll at the end of the exit ramp.

Evan's eyes had a faraway look to them, as if he were seeing something beyond the road in front of him.

"I think there's something I want you to see," he said.

"You think or you know?"

He didn't answer. I saw a sign reading *Route 66 Roadside Attraction!* On the horizon ahead, a blob of pale blue began to emerge against the green landscape. Squinting into the sky, I gradually realized it was a whale. A giant metal whale beached alongside a small swimming hole. Cartoonish eyes and a gaping mouth big enough to walk in.

"What *is* that?"

Evan pulled in and parked. He smiled as he shut off the engine. "It's why we're here."

I climbed out of the truck, gaping. The little swimming pond was cut from the natural earth. The whale was about twenty feet long. Its mouth yawned open, inviting kids to come inside and play. A slide started at the pectoral fin, winding out and dropping into the water below. A small diving platform had been built on the whale's tail. Though the sign had made it sound like a somewhat famous Oklahoma landmark, there was no one here swimming or picnicking in the summer heat.

I looked over at Evan, shielding my eyes from the sun. "We're taking a break from our run from the law to have a swim?"

He grinned. "Why not? Seems like a good place for it." He reached behind to take hold of his collar and then stripped off his shirt.

I hadn't seen the whole of his naked torso in four years. My breath stuck in my throat as my gaze traced the tight lines of his abdomen and swept over the broad, smooth plains of his chest. Evan's eighteen-year-old physique had been impressive enough, but now it was the solid, powerful body of a man in front of me.

Dry-mouthed, I sank down on one of the multicolored benches lining the swimming hole's tiny, makeshift beach.

"Aren't you coming in?" he asked, now stripped down to his boxers and taking off his watch.

"No bathing suit," I managed. "I'm good right here, thanks."

He flashed me a smile, either oblivious to my torture or enjoying it. "Suit yourself."

He waded down the little man-made beach in long strides, his skin bronzed in the sun, then dove in. With long-armed strides, he swam to the center of the swimming hole and treaded water. The fading sunlight glinted off his hair, turning it gold.

"Want me to time you?" I called. "For old time's sake?"

"Sure," he said.

I took the wristwatch he'd set atop the pile of his clothes. It was an old watch; I guessed the waterproof one I'd bought for him before prom hadn't survived our separation.

I waited for a new minute to roll around. "And…go."

Evan disappeared beneath the surface, and the seconds began to add up. This was nothing like Funtown. This pool was a natural hole in the ground. No lights, no white cement, no clear blue water. Evan went under and vanished.

One minute. My leg jounced and I gnawed my lower lip.

At two minutes, I got off the bench and knelt in the grass at edge of the pond. I kept half an eye on the watch and the rest of my vision trained on the still, murky water.

Three minutes. My heart crashed harder in my chest with every passing second.

At five minutes, I was sure he was dead. My free hand reached to splash the water gently. Then harder. Then frantic.

Evan rose to the surface, sucking in huge droughts of air. He wheezed and gasped, and I felt a little less guilty for freaking out and making him come up. He sounded like he was choking.

"Are you okay?" I asked.

When he'd caught his breath, he jerked his head back to get his hair out of his eyes. "Yeah, I'm good. What's wrong?"

"Nothing, I…" I stood up and retreated back to the bench, feeling stupid. "Nothing."

Evan glided toward the beach. His feet found the bottom and he strode up the sand toward me. "Jo? You okay?"

"I didn't like that I couldn't see you."

Evan's thoughts were so visible on his face, I felt like a mind reader. He was touched I cared, and sorry to make me worry. "I'm sorry, Jo."

"It's fine in a pool where I can see you. But out here…" I lost my train of thought watching the water droplets bead on his chest. Desire sunk deep in me. I'd forgotten how potent it was—a sweet ache in my lower belly like a warm, heavy stone.

I looked to see Evan's eyes on me, amused. My cheeks flushed red. "What?"

"Nothing," he said. "Are you hungry?"

"When am I not?"

I surreptitiously watched Evan get dressed. He looked so hearty and hale. Golden. By contrast I felt scrawny, pale and extremely unsexy in my tank top and loose cargo pants. I wished I'd covered up my arms, which were thin and marked with fading bruises.

Evan took our lunch stuff from the truck. We laid out the red-checkered quilt, and set up the picnic with the sandwiches, chips, ice tea, and fruit we had bought at the grocery store in Davis. I was ravenous and we both ate without talking.

Full and content, I finally closed my eyes and turned my face to the sun, basking in something that felt close to peace. When I opened my eyes again, Evan was looking at me over the remains of his lunch.

"What are you thinking about?" he asked.

I looked around at this peaceful little oasis in the middle of a flat and endless countryside. "I feel good."

My gaze landed on the big blue whale with its smiling mouth and hand-drawn cartoon eyes. "I had a whale like that when I was a kid. A stuffed animal, I mean. My mother gave it to me. I loved that thing. I carried it with me everywhere I went. I called it…"

I turned my head into the memory. "Moby," I said, shocked that it came to me. "Mama gave him to me and said I should call him Moby. Because it was the name of a whale in a famous book I would read someday."

My breath caught as the memories emerged out of the gray fog and into bright, vivid color. I let out a surprised laugh and looked at Evan in wonder. The memories coming one after another, piling up.

"She was always encouraging me to read, my mother. I remember when she said it was the best way to explore the world when you couldn't go anywhere. Her light was on so bright that day. *You're never stuck anywhere if you have a good book*. Those were her exact words. I remember them. And her voice and her smile…"

I laughed, took a deep breath, and dried my eyes on a napkin. "I can't believe it came back."

Evan wordlessly reached over and held my hand, and we sat that way for a long time, basking in the sun, and me basking in the little piece of my mother I could now remember.

Eventually, Evan took another dip. He didn't hold his breath again, joking his full stomach would anchor him to the bottom. The sun was dipping toward the horizon as we packed up and left.

As we drove away, I watched the blue whale in the rearview mirror. Fingertips touching the reflection as it grew smaller. I wished I had my cell phone so I could've taken a picture of it. Instead I held it in my memory, like a poem, written vivid, bright blue words.

CHAPTER
28

EVAN

We arrived in Tulsa around five o'clock and found a roadside motel with vacancy.

"I only have one room left," the desk clerk said. "No smoking, king bed."

I looked at Jo, half-expecting her contented, peaceful expression to darken with suspicion about the sleeping arrangement. The last thing I wanted to do was extinguish the happiness she'd found at the Blue Whale. It had shone so bright in her eyes for the entire drive. Her smile was easy and she laughed a lot. As we walked from the truck to the motel office, I saw she was standing up straight, not hunched-over and hugging her sides.

"You all right with one bed? We can go somewhere else."

"No, it's fine."

I took a shower to wash the swimming hole water off my skin. When I came out of the bathroom, Jo was watching the news.

"What's the latest?"

She snapped off the TV. "They're in pursuit. They're hinting that you may have kidnapped me."

I ignored that last part. "They won't catch us."

"How do you know?"

"Because I won't let them."

Jo let it go. For now. I knew the further north we went, the more questions she'd have. I prayed that by the time we reached the Center, she'd trust me enough to accept the answers. I prayed I'd *have* the answers at all. So far, much of what drove us lurked just outside my reckoning.

I went out to bring us back some Chinese takeout dinner then Jo took a turn in the shower while I half-watched some ancient *Bonanza* rerun on the TV. I tried not to imagine Jo in there, naked, the water streaming over her skin as she ran her hands over her body that was slippery with soap…

I groaned and adjusted my groin. *Jesus, not now.* Not until she was ready and rested. Maybe never. Maybe after she'd been through so much horrible shit in these last four years, sex was the last thing on her mind. I couldn't blame her.

But God, I wanted her. When the bathroom door opened and Jo emerged in a cloud of steam, I wanted to grab her and throw her down on the bed and fuck her senseless. Or make love to her, slow and gentle. Whatever she wanted. Anything she wanted.

She was wrapped in a towel, covered from her small, perfect breasts to her upper thighs. Her wet hair spilled down her pale shoulders like black silk. From my perch on our lone bed, I looked away, shifting my legs to hide the erection straining against my jeans.

Jo rummaged in her small bag. She fished out some panties, a pair of shorts and a shirt. My shirt. The old blue and black plaid flannel I'd given her in high school.

Holy shit, she still has that?

I remember she asked me to sleep in it so that it would smell like me when I gave it back. That had been one of the biggest moments of my life, that little request. And now here…I knew she packed hardly more than three items of clothing when she left Dolores. My shirt was one of them.

Clothes in hand, Jo retreated back to the bathroom. I heard running water, the sound of teeth being brushed. Somehow, being in her personal space, listening to all the private, before-bed rituals, was a turn-on.

When she came out of the bathroom, she smelled like some sweet lotion and she was wearing my shirt and…

Goddammit, Jo…

I kept my eyes on the TV as she opened the bedside table drawer, fumbled around and came up with the motel notepad and pen. She folded back the covers and settled onto her side of the bed. Only a foot of white space between us that felt roughly the size of Texas. She tapped the pen against her lips—unaware of what that did to me—then began to write. In fits and starts at first, then with some continuity. Then a break. A word crossed out. Then more writing. *Bonanza* blared on the TV.

"Poem?" I said during a commercial break.

"Maybe," she said. "It's been so long. I'm rusty as hell."

I remembered she said she hadn't written anything in a year. Today was racking up victory after victory.

"What's it about?" I asked. She hesitated and I quickly added, "You don't have to tell me."

"It's about the pool. Our pool. In Planerville. I think about it a lot."

So did I. The pool, where we swam and got to know each other. Where we kissed and touched and she let me put my mouth between her legs. My life happened in that pool. Every memory of every minute spent in its waters was precious to me. Including the time she thought I'd been drowning.

Jo studied the scribbled words on the pad. "Timing you underwater today brought it back. How it used to freak me out when you'd stay under for so long. I guess it still freaks me out."

I struggled to find something to say that wasn't a hoarse request to touch her. Or that she would touch me. End this torture already.

Give her time, give her space…

It was a monk's mantra and I was no monk. A virgin, yes, but if I was supposed to be nervous or anxious about that, I wasn't. I just wanted her.

Her head bowed under the silence. A little sigh made her shoulders slump. She set the pen and paper aside and turned off the lamp. She lay on her side, her back to me, and pulled the covers up over her shoulders.

I clicked off the TV. The only light came from the street outside, filtering wan and yellow through the curtains. I slid off my jeans. In t-shirt and boxers, I crawled under the sheet on my side.

Minutes passed.

"Evan?" Jo's voice frail in the dark. "Do you ever…" I heard her swallow hard. "Do you think about us? What we had?"

My chest ached at the longing in her voice. The fearful tentative reaching across the space between us.

"Every minute," I said. "I think about us every minute of my life. All I do is think about us."

She rolled over to face me. In the dim light, I could see the tears glittering in her eyes.

"I get it," she said. "I know why you're over there and I'm over here. I do. I feel like there aren't enough showers in the world to wash the last four years off of me."

I half sat up, stunned. "No. That's not why—"

"Then why won't you touch me?"

"I didn't want to pressure you. You've been through so much and I wanted to give you space."

"I don't want space. I don't want to be apart from you. Not for another damn minute."

Thank god. Oh fuck, thank god.

"Come here," I said gruffly. "God, Jo, come here."

We met in no-man's land, moved into the middle of the bed. She came crying into my chest. I held her tight, her body small in my arms and shaking with sobs. I wrapped myself around her. Her tears soaked the front of my t-shirt as I fought to keep my own sobs back. Someone had to be strong here. But the reality of her in my arms was breaking me down. The scent of her washed hair and the warmth of her skin. Moment by moment, inhale by exhale, every heartbeat of hers against mine erased our separation. The lust consuming me all night revealed for what it truly was: my need to be with Josephine for the rest of my life. Not only her body but everything that she was: her scribbled words, her lonely heart and her victorious happiness.

I stroked her hair as she clung to me. Her tense, tight body relaxed into mine. Fitting with me. A perfect mesh of flesh and bone.

She drew her head back to look at me in the dark. I heard her breath catch in a tremulous intake of breath.

"I want to kiss you, Evan. Do you want to kiss me?"

"More than anything," I said, in love with her brave honesty. "But if I kiss you I won't want to stop."

"I don't want you to stop. Have you still never...?"

I nodded, hard and aching for her. "I've been locked up. And when I got out, all I wanted to do was find you."

"You found me," she said, pressing her body tighter to mine. "I don't know how, but you did." Her hands slipped around the back of my neck. Her fingers played in my hair, then slid around to my jaw and along the edge of my mouth. Her soft eyes followed the trail of her fingertips, an intimate reacquainting.

"Kiss me, Evan. Please. Please…"

I gently laid my lips on hers, intent on taking it slow. But Jo's mouth parted for mine. A little gasp in her throat and that's all it took for my restraint to burn to ash. We fell into each other, a tangle of arms and legs, greedy kisses and hands seizing back the four years stolen from us.

My hands surged into her hair, angling her head into my kiss. I wanted to devour her. Her tongue stroked mine and her teeth grazed my lips. Her hands moved down my chest, over my abdomen, down to stroke my aching erection.

"No, wait." I captured her wrists and pressed them on the pillow above her head. "I'll never last."

"I don't care. This is for you."

"The hell it is. It's for us. We've waited too long."

"Turn on the light," she whispered. "I want you to see everything."

I clicked on the lamp and groaned at the sight of her dark, damp hair fanned over the pillow, her eyes half-lidded and her mouth parted. Her lips were red and swollen from my kisses.

"Slow," I said, more for myself than for her.

I moved my mouth down her throat, kissing a path along her warm, soft skin. I unbuttoned her shirt—*my* shirt—enough to lift it over her head. Then her breasts, small and perfect, were in my hands. Solid, real flesh, not a fantasy to keep me going in prison. A low moan issued from deep in my chest. She shuddered and arched into me as I bent to kiss a hard nipple. I teased and sucked at it, then moved to the other. Her hands made fists in my hair as I bit to the threshold of pleasure and pain, then soothed the sweet ache with my tongue.

"God, you're beautiful," I said hoarsely, resting my forehead between her breasts to catch my breath. "You're so fucking beautiful. And mine."

"Yes," she whispered with no breath at all. "Yours…all yours."

I reared back on my knees, trailing open-mouthed kisses down her stomach and over her underwear. I hooked my fingers in the waistband and tugged them off her hips.

"Four years," I murmured, flicking my tongue over her. "Four years I've waited to taste you again."

She moaned as I spread her open gently and moved in, sucking and licking her sweetness. She propped herself on her elbows to watch me, then fell back writhing. Her hips rose and fell against my mouth. I was relentless. One crashing orgasm hit my tongue, then another. I would have kept going but she reached down to clutch my wrists.

"God, Evan, no more... I can't..."

"Come here."

I rolled to my back and pulled her toward me. Up and onto me. She straddled my hips, her wetness sliding over my boxers and nestling my erection. I pressed one hand to her cheek, the other at the small of her back, wanting to slow down and savor this, make it last. She pulled my t-shirt off and laid her hands gently on either side of my chest. The frenetic energy between us simmered.

She bent down, kissing me. Her breath hot in my ear. "How do you want me?"

"Like this. Facing me. I want to look up and watch you come. And I want to kiss you the whole time."

I pulled her mouth to mine, my tongue looking for hers. My other hand slid down her breasts and stomach to where her thighs were spread. I slipped two fingers into that wet heat and she cried out to my mouth as I groaned back into hers.

"Jesus," I gasped, fighting for control as the need became unbearable. "You feel so fucking good..."

Her head tilted back. My mouth sucked at her throat while my fingers stroked her to another release. I wanted to give her everything, make it as good as possible, because I didn't think I'd last long. Already I was losing control.

"I need you, Evan. Now. Please..."

She stripped off my boxers, her gaze hungry and appreciative, roving up and down my body.

"I need a condom," I said, cursing myself for leaving them in the bathroom. The ten seconds it would take to get them was too long.

Jo shook her head, her hair spilling down over her pale skin. "I'm on the pill. And I'm clean. I promise. In the hospital, they tested me…"

"I believe you," I said, my heart pounding even harder at what she was telling me. "Is that what you want?"

"I want you to feel everything," she said. "And I want to feel everything. Skin to skin. I want to feel you come inside me."

Jesus, her words alone were sending me to the brink.

I lay back as she came crawling up, her knees on either side of me. She hovered there, an agonizing, savoring moment.

I gripped her hips, my heart bursting out of my chest. "Now, Jo. Please…"

She laid her forehead on mine, her hair falling down to curtain us. "Yes, now. Now…"

Her mouth settled on mine, lips parted and trembling. I tasted her air, then she sank down on me with a little cry of purest want.

A sound came through my throat I'd never made before. Sensations I'd never felt in my life: wet heat, tightness, hardness and softness. Then I was deep inside her, enveloped in her body, trembling at the power of a thousand unknown emotions sweeping through me.

"Evan," she said against my mouth. "Are you ready?"

I nodded. She began to move and my body moved with her. It knew what to do. It was so easy. I fell in sync with her rhythm, clutching her thighs and driving up hard into her. Every one of my thrusts a question and every rolling grind of her hips the perfect answer.

"Does it feel good?" she breathed.

"No." I wrapped my arm around her waist and rolled with her, got her under me without breaking our rhythm. "There's no word for how this feels."

Her head rose, craning for my kiss. I sank into her mouth, the wave of my body crashing on hers again and again. I braced my weight on one elbow, my other hand found hers and laced our fingers above her head. I breathed her breath, tasted her sweat, kissed away the tears seeping from the corners of her eyes. She wrapped her legs around my waist, holding me tight as my thrusts went deeper, harder. I could feel her coming and I struggled to hold on, to wait for her.

Her body tensed beneath mine and I broke our kiss to watch the beauty of her coming undone. Her green eyes widened with a sudden rush of pleasure. First a gasp then an uncontrolled cry tore from her. She'd hardly begun to subside when I felt my thundering release let go, spilling deep into her. She took it, took all I had to give, until I was drained and spent, lost in the pleasure of it. Lost in her, completely.

It seemed we sank deeper into the bed then, heavy and satiated—for now—and sighing over and over that we'd arrived here at last.

And I knew then, without any dream or hunch to tell me, that Jo was the first woman I'd ever sleep with, and also the last.

CHAPTER 29

JO

Evan collapsed over me, breathing heavily against my neck. I held him close as the pulsing ribbons of my orgasm tapered away, leaving me drained yet electrified, both spent and wanting more.

Even with his weight pressing me down and his sweat mingling with mine, it still felt unreal. He was here. With me. We were together.

He wants me.

It wasn't only time and geography that had separated us. I had spent four years in a prison of my own. My time with Lee left me feeling worthless. I couldn't even contemplate having Evan in my life again. Someone so clean and good… How could he want me?

Yet here he was. And here I was the first woman he'd made love to. He waited for this. Wanted this. As he'd pressed and pushed into my body and back into my life, my reflection in his eyes was one I could finally bear to look at. Even admire.

"I can't move," he said, his voice muffled.

I laughed, running my hands over the hard muscles in his back. "Don't. Stay here forever."

He raised his head to look at me.

I brushed back the hair falling in his face. "What is it?"

"We're here. This happened. And you're with me, Jo. More than anything else, you're here with me."

"I can't believe you waited so long," I said, nuzzling his neck. "For me."

He moved off of me, carefully pulling out with a small groan. I missed him immediately.

"Of course I waited for you. I was locked up. Who was I going to fuck in prison? Don't answer that."

I laughed, warm all over, and snuggled closer to him.

"Even had I been free, it wouldn't have mattered. I couldn't think about any other woman. All I cared about was finding you."

"How did you find me? The dream...How does it work?"

He gazed at the ceiling, thinking. "I can't remember all of it. Just bits and pieces. The best way to describe it...it's like déjà vu. When I felt like I'd been on a road before, or had seen a sign for a certain town, I knew I was on the right track."

I didn't push him for more. On the road, I'd been unnerved by the doses of unreality and Evan only giving me information on a need-to-know basis. But now I trusted him. I loved him for who he was. I wanted to tell him, but the words stuck in my throat, trapped by fear of what lay ahead.

He kept saying I would be safe and he would be free. Free of what? Some shadow that trailed us, and not the police either. I couldn't see it, but I felt it, and that night, I didn't want to think about it. That night was just about us. I'd been scrambling for purchase on the edge of a great cliff. Evan had reached down and pulled me up. Now I was in his arms.

Evan turned off the lamp. Wrapped tightly in him, I drifted into a satiated sleep. When I next woke it was some hours later, in the deepest part of the night. Evan was still wrapped around me. My back to his chest, his arms around me, our fingers laced together and our legs entwined. His breath warmed the nape of my neck. The motel room's AC unit was humming, yet I felt the sweat where our skin touched. I wanted more of it. More sweat, more kisses, more shared breath. I wanted him inside me again. Wanted to take every bit of his male essence until he was spent and I was full.

But Evan came awake before I could move. I felt him raise his head, his body suddenly tense, and tight. Alert.

"What is it?" I asked.

He didn't reply, but disentangled himself from me and went to the window. From where I lay, it was dark and silent outside, but I saw Evan's shoulder muscles tense and his hands clench and unclench.

"Evan?"

He turned from the window, picked up his boxers and jeans from the floor and pulled them on. "I have to go."

My heart clanged dully against my ribs. "What do you mean, *you have to go?* Go where?" I turned on the lamp and looked at the digital clock on the bedside table. "It's two in the morning."

He put on a t-shirt then, sat on the edge of the bed and yanked his boots on. "Listen to me, Jo," he said. "There's a bus stop on the corner. You can see it from the window. If I'm not back in three hours, you need to take that bus east. Get off at the truck stop on the edge of town by Route 412."

"I need to *what?*" Dread settled into my gut, choking my air.

"The truck stop has a diner. Get a table and wait for me."

"*Wait* for you? And where the hell will you be? No, don't answer. Fuck that, I'm coming with you." I threw off the covers and looked around for my clothes.

Evan strode to me and took hold of my shoulders. "You have to do as I say, Jo. Promise me."

"No," I thrust him away. "No promises until you tell me what's happening."

"I think it was the toll road. I think my truck got flagged when I paid the toll coming off the highway."

"You *think* or you know? Evan, quit fucking around and—"

He took my face in his hands, his eyes boring into mine with an intensity I'd never seen before. "I'm not fucking around. You stay here until five. If I'm not back by then, you get to that diner and you wait for me there. Promise me."

A thousand different ways of saying no flooded me, but I only stood mute as he shrugged on his jean jacket, put on a baseball cap and grabbed his keys from the table. I stared as he pulled out his wallet and threw what looked like a couple hundred dollars in cash on the bed.

"Bus fare and anything else."

"Evan."

He came to me, tucking his wallet in his back pocket. His hands went around the back of my neck, his thumbs under my chin. "Five o'clock, Jo. Not a minute later. All right?"

I nodded, unable to speak. He crushed his lips to mine in a hard, bruising kiss. I clutched at his arms to keep him there, but he tore away and was gone.

I stared at the empty room that seemed even emptier without him. The sheets were tangled on the bed where we'd made love. Evan had been there with me, and now…I shivered.

Waiting and doing nothing felt wrong and useless. I dressed, then packed up our belongings into his large duffel and my smaller one. As I stuffed the cash into my bag, I thought I could hear Lee's voice:

He fucked you and left you some money…

I silenced the insidious thought and started pacing. I peeked out the window but the night was dark. Here, at the edge of the city, at this late hour, few cars passed by the motel. No flashing police lights that told me it was over. Just…nothing.

The minutes added up so slowly, I thought I'd be insane by five o'clock. It finally arrived and no Evan.

5:01

5:03

For the last three hours, time had crawled, and now I felt it racing out from under me.

5:05

This was too much like the night of our high school prom.

At six minutes after five I gathered up our bags, my hands shaking so bad I could hardly grip them. I put them down again. I couldn't do it. *Not yet,* I thought. *A few more minutes. I'll give him a few more minutes.*

At ten after, I battled through the paralyzing fear to keep my promise. I went to the bathroom to splash cold water on my face. The water was bracing and I pulled in deep breaths as I stared at my reflection. *You can do this,* I told the girl in the mirror. *You promised him.*

A key rattled in the door. The door opened.

I froze.

"Jo...?"

My heart stopped, then took off at a gallop. I tore out of the bathroom, my eyes falling on the clock. Eleven minutes after five.

Evan was out of breath, his hair falling over his face. He brushed it back and relief softened his frantic expression. Then it hardened into something pained and scared and beautiful.

"You're late," I whispered.

He strode to me in four long steps and gripped my shoulders. "You should've left at five. I told you if I didn't come back—"

"No!" I cried. "There is no *you not coming back.* You have to come back to me." Tears flooded my eyes, choked my throat. "You always have to come back to me, Evan. Do you hear?"

He hauled me to him, crushing me against the solid strength of his body.

"Promise me," I whispered against his shoulder. "Swear it. Swear you'll always come back to me."

"I swear," he said, holding me tight, melting against me. "I swear, Jo. I will always come back to you."

I wrapped my arms around his neck and pulled him to me, opening my mouth to his kiss, taking him in as deeply as I could. I had my own premonition then, one that felt as powerful and real as anything Evan might experience: I was meant to kiss him and only him for the rest of my life.

Evan pulled away, his breath coming hard. "We have to go, Jo. We have to go right now."

"Why? What happened?"

"I'll explain on the road."

Our bags in hand, Evan cracked open the door to the motel. The sun was up now. He peered out, looking left and right. When he was satisfied the coast was clear, he beckoned for me to follow him. I felt like a burglar sneaking away with a bag of loot as we crossed the parking lot toward the main drag.

I gave a little cry as Evan yanked me behind the wall of the bail bonds/ fast cash place beside the motel. Over his shoulder I saw a squad car roll into the motel parking lot. My heart crashed against my ribs.

"Are they here for us?" I whispered.

He nodded and took my hand. "Come on." He led me through parking lots and empty lots behind the little strip mall, until a chain-link fence topped with barbed wire forced us back to the main street.

"What happened to your truck?"

"I ditched it," Evan said, glancing over his shoulder. "Literally. I drove it south about twelve miles and straight into a ditch. Then jogged back here. It won't fool them for long but it might buy us some time."

"I'm sorry. I know you loved your truck. *I* loved your truck."

He glanced sideways at me, his smile warmer now. "Small price to pay."

We boarded a bus and rode it out to the truck stop diner. Looking over our shoulders every minute, we bought a couple of tuna sandwiches and bottled water for the road. Then we hurried out to the truck bays where long-haulers were refueling or chatting amongst themselves. Evan took my hand and led us to the front of the lines, to the trucks that were going to pull out of town first.

"Which one?" I asked.

"Someone going north. To Kansas City."

"Are we going to Kansas City?"

"No." Evan searched the line. "How about him?" He nodded at a guy climbing into a chicken truck. The smell carried on the heat and feathers fell like snow from the cages.

I made a face. "Hell no. I'd spend the whole time itching to crash it and set the chickens free."

"We're running out of time."

My eyes picked out a short, stout trucker with a beard, plaid shirt, and a beat-up old cap his head. He was refueling a tanker. "That one," I said and took Evan's hand. We headed over slowly, trying our damnedest not to look guilty and in a raging hurry. I made sure my hair covered my scar as we approached.

"Good morning," I said brightly, as the driver was climbing back into his cab. "Nice tanker." I jerked my chin at his rig. "My cousin Gerry used to drive one just like it."

"Oh yeah?" The trucker eyed us up and down, and the bags in our hands.

"You heading north by any chance?" Evan asked.

"I am."

"Do you think you could take us a little ways?"

The trucker rubbed his beard reluctantly. "Where you off to?"

"Kansas City, sir," Evan said. "We got family there." His eyes flicked down the long line of trucks and I saw them widen slightly. I refused to look but kept the smile plastered to my face.

"My mother," I piped up. "Our car broke down in Dallas and we've just been trying to keep going ever since."

The trucker took off his cap, scratched his head with agonizing slowness, before putting it back on. "I'm going through Wichita. I suppose you can ride with me for a spell."

"Thank you, sir. Thank you so much."

We ran around to the passenger side and practically dove into the cab. Evan studied the long, rectangular rearview, his teeth clenched. No flashing lights, but I thought I saw a patrol car way down the line. My heart hammered waiting while our guy settled into his seat, utterly unhurried, checking his gauges and testing his radio and whatever else truckers did before actually trucking.

The guy's cab was clean and uncluttered, except for the remnants of a few fast food meals. No cigarette butts choking the ash tray, no nudie pics plastered on the dash and roof, unlike Gerry's old rig. We had room to stow our duffels at our feet. I sat between the two men and Evan kept an arm wrapped tight around me. I could hear his heart thudding too.

"I'm Cal," our trucker said as he finally started up the engine. It hissed and growled, each shift of gears lurching us forward as Cal slowly—so damn slowly—maneuvered the truck out of the parking lot. "You two got names?"

I froze then blurted, "Jack and Diane."

"Pleasure to meet you, Jack and Diane. Ha! Like the song?"

Evan coughed and I forced a light laugh. "I know, right? Coincidence. Our friends are always giving us crap about it."

Cal smiled thinly and I decided to shut the hell up before I overdid it.

"Haven't had hitchers in a good long while," Cal said.

"We really appreciate it, sir," Evan said.

Cal waved off gratitude with one meaty hand. He pulled out of Tulsa and I felt the tension in Evan loosen. Cal was a quiet guy. Or maybe he wasn't used to having company. Either way, he didn't say much during the ride, and we didn't offer any conversation.

Having seemingly escaped the police, my adrenaline drained out, leaving me tired. Or maybe it was last night's lovemaking. I snuggled up to Evan. His left thigh was pressed against my right and even there, in the cab of some stranger's truck, with the cops on our ass, I had to fight to keep my hands to myself.

You're being ridiculous, I thought, then took it back. It wasn't ridiculous to want Evan so badly. It was ridiculous that we'd had to wait so long.

An hour passed, and the silence was too much for even Cal. We made small talk, and he slowly warmed up to us. We learned he'd been a trucker about six years. Mostly tankers, and mostly dairy, though sometimes he did gas and oil. I was telling him about Gerry, and how he'd be gone for long stretches at a time.

"Yeah, that sounds about right," Cal said. "I gotta wife and kid—a daughter—back in Oklahoma City. Don't see them half as much as I'd like. I'm on the road nine months out of the year."

"Must be hard," I said.

"Sure. But you gotta do right by your women. Ain't that right, Jack?"

Jack smiled and held me closer. "Yes, sir."

The CB crackled. A trucker came on, speaking the coded language of the road.

Cal took the hand-held with its spiraling cord down from its place near the sun visor. "Five-by-five, go ahead."

"Did you clear Tulsa?" the other trucker asked.

"About an hour out," Cal replied.

"Lucky you. I'm stuck high and dry. Bear trap on the 412."

I squeezed Evan's hand. I only spoke a little trucker from my time with Gerry. Bear trap meant police had set up a roadblock or check-point.

"What are they looking for?" Cal asked, giving us a sideways glance.

"APB out on some folks. Two kids. Girl's dark, got a scar up her face. Guy's blond, tall."

Evan tensed and his arm around me tightened.

"That's all we got so far," the trucker on the CB said. "But it's jamming up the works something fierce. Was wondering if you got out okay."

"I'm rolling," Cal said, his hand on the steering wheel clenched until his knuckles went white. "I'm 35 north. Just past Billings."

I exchanged glances with Evan, neither of us missing that Cal was broadcasting his locale.

"You stay ten-ten," Cal said into the mouthpiece. He lowered it from his chin but didn't hang it up. He kept it in his hand and without saying a word, he drove to the side of the road, slowing his rig with a hiss of the air breaks, and then stopping.

"This is far as we go," he said finally, not looking at us. "I don't want trouble."

"Neither do we, sir," Evan said sincerely. "We're very grateful. More grateful if nobody knew we were here."

Cal stared straight ahead. "You got yourselves in some trouble, did you?"

"Yes, sir."

"What for?"

When Evan hesitated, I faced Cal, knowing that he was a good man, and being honest with him might serve us better than lying to him. "I was in a bad place, sir, and Evan pulled me out. We didn't mean to hurt anyone who wasn't also trying to hurt us."

Cal peered at Evan. "That true, son?

"Yes, it's true, sir. I hurt someone who was trying to hurt her. And I'd do it again if I had to. To protect her."

Cal took in my cheek and Evan's arm around me. "Less I know the better. I can't take you no further. But I haven't seen you."

"Thank you, Cal," I said as Evan gathered our bags and opened the door on his side.

Cal made a small grunt in return, eyes straight ahead, as if looking at us too long made him guilty. Before we shut the door, he leaned over the bench seat and said, "Son, you stay out of trouble best you can, yeah? Take care of your girl and don't do nothing stupid."

"No, sir."

Cal nodded, reluctantly satisfied. Evan shut the door and we watched the tanker roll away.

When it was gone, the road was empty, lonely in the new, hot morning. The sun beat down on the deep green tangle of trees. A river coursed slowly beneath the highway, colored a sicker, muddier green.

Evan scanned our surroundings. "We should get off this road. Stay out of sight for a while before we try hitching again." A truck trundled toward us on the highway. Evan shouldered our bags. "Come on."

When the truck passed, we crossed the road and headed west along the banks of the river. After three quarters of a mile, the river curved away from the highway and swelled into a brighter green, cleaner and clearer toward the opposite shore. Here I felt safer. Hidden. Any sound from the highway was lost in the river's slow flow and the birdsong ringing out from the forest around us.

We found a dry patch of beach and Evan laid out the red-checkered blanket. We didn't have much food packed in our bags but we ate our sandwiches and drank from water bottles.

Evan's blue eyes were on the river, lost in thought or something only he could see. I studied him a few moments, then asked, "What do we do now?"

"I need to go under," he said, jerking his chin at the water.

"Here?" My stomach sank. "I hate it. I won't be able to see you."

"Come with me. Hold my hand. I have to do it, Jo. I need more minutes."

I nodded reluctantly and got up. We stripped to our underwear. He dug his old watch out of his bag and put it on my wrist. It was far too big for me and I held my left arm high to keep it dry. Evan held my right hand and we waded in. The water was warm and muddy at the shore but dropped swiftly to some depth I couldn't see. I brushed my toes on the soft, almost slimy silt beneath me. Evan held my hand tighter.

"I won't let go. I promise. But let me stay until I have to come up. All right?"

I nodded, and I readied his watch. "Go," I said, hardly a whisper.

Evan went under, the murky water concealing him from me but his hand solid in mine. The minutes began to add up, and my anxiety mounted. Four minutes came and I expect him to rise up, gasping. He didn't. Five minutes.

Six minutes.

"Six fucking minutes, Jesus, Evan," I whispered. It took everything I had not to haul him up. My hand on his tightened and I felt an answering squeeze.

At seven minutes, I was clutching his hand so tightly my bones ached. His hand tightened too and I felt him struggle to stay down. I reached my limit and was about to yank him up when he broke the surface in a splash of water.

I noted the time: 8.02 seconds

"That's impossible," I whispered. Then my relief and amazement morphed to panic. Evan clutched his chest, sucking in lungful of air in between deep, harrowing coughs, his feet stumbling for purchase on the riverbed.

"Evan!"

In a panic, I dropped the watch into the murk as I hauled him toward the shallows. He had one hand pressed to his chest while with the other he hung on my shoulders, wheezing and gasping. His face was a grimace of pain and a scream for help welled up my throat. It took us an eternity to reach the shore where Evan collapsed to his knees, shoulders hunched. Slowly his gasping breaths grew deeper and his hacking coughs subsided.

He lifted his head and croaked, "How long?" he croaked.

I gaped. "Are you insane?"

"How long?"

I sat back on my heels beside him, the warm water lapping at my thighs. "Eight minutes. And two seconds," I added, my voice rising with every syllable. "How's that? Eight minutes, two seconds. Is that good enough? Want to try for nine? How about *ten*. You got ten fucking minutes in you, Evan? Will that be enough?"

He shook his head, recovered now, his breathing deep and even. "I'm sorry I scared you."

"Good." I got to my feet with a splash. "Because you're not doing it again. I dropped your watch in the river and I'm fucking *glad*. Never again, Evan. Never. Again."

Evan got to his feet. He said nothing, but his expression was suddenly hungry. Almost feral. I took a step back even as a flush of heat swept over me.

"Why do you do it? Tell me why you have to go under so long."

"I don't know yet," he said, and put his arms around me. I stiffened at first, wanting to shove him away. But his wet skin was all along mine. He was strong and smelled green and I wanted him close.

"You don't know?"

"No," he replied, his hands sliding up and down my back. "But it's important. I can feel it."

"I don't understand," I said, pulling his hips close against me. "And I hate it."

"I'm sorry," he said, his voice gruff, his lips brushing the hollow beneath my ear, then grazing with his teeth.

"You scared me." My body was betraying me, burning up my anger and turning it to desire. I could feel his body tense against mine, a hardening between his thighs.

"I said I was sorry." He stroked my hair, his mouth seeking mine. Rough and deep.

"You're not sorry," I managed to say around his biting kiss that was stealing the strength out of my legs. I had another smart remark on deck but the words died as Evan gripped my hair, his eyes burning blue fire. And I could feel it in him—he was about to unleash himself on me. The exhilaration of being under for eight damn minutes had somehow morphed into a ferocious need.

My own desire was burning white hot. Not only because of Evan's hands and mouth on my body, but because that primal lust I felt in him was mine. I'd put it there.

He wants me…

"Are you ready for me?" he growled against my lips.

I arched my neck as he burned a path down my throat with his mouth. "See for yourself."

Rational thought flew out of my head as Evan's hand slipped between my thighs. His fingers dipped beneath the hem of my underwear. He cupped me, his fingers deliciously rough as they slid across my sensitive flesh.

"You're ready," he said.

"Yes," I breathed. "And this time…"

"Hard."

Yes.

Last night's gentle lovemaking had been beautiful. Evan's hands had been gentle with me, his chest and arms soft as he held me. Now I wanted to taste the power of his body. I could feel the force of his need coiling in his muscles, humming along his skin like a live current. I wanted to feel that raw, pulsing strength, wanted every inch of him pounding over me and inside me until he broke me apart.

He removed his hand from between my thighs and picked me up. I wrapped my legs around his waist as he carried me back to the blanket. He set my feet down, then his hands snaked into my hair as he yanked me to him in a crushing kiss. A thrill of electric lust coursed through me. This was exactly what I wanted. And he knew it.

His hands unclasped my bra, tore it off, and then slid my panties down my legs. My stare was unabashed as he stripped off his boxers, another rush of wet heat between my thighs at the sight. My body was ready for him.

Evan laid me down on the blanket. He hooked my leg on the crook of his arm and took hold of my hips. I expected him to drive into me with one fast thrust, to unleash the pent up fury I felt in him. Instead he entered me slowly. I cried out at the intense pressure, so hot and heavy and good. Then he was done being gentle. He began to move in me. Hard.

"Oh my God," I moaned, clutching at the blanket, trying to anchor myself against his deep thrusts. A warm, throbbing glow began to build in me. Evan took up my other leg. Now I was folded in half, both my calves resting on his shoulders. Evan sank even deeper inside, his hands planted on either side of me, holding his weight. It was exactly what I wanted. It was nothing I could have imagined.

"Too much?" he managed to gasp. "Tell me and I'll stop."

"God, Evan," I breathed, clutching his neck, my nails digging into his skin. "It is too much and don't you dare stop."

He let go then, threw it all off. I slipped beyond reality, into another dimension where only sensation existed. No thoughts or coherencies, only the rapidly increasing movement, gasping breaths, growled curses and whimpering cries. His body so powerful against mine, and so deep. I threw back my head and came harder than I ever had in my life—a rolling wave, thunderous in the black backdrop of my eyes. My arms stretched over my head, fingers clutching the warm sand beyond the edge of the blanket.

Evan was close behind. He drove into me, slick with sweat between my raised legs, opening my bent body to him. He grunted through clenched teeth, then let out a guttural sigh as he emptied himself into me with a few final thrusts.

I opened my eyes. Evan was hunched over me, the sun outlining him in a halo of gold. Still inside me, he eased my shaking legs to the ground. Sweat meandered along the bronze planes of his back and his hair stuck to his nape.

I felt him come down, come around in a daze. He pushed up on an elbow to look at me, his hungry, almost feral expression softening.

"No way you've never done this before last night," I declared, breathing hard. "No chance."

He laughed and wiped his sweat-and-river dampened hair from his eyes. "Not really something a guy's going to lie about."

"Then you're a natural."

"No, it's just you."

I sat up, blinking in a sort of daze myself. "How did we end up like this?" I asked, indicating our nakedness. "I was pissed. And scared. And then..."

"Life or death," Evan said. "Being close to death makes us appreciate life and drive toward things that make us feel alive. Like sex. Sex makes you feel alive." He flashed me a smile. "Doesn't it?"

I didn't smile back. "Were you close to death under there?" I jerked my head at the river. "I felt like you were."

"In a manner of speaking. Holding my breath for so long, not taking in air, not feeding my body? That's a kind of death, isn't it?"

I shivered despite the growing heat of the day. "Is that why you do it?"

"No. I don't know." Evan turned to watch the river. "The Native American legends say in dreams, the spirits of the dead can communicate with you. Guide you from the other side. Being close to death brings you closer to them. You can hear them better when you're close."

"Do you believe in that? Native American legends about guiding spirits? Is that...why we're on this trip?"

I tried that one on for size in my own mind. It didn't make sense but it didn't *not* make sense either. This whole journey felt like that: a crazy race toward some mythical 'center' that no sane person would go along with, while at the same time it felt like exactly the right thing to do.

He turned to me, naked and beautiful in the sun. "Maybe. I don't know, Jo. The only truth I have is that it's for us. Everything I do is for us. For you. Is that good enough for now?"

"I guess so," I said. "For now."

"Thank you, Jo. For trusting me."

"I do trust you. With my life."

And that was the truth, and I sucked in a breath as the utter distinction between how I felt with Evan and how I'd lived with Lee struck me.

"What are you thinking about?" Evan asked.

"Nothing," I said. I gave myself a shake. "Not something you probably want to talk about at this particular moment, anyway."

Evan pulled to him and I lay down with him on our blanket, my head pillowed on his shoulder. "Tell me. Whatever you want to say, you can say it."

"It's not pretty. Maybe not the time or place…"

"Tell me, Jo."

"I was thinking about Lee." I felt Evan tense beneath me. I smiled a little. "Told you."

"No, go ahead. I want to hear it. I want everything you give me."

"I was thinking how different I feel with you. He made me feel worthless. So did Jasper…

"You are not worthless," Evan said roughly. "The very last fucking thing you are is worthless."

"I know I'm not. Not anymore. And not because you told me, but because you give me the strength to believe it for myself," I said, running my fingertips over his chest. "You make me feel beautiful, Evan. And whole. And alive. All that old, tired pain from Jasper, and the new pain of my time with Lee…When I'm with you, it disappears." I lifted my head to look at him. "How do you do that?"

Evan shook his head slightly. "There's no mystery, Jo. I love you."

I felt the soft warmth of those words strike my chest and then sink in. "You love me?"

"Can't you feel it?"

I nodded, tears filling my eyes. "I hoped…that you did…"

Evan's eyes shone, submerged and blue like our pool.

"Oh, sweetness, I've always loved you. Since high school. Since the day you told me about your mother and your scar…And I had just told you why I'd been at Woodside and you didn't laugh at me or call me crazy. You believed me. Or maybe you didn't, but you *accepted* me. And that had never happened to me before."

He sat up on one elbow, intent now.

"But more than your acceptance, I fell in love with you for you. Not just because you were the first girl I'd ever kissed or touched. I fell in love with your strength and your fire. You'd been through hell," he touched my scar, trailed his finger down it lightly, "and you never gave up." His fingertip touch became his whole hand as cupped my cheeks. "I love you, Josephine. I do. And I'll never stop."

My tears rolled down to his hands holding me. He drew me toward him for a kiss, and as his lips touched mine, I whispered, "I love you, Evan. I love you, and I'll never stop."

And it felt like vows, our words. As if we'd bonded ourselves together at that riverbank, with the sun shining gold and hot above us. We kissed and kissed, and Evan sighed into our kiss, as if he were utterly content. And me...I felt happy. Because of Evan. Evan breathed his love into me, and I was happy.

CHAPTER 30

JO

We left the river at mid-afternoon, thinking our luck would probably run out if we lingered any longer. I could've stayed forever, naked with him in the sun, but Evan was getting that look again, his facing filling up with that unnamed sense of urgency. It was time to go.

We washed up as best we could in the river, dressed and hiked back to the highway, the clouds thickening above us in the hot, heavy air. We hitched into Wichita, catching a ride with a traveling auditor who specialized in helping small businesses sort out their tax problems. It wasn't the season for it he said, but he still got a few calls. He said we got lucky he came along. I thought we did too, since this guy wasn't a fan of news radio and hadn't heard the APB for two hitchhikers wanted by the police. Hitchhikers who looked exactly like his two passengers. He chatted nonstop, thrilled to have the company, and when we got out of his sedan in Wichita he seemed disappointed to see us go.

We kept to the streets at the edge of the city until Evan found a motel he thought was close enough to transportation, but obscure enough to avoid notice by the police.

A bored-looking, dark-haired guy in his mid-twenties sat behind the glass at the front desk, his attention fixed on the iPad propped in front of him.

He was into deathcore metal music videos, judging by the sound of cranking guitar riffs and screaming lyrics. If I had to guess, I'd say he was the son of the motel owner, forced to work at the family business all summer.

As usual, Evan paid cash for a room on the first floor, near the back. A thrill shot down my spine when this time he insisted that the room have one king size bed.

"I smell like algae," I said as Evan unlocked the door. "I need a shower. And food."

"I want a shower too, but you go first. I'll get the food. I'm starving."

"It's what happens when you exert yourself so hard," I said, when we'd stepped inside.

He pulled me close. "I'm going to *exert* myself against you all night," he said, and laughed when I rolled my eyes. "Oh come on, that was a great line, right?"

"That was a terrible line," I said, giving him a playful shove. "Food. Go."

"Preference?"

"Anything. You pick." I was halfway in the bathroom when I stopped. "Shit, I'm way overdue to call Del. She's got to be worried sick about me by now. Can I do that without getting her in trouble?"

"I'll ask the front desk guy where there's a RadioShack or something," Evan said. "I can get one of those prepaid cell phones, you know? The kind you can just throw away when you're done?"

"A burner," I said. "Are they expensive?"

"I don't think so. I have enough. Which reminds me."

Evan pulled out his wallet and emptied out money onto the bed. Then he went to his duffel and pulled out another small leather portfolio. Another few hundred dollars joined the bills on the mattress. I watched as he counted and separated the cash into two piles.

"What's this?" I asked.

"Your share."

"My share?"

"About four hundred each. We're in this together right? I don't want you to feel you have to ask me for anything. If you want something you should have it."

"Thank you," I said quietly.

Evan moved to kiss me softly. "Be safe. Keep the door locked. I'll be back in an hour."

"That's right," I told him. "One hour. Not a minute later."

He kissed me again. "I will always come back to you."

I was out of the shower and dressed in my sleep shorts and a tank top when Evan returned. He'd found a mom-and-pop barbecue joint by RadioShack and his arms were laden with bags of barbecue chicken, coleslaw, biscuits, and mashed potatoes. After we stuffed our faces, Evan rifled in the RadioShack bag and handed over the prepaid cell phone.

"What if this doesn't work?" I said. "What if it gets us caught or gets Del in trouble?"

"Do you trust her?"

"Absolutely."

"Then call her. Keep it short. Tell her you're okay and nothing else. That'll keep all of us safe."

I nodded and heaved a breath. Evan went to take a shower, giving me privacy.

I punched in the number.

"The Rio, Del speaking."

"Del, it's Jo."

"Jo?" My best friend sucked in a hissing breath, her professional, phone-answering voice morphing to a whispered shriek. "Baby, where the hell are you? The cops are crawling all over, asking about you. Are you okay? Tell me that first."

"I'm okay."

"Praise Jesus," she said, and then in the next breath, "And I don't think I have to tell you what the cops are asking *about*, do I?"

"No, you don't. I know exactly what they're asking about, and Del—
"

"Then don't say another damn word, honey," Del said sharply. "Not one word. I'm not bugged but God knows what kind of CSI trickery they may try to pull on me."

"Okay, right. You're right. I'd hate to get you in trouble for talking to me."

"They can't arrest me for talking. I don't know nothing and you ain't saying nothing. Just checking in."

"Yes." I allowed myself the smallest breath of relief. "That's what I'm doing, Del. Checking in. I wanted to hear your voice."

"Me too, honey. I been worried sick. I seen on the news about a guy named Salinger? Patty Stevenson's been flapping her gums that he was in the diner the afternoon Lee's house went up in smoke. She's telling everyone you were talking to him pretty cozy. The cops say you're with him now."

"Yes, Evan. I'm with him."

"Voluntarily, girl, or what? I need the truth because the news sure don't paint a pretty picture of him."

"Of course voluntarily," I said, sitting up. "Just what the hell are they saying?"

"He busted out of prison, for one thing. Escaped con."

"That's true. But he never should've been in there in the first place."

"And secondly they said he's a mental case. He spent time in an institution."

My face flushed red. "That's true too, but that doesn't make him... Look, Del, don't believe anything you hear about Evan. Okay? For my sake. He's the best man I've ever met in my life. He would never hurt me. I didn't jump off one sinking ship onto another, I promise."

"If you say so, then amen, girl. I believe you."

"And what about the police? They're on our tail pretty hard."

Dell's voice dropped to a lower register. "It's not good, honey. It's an all-out manhunt for you and your boy. They're sure Lee didn't die in that house fire. They're *sure* about that."

My voice was faint. "It was an accident."

"Stop right there. I'm not going to ask a thing about Lee and I don't want you to tell me anything either. I just wanted you to know the *gravitas* of the situation over here. But I will say this so you don't have to: I know you ain't going to hurt anybody on purpose. Some folk like Lee... Well they just have to lie in the bed they made themselves. Or the grave. But the more you run, honey, the harder it's going to be to tell them whatever it is you got to tell them."

It's going to be impossible, I thought with a pang of dread. I looked to the bathroom door where the shower was still running. If we were caught, Evan would go to jail for life.

And if you're not caught? What happens when your money runs out and you reach the center, wherever that is? What happens when this road trip ends and there's no more road?

"Do you remember what we talked about before I left?" I asked Del. "About the money you were helping me to save up?"

"I sure do, honey-pie. And my offer still stands. You tell me when and you tell me how and I'll make sure my boy comes through for you. For both of you."

A flood of relief and love for my friend swept through me. "You're going to get in trouble for saying that, Del," I said gruffly.

She snorted. "Small price to pay if you're safe, baby. Finally safe."

"I am."

"Go on, then. Check in if you can, and I'll be watching on the news for you and praying."

"I love you, Del."

I heard her sniff on the other end of the line. "That better mean you love my fabulous ass, and not goodbye. Better not."

"Not goodbye," I said. "*This* is goodbye. I gotta go, Del."

"You take care, honey. Love you."

I hung up with her and wondered if I had actually spoken to her for the last time.

I felt my face grow hot at what they were saying about Evan. Even if we sorted this all out and convinced them Lee's death was an act of self-defense, Evan could never be a firefighter with such a terrible record. Impossible.

Unless he became someone else.

If Del's contact could get us new IDs then Evan could start all over again. He would be free, just like he said.

Bolstered my plan, I ate the rest of my potato salad and washed it down with Diet Coke. I was still hungry. All of my appetites, it seemed, had returned with a vengeance.

Evan emerged from the shower with a towel slung low around his waist. I stared at his naked abdomen, the six-pack of ab muscles tapering into a delicious V. A lethal combination guaranteed to turn a woman—at least this woman—into a rabid sex fiend.

Evan was oblivious to my drooling. He stood toweling his hair and asked, "How did it go? How's your friend?"

"Fine," I said. I told him about the fake IDs. "If this is how we can start a new life together, we should take it, shouldn't we? We have the money."

"Not yet," Evan said. "We can't go back to Louisiana yet. We head north. To the Center. To go back now would be…wrong. And dangerous for your friend, too."

"Then we'll go to the Center…" The word sounded strange in my own ears. "And then make our way back to Louisiana to get the IDs from Del. Deal?"

Evan went back into the bathroom without agreeing. "Did she say anything about us?" he called. "What the police are doing?"

"I believe *all-out manhunt* were her exact words."

Evan remerged without the smaller towel. "I figured as much. About the manhunt. We need a car. Tomorrow, let's see if we can't find a salvage yard or something. I'll bet there's a junker somewhere I can buy for cheap and fix up."

"We only have eight hundred bucks between us. We can't afford the IDs from Del's friend if we spend too much on a car."

"We'll get a super cheap car," Evan said, a small smile on his face. He still hadn't put any clothes on. "Our getaway car. But that's tomorrow."

I rose off the bed and stood in front of him, my hands resting on the cut of his hips above the towel. "Okay fine." I tugged the towel off and let it drop to the floor. "Tomorrow, the getaway car. Tonight..."

"Tonight we lie low," Evan said, backing me to the bed. He lifted my tank top off over my head and flung it away, and laid me down. His mouth burned a path between my breasts.

"Yes," I said, drawing out the S in a hiss as ripples of heat skimmed over my skin.

"Very low." Evan said, trailing his mouth down my stomach now, and down… "Can't let anyone know we're here. You need to stay quiet, Jo. Very, very quiet…"

I tried my best. But by the time Evan was done with me, I was pretty sure the entire tri-state area knew exactly where we were.

Lying in the drowsy, delicious aftermath, I thought getting caught would've been a small price to pay for that last shuddering orgasm. It would be worth the pleasure of being held by Evan afterward, how he looked at me and kissed me, the things he whispered as sleep came for us.

But bad dreams ruined my sleep that night. Filled it with sinister laughter, flashes of bloodstains spreading over carpet and Lee's dead body at my feet.

Don't test me, woman.

He used to say it all the time, usually right before working himself into a fit. *Don't test me, woman, if you know what's best for you.*

In my dream, dead Lee sat up, like a vampire rising from a coffin. His dented head leaked old blood, and he cackled through teeth rotted by drugs.

Don't test me, woman. You made this mess. He picked up the bloody skillet from the floor beside him. *Clean up your mess, Jo, if you know what's best for you.*

CHAPTER 31

JO

I woke up shivering, a nasty dream hovering at the edge of my memory. Evan, still half-asleep, folded me into his arms until I was warm again and the dream forgotten.

With no cell phones or computers, we were Internet-poor and I never realized how much I took information for granted. All the information in the world, usually at my fingertips, now out of reach. Evan needed to find a salvage yard, we both needed a laundromat, and we hadn't the faintest idea where to find either one. The scuzzy-looking guy at the front desk wasn't much help, so Evan and I took a walk.

The laundromat was easy but we quickly realized we needed every stitch of clothing washed—including what we were wearing. We found a secondhand clothing store and I bought a tank top and another pair of cargo pants. On my way to the register, I spied a sundress in lavender and turquoise. It was rayon—cheap material, but soft. And only ten bucks. I bought it with the money Evan had given me and stuffed it in the bottom of the bag before he could see it. I didn't have any plans for when I'd wear it, only a vague idea I wanted to look pretty for him sometime.

Evan bought a pair of jeans and a few t-shirts, but I could tell he was trying to conserve money. Our eight hundred bucks seemed like a lot until we had to buy a car with it. I don't think either of us had high hopes we'd find even the most decrepit junker for much less than that.

While our clothes were being laundered, we ate lunch at a little Mexican place, taking a corner far from the windows. When he went to pay, Evan struck up a conversation with the guy behind the register. The guy told Evan about a salvage yard that sometimes sold used cars. South end of town, a few miles out. We thanked him for the tip, took our newly-laundered clothes back to the motel and headed out.

On the bus to the salvage yard, I was conscious of eyes on me. Evan kept the bill of his baseball cap low over his eyes, but there wasn't much I could do about my scar except keep my hair over it. Around Evan, I often forgot about my face. Now it was a dead-giveaway to any regular news-watcher or police-blotter devotee. I rested my cheek against Evan's chest to hide my scar and to listen to the rhythm of his heartbeat.

Evan's pulse was steady. He was cautious, but not wound up. I decided to use his intuition as my barometer: if he were worried, I'd get worried. Until then, I'd enjoy being with him. Touching him whenever I wanted. Feeling his body next to mine.

The salvage yard was an acre-and-a-half of dented metal. Row after row of beat-up junkers sprawled under the overcast, humid sky. The smell of gasoline from a burn pit reminded me of Lee, setting my teeth on edge. A shadow of last night's dream passed my eyes and was gone again.

Evan took my hand and we walked to the front office—a trailer near the fenced entrance. A young, twitchy-looking guy with the name Travis on his shirt rubbed his greasy, stubbly cheek in thought after Evan made his request.

"How much you say you looking to spend again?"

"As little as possible," Evan said. "I can fix something up too. If you got the car, I can get the parts and put something together myself."

Travis scratched behind his neck. He eyed me up and down in a way I didn't like as he haggled with Evan. At last he offered a twenty-five-year-old hatchback. It was missing a timing belt, needed new spark plugs, a new alternator, plus a bunch of other issues that made it sound like a corpse and Evan would have to be Dr. Frankenstein to get it off the slab.

"I can let it go for four hundred bucks," Travis said. "Parts would be another hundred or so from Mike's place up the road. But tell him I sent you and he'll give you a deal. You can do the repairs here."

Five hundred dollars sounded like too much to me, but Evan shook hands with Travis, deal done. An hour later, I was sitting on an overturned bucket in the salvage yard, watching Evan try to work a miracle on the car. It must have gleamed white once. Now it sulked a yellowish pale grey. I showed it some mercy and dubbed it Snowball.

I watched Evan work on the car, admiring how the muscles in his arms worked to lift, twist, and screw in bolts. He reached back to wipe his hands on the grease rag he kept tucked into his back pocket, which drew my attention to his ass.

Evan Salinger had a seriously fine ass.

"See something you like?" he said, grinning, without looking up from his work.

"Several things," I said. "Are we almost done here? I feel like we've spent too much time in one place."

"Almost done."

I squinted at the skies, trying to guess the time. Two o'clock or so. I had no way to confirm since I'd dropped Evan's watch in a river. Evan seemed to be in no particular hurry. Nor was he concerned that our escape fund was down to three hundred bucks.

"Where to next?" I asked. "We've got Snowball, a beautiful piece of automotive engineering, but now we've got a cash flow problem."

"I think we'll be okay," Evan said, and grunted as some bolt or screw gave him a hard time.

"Less than three hundred bucks." I chewed my thumbnail. "How many days can we make it on that? Are we going to *Thelma and Louise* it? Start holding up liquor stores?"

"I'm not a thief and neither are you."

"That's a non-answer if I ever heard one."

He emerged from under the hood. "We'll be okay," he said again. "And if not, we can always make a few bucks freelancing at a strip club."

"Sorry to burst your bubble, but I'm a terrible pole dancer."

He slammed the hood down. "I beg to differ."

I groaned. "Cute."

Evan chuckled and tossed me the car key. "Give her a try."

The hatchback smelled like cigarette butts and dog hair. I turned the key and the engine sputtered to life.

"It's alive!"

Evan leaned on the window frame with a satisfied smile.

"You're pretty handy," I said, getting out so he could take the wheel. I was honestly impressed this piece of shit car was jugging away. "I think you have a future as an auto mechanic."

"I'm a mechanic in this life. A firefighter in the next."

"What does that mean?"

Evan hooked an arm around my shoulders. "You're calling her Snowball?" He studied the little white car. "Ironic. I'll be shocked if she can hit fifty without overheating."

"Damn, you got it running," Travis said from behind us. I untucked my hair from behind my ear and let it cover my cheek before I turned around.

"She's running," Evan said.

"Maybe I gave it to you too cheap." Travis wore a fixed smile. His expression reminded me of a weasel or an opossum. I itched to get out of there as fast as possible.

Evan extended his hand. "Thanks again. And for the use of your yard. I appreciate it, man."

"Sure, sure, no problem," Travis said keeping his hands jammed in front of his pockets. "You're on your way then? Where you headed?"

"Here and there," Evan said flatly. He nodded his head at me and flicked it toward the passenger door. I was halfway there. "Take care, now."

We drove off the lot with Evan watching the rearview mirror almost as much as he did the windshield.

I kept an eye on my side mirror. "Do you think he knows?"

"I don't know. I think he's mostly pissed he sold the car for cheap. But he got a little curious at the end."

We drove in silence for ten minutes. I didn't know Wichita, but I assumed Evan was taking us back to our motel.

"It feels like we're going the wrong way," I said.

"I know. I think we're..." His words tapered off as his eyes narrowed at interchange. He hit the blinker and took the exit for I35 South.

"*South*? Where are we going?"

Evan said nothing but drove for another few minutes. South, when he'd been so insistent we stay north. Always north. Then I saw the sign. A tall blue rectangle with the word *Joyland* tumbling down its length. A curving arrow between *joy* and *land* pointed toward the park entrance.

"I've been here before," I said as Evan turned Snowball down the overgrown, pot-holed drive.

"Looks like it's been closed for years," he said.

"But I was here." I stared out the window, my mouth slightly parted and my hand reached for his. "My mother took me here."

He gave my hand a squeeze as he parked the car. "Come on."

We walked hand-in-hand through the old amusement park. In the falling light of the afternoon, the park was a quiet and lifeless ghost town. The rides sat motionless, peeling paint and rust. The game booths were either shuttered up or gutted completely, shelves robbed of their prizes. Food carts lay overturned among weeds and dried leaves choked the pathways.

I stopped walking and closed my eyes. My ears imagined children laughing, the metallic grinding of old rides and carnies cajoling passerby to try their hand at a game of chance. I smelled cotton candy and popcorn and hot dogs, kettle corn and barbecue sauce. A cloud of carnival perfume wafting in the still dark air of a summer night.

Colored lights flashed behind my closed eyes and I felt my mother's hand in mine. Now it was her laughter I heard. She laughed as she pulled me by the hand from one game or ride to another. Her lights were on and they shone brighter than all the bulbs of the midway.

I opened my eyes. The park was a burned-out dream. Only rusted metal and rotting wood hung their scents in the air. Evan's hand held mine now.

We walked on, leaves crunching around our feet. We came to the sign with the clown, his smile manic as he beckoned visitors deeper into Joyland. I remembered him. He was rusted now, his stance tilted on one broken leg. His paint was chipped, the primary colors faded by a decade of sun. But my memory restored him, brought back his conical cap and polka-dots.

"Mama told me to close my eyes," I said. "*Open your mouth and close your eyes.* She put a pinch of cotton candy on my tongue. I'd never had it before. I remember thinking it tasted exactly like its name: a cotton ball of sugar that melted away."

Evan smiled at me but said nothing.

"I wanted more and my mom laughed and held out a plastic bag full of it. I tore out a pink hunk and crammed it in my mouth. Instead of telling me to slow down or take smaller bites, my mother laughed and hugged me and pulled me toward the Tilt-a-Whirl. My stomach lurched the whole ride. I was woozy afterward, so we washed the cotton candy down with ice cream sodas and I crashed on the car ride home. Dozed in the passenger seat with my head cradled in the seatbelt. Patsy Cline's 'Crazy' was on the radio and my mother sang along. She had a beautiful voice..."

Evan gave my hand a gentle squeeze. "Then what happened?"

"I pretended to be asleep when we got home. So she'd have to carry me to bed. She knew I was faking but she played along. She tucked me into bed with my blue whale in the crook of my arm. She kissed my forehead and said, 'This was a good night, Josie.' I couldn't pretend to be asleep anymore. I put my arms up around her neck, held her tight and said, 'No, it was the best night.'"

I breathed in the night air, let it out, waiting for the memory to fade back to gray. It didn't. Joyland was a ghost town around us, but in my mind it was bright and brilliant, full of color. And my mother was closer now, too. I could see her face so much clearer now.

I looked up at Evan in the darkening night. "How are you doing this? How do you know to take me to these places?"

"I don't," he said.

"Evan..."

"Does it make you happy? To be here?"

I stared. "Well...yes, of course. I'm getting my mother back. Little by little. It's like a miracle. But, Evan—"

"Then that's why. As for how...?" He shrugged. "I don't know to take you to these places, Jo. That's not how it works. I dreamed it but can only remember little pieces. It doesn't come back to me until we're in the moment. I wait and listen, and when it comes, I follow."

I nodded, not sure what to say. However, he was doing it, he was giving my mother back to me, piece by piece. A gift more valuable to me than

I had the words to express right there, in the falling dark.

Evan moved close, touched my cheek softly. "More than anything, I want you to be happy. If there's a driving force then that's it. Your happiness."

He held me close, wrapping me in his warmth just as he had four years ago.

I leaned into him. "I'm happy. More than I've ever been."

"Then I'm taking you exactly where you need to be."

CHAPTER 32

EVAN

I woke up with a gasp, and half sat up, the dream slipping away before I could grasp all of it. As usual. But this time a few fragments lingered; names and objects.

The burner phone.

Rapid City.

The detective.

Step by step instructions without a diagram of the finished product.

The clock said two a.m. Jo slept peacefully. I slipped out of bed and took the prepaid phone from off the nightstand where Jo had left it. She was planning on throwing it out but didn't want to leave it in the hotel trash.

As quietly as I could, I stepped outside the motel door, watching to see if Jo woke at the sound. She didn't.

I stepped out onto the tiny porch outside our room, made a call to information, then a second call. At this late hour, I got an answering machine. I left my message and hung up. The instant the call ended, I felt a chill sweep over my skin. I peeked into our room. Jo was stirring in the bed. I hurried back inside, and tucked the phone into the inner pocket of my duffel with plans to ditch it somewhere safe tomorrow.

I slipped back into bed with Jo and wrapped my arms around her. She sank deeper into sleep, and I followed soon after, easily. I hated hiding anything from Jo but my mind was at peace because I had done the right thing even if she'd never see it that way.

I woke at dawn, wrapped around Jo. Her naked back against my chest and a thin sheen of sweat between us. She smelled like tangerines: sweet but tart. I smiled into her hair because she tasted the same: sweet and tart. She stirred, rolled in the circle of my arms to face me. My fingertips ran along her scar. While I hated where it came from and the pain it carried along its pale seam, I loved it as a symbol of her survival. A battle scar.

Her smile flickered under my fingertips. She kissed me, then declared the coffee in the motel was shit.

"Is that a subtle request?" I laughed.

"It's concern for your well-being. I'm not too friendly without coffee."

"You seem pretty friendly to me," I said, kissing the hollow beneath her ear. "But I'll get you some coffee anyway."

She folded back the covers and sat up. "You're a saint. I'll hop in the shower and get us packed up."

I got dressed and Jo bustled around the room, humming to herself as she collected our belongings. Since Joyland last night, she looked as if another heavy weight had fallen off of her, or a shadow had lifted. I wondered if she'd look this content in our own space. Our own home instead of some dingy motel. I drank in the beauty of her, then went out.

I double-checked the door, making sure it was locked behind me.

I should've told her to put the chain on.

I was only gone fifteen minutes. Shoving the pair of coffees in the crook of my elbow so I could get the room key, I noticed the door was cracked. Then I heard a muffled cry inside. I dropped the coffees and shouldered the door open like a battering ram.

The guy had Jo up against a wall, a hand over her mouth as she writhed and twisted in his grip. I was on him in a second, tearing him off of her and hurling him to the floor. Only then did I register him as the front desk clerk, the scrawny guy who had checked us in the night before.

"Evan, behind you," Jo cried. "There's one m—"

I whipped around as a second guy took a swing at my face. He popped me under the left eye. Adrenaline and rage surging in my limbs, I seized him by the shirt front and threw everything I had into my punch. Pain flared along my knuckles as they struck his jaw. The guy's head whipped left and blood spattered. His body followed his head and he hit the floor with a groan.

Jo screamed my name and then a stabbing shard of pain dug into my side. The desk clerk had landed a kick to my kidney. I whirled around with a right jab to his gut and he doubled over.

The second guy had pulled himself into a crouch and was scrambling for the door. He'd call for help or the cops and we'd be fucked. I started after him but froze when I heard a clanging *thud* and a choked cry behind me.

Jo was standing over the desk clerk, the bedside lamp in her hand. The clerk was out cold, a lump rising on his brow. Jo's face had drained of color and her eyes stared wide.

"Oh my God, is he dead?" she whispered.

The clerk's scrawny chest rose and fell with a soft moan.

"He's not dead," I said, taking the lamp from her hand. "Did they hurt you? Did either of these fuckers hurt you?"

She shook her head. "They knew about us. That one..." She pointed at the clerk. "He said he knew who we were. Said we probably had money from robbing a bank or something." She looked wide-eyed at me. "He said he called the cops but he wanted a re-reward first. Our money. I told him we had nothing but they didn't listen."

"Shh." I held her close to me for a moment, holding her together. "We have to go. We're leaving right now."

Our things were scattered all over—clothes and sundry items littering the bed and floor. I started grabbing everything I could see and stuffing it into my duffel, expecting the cops to bust in the door at any minute.

Jo hadn't moved. She stared down at the unconscious clerk murmuring, "Something's not right."

"Get your stuff, Jo," I said.

"In the kitchen," she murmured. "Lee...He hit me in the kitchen. But I was holding..." Her gaze lifted and met mine. "No, you were holding it. The skillet. In the living r—"

"*Josephine!*" I barked.

Her eyes cleared and she shook her head, coming back to now.

"Get your stuff," I said. "We're leaving right the fuck now."

She spurred into action, helping me grab the rest of our things, and we ran from the room to the parking lot. I didn't see the clerk's accomplice, and I prayed he took off in the opposite direction. If he had the make and model of our car and the license plate, we'd be screwed. In the far distance, I heard the sound of sirens.

I tossed our bags in the back seats as Jo scrambled in. She was still buckling her seatbelt as I hauled the little car out of the parking lot. I forced myself to drive the speed limit down East Douglas, hopefully blending in with morning traffic. I glanced at the rearview and saw a patrol car screech into the hotel driveway, only a block and a half behind us.

The damn hatchback started to stall at the first stoplight, but after a few pumps of the gas, it lurched through the intersection. The I35 interchange was just a few traffic lights ahead. I prayed for the signals to stay green. Snowball did fine on the move. She'd stall in stop-and-go traffic.

Our luck held and I turned onto the entry ramp. Only when we were heading north at 55 miles an hour did I breathe a shallow sigh of relief. No cops in the rearview mirror, but that might not last. I didn't dare push Snowball over 55 or she'd overheat.

"Are you okay?" I asked Jo. "Tell me the truth, did either of them touch you?"

Her hands trembled in her lap but she seemed okay. "No. They were after our money. You came in before they got it but…Oh shit, Evan, the burner phone. Where is it?"

"Gone," I said. "I took care of it."

"When?"

"Last night."

Jo exhaled.

So did I.

CHAPTER 33

JO

Snowball took us north for about four hours, then the temperature needle began to climb. As we drove through a tiny town called Franklin, just across the Nebraska border, the car was threatening to stall at every stoplight and smoke was coming out the air vents.

Evan pulled into the parking lot of the first motel he saw.

"Think it's safe?" I asked.

"We don't have much choice. The car's not going to make it any further today. Better to hole up here than get stuck on the side of the road."

He parked at the rear of the motel, backing it into the spot to hide the license plate. Buying Snowball from Travis at the salvage yard hadn't exactly been the most legal of transactions and God knew what would come up if some cop decided to run the plate.

Franklin, Nebraska reminded me of Planerville, only with more personality. And a certain pride: though our motel was cheap, it had a quaint, clean dignity. The lady behind the front desk—Mary Ellen Hildebrand—was pushing sixty and looked the embodiment of the perfect grandma. Her sweet demeanor and welcoming courtesy calmed my nerves.

Mary Ellen hollered at her husband Hank—a picture-perfect grandpa—to man the front desk so she could show us to our room, pointing out some of the old architecture of the place as she went.

"We had the pool put in some ten years back, though I'm afraid to say it's not heated. But Lord have mercy, who needs a heated pool with the summer we've been having?"

"I agree," I said, shooting Evan a wry look. "Who needs a pool?"

Once unpacked, Evan said he'd go find a deli and get sandwiches.

"One sandwich," I said. "We'll split it."

He didn't argue. We were running out of money. I thought about calling Del to wire me the four hundred bucks I had in her "bank," but feared that would implicate her and get her arrested.

I watched the door every second Evan was gone, jumping at sounds. He came back just as jumpy, and we ate in silence, lost in our own thoughts.

Mine were back in Wichita. At the break-in. Some flash of…something that struck me the moment that lamp hit the hotel clerk's head. I couldn't grasp it, and wasn't sure I wanted to.

Evan turned on the TV and we snuggled up to watch reruns of *The Munsters* and *Beverly Hillbillies*. The *Hillbillies* episode revolved around the Clampett family taking a trip to a local fairground. It reminded me of Joyland and despite the horrible scare we'd had in Wichita, I reveled in my restored memory.

Evan shut off the TV. I raised my head from the crook of his arm to look at him. "Tell me something about your childhood. Your happiest memory."

"My happiest memory." He rubbed his cheek, fingers rasping over the stubble. "Renting a tuxedo to go prom with you."

"You weren't really a child then."

"No, but it was my happiest memory of being taken care of by my parents. Of them providing for me."

I snuggled closer to him. "Explain."

"Well, Norma insisted that I have a suit just as fine as Merle or Shane's. She made sure of it. She even bought me a corsage to give to you because I hadn't thought of that."

"She did?"

"She sure did. Merle trampled on it, of course…"

"Weird how your best memory comes from the worst night of my life?"

"It was my worst night, too. But the day was awesome. That whole week was amazing. Things were still shitty with Merle and Shane, but I felt closer to Harris and Norma. Norma, mostly. For a whole week, I had a real mother and father. And come the weekend, I was going to have you. You were going to wear a beautiful dress for me, go to the dance with me. You'd walk in on my arm in front of the whole school and I knew you'd look astonishing. And after, we were going to be together. I was going to make love to you. I just… I'd never been so happy. I'd never felt so close to normal in my life."

"We were robbed," I said, my eyes stinging. "They took you from me. They tore us apart." I turned in his arms. "I really wanted our future. The Grand Canyon. Are we still going to have that, Evan? Is it part of whatever plan you have for us here?"

"I can't see that far ahead. I think the Grand Canyon is out there, waiting for us, but it isn't time yet. We have to reach the Center before we can go home."

Home. I hadn't known such a place since I was a little kid, and those memories were still lost in the gray fog. The home I'd known when I was thirteen was tainted and poisoned by Uncle Jasper. I couldn't define home until I exorcised him from me. Not only him, but my mother in the bathtub, knowing my scarred face had driven her to suicide.

I shivered, and Evan's arm around me tightened. "Let's get out of this room," he said.

"And go where?"

"I'm taking you on a date."

"A date?"

"We were robbed on prom night, right? So let's take it back. Will you have dinner with me?"

"Do you think it's safe?"

"Safe enough. I want to take you out, Jo. Nothing fancy. Just somewhere nice."

A smile spread over my face. "I'd love to."

We showered and got dressed. Evan wore jeans and his nicest shirt— one of the newer t-shirts he'd bought at the second-hand store in Oklahoma. It was the same pale blue as his eyes, and it stretched over his chest and arms rather nicely.

I put on the lavender dress I bought back in Oklahoma too, and brushed out my hair until it shone. I had no makeup of any kind—I left it all behind in Dolores. I was conscious of my scar and how it interrupted my face. But the way Evan looked at me when I stepped out of the bathroom, butterflies took flight in my stomach.

"You are so beautiful," he murmured.

We left Snowball to rest and walked down Franklin's tiny Main Street. We found a diner called Smokey Joe's, a throwback to the drive-thrus of the 1950's. Lots of red paint and white faux leather seats. Old electric guitars and record LPs hung on the wall, along with scenes from movies like *American Graffiti* and *Grease*. A jukebox stood in one corner, Elvis crooning about his blue suede shoes. The scents of grilled burgers, coffee and ice cream hung in the air, and I felt like we'd stepped backward in time.

It felt safe here.

We ordered burgers, onion rings and chocolate shakes, spending more money than we probably should have. But Evan was right: this was the date we never had. We talked and laughed with our feet tangled together under the table and our hands locked on top.

"Dance with me," Evan said.

"Here?" I glanced around. The restaurant was half-full of diners— families and regulars taking advantage of a beautiful clear, summer night.

"Right here."

Evan went to the jukebox in the corner and a moment later, Patsy Cline's hauntingly beautiful voice filled the room, singing 'Crazy.'

He grinned and held out his hand. We danced in the narrow aisle next to our table, while a few patrons turned to watch. I knew it wasn't wise being that conspicuous, but right then, with my head against Evan's chest and our bodies swaying together, strangers smiling on us, everything bad and scary retreated.

Back at the motel, Evan was pulling the room key from his pocket when I stilled his hand. If this was a date, I'd do it right.

"I had a good time tonight," I said, leaning against the door. "Thanks for dinner. And the dance."

"You're welcome," Evan said, catching on. "I had a good time, too."

He bent and softly brushed my lips with his. A first date's goodnight kiss, sweet and perfect. I could taste a little chocolate milkshake on his mouth.

"Would you like to come in?" I asked.

"I would," he whispered. His next kiss wasn't gentlemanly. It sent ripples of heat through me.

I managed to get the key in the lock and draw Evan inside. He shut the door and then I was in his arms, his mouth moving over mine with delicious intention.

Our kiss stayed unbroken as we shed our clothing. The only sounds our rasping breaths, his belt buckle jingling, clothing rustling and falling away. Evan laid me down on the bed, his body wondrously heavy over mine. He kissed me everywhere, touched me a thousand times until I was lost in him and he in me.

When I slept, my dreams were only of him.

I woke in the deepest part of the night. Evan was untangling his limbs from mine and folding back the covers.

"What is it?" I whispered.

He kissed me softly. "I'm going to the pool."

"Why?" But I knew why.

"Stay here," he said. "Sleep. I'll be back soon."

The door clicked shut behind him. I lay down and tried to fall back asleep but couldn't. He needed someone to time him. He couldn't count seconds under water, it would ruin his concentration.

The alarm clock on the side table was one of those old fashioned kind with the two little bells on the top and a winding key on the back. It was practically an antique. Hank and Mary Ellen must put a lot of faith in their guests. I vowed to take special care of it as I padded down to the pool.

The night was hot without a breath of wind. The hotel made an L shape and the pool was a kidney bean within its courtyard. All the windows facing the pool were dark. I hoped they'd stay that way.

Evan was in the water, his face in profile to me, his expression serene.

He only glanced at me as I came to sit on the edge.

"You ready?" I asked.

"I am."

He began to take short, shallow breaths, huffing oxygen deeper and deeper into his lungs. One final, deep breath without an exhale and he went under.

I stared at the little face of the alarm clock and watched the seconds add up. Then the minutes.

Five minutes. Six minutes.

Seven…

I gnawed my lip almost until it bled.

Eight minutes. Through the rippling water, lit from within, I could see Evan's arms moving. He was having to fight to stay under now.

Nine minutes, and I started to shake.

Nine and half minutes, and Evan broke the surface, gasping and clutching his chest.

I carefully set the clock far from the pool's edge, then slipped into the water. It sucked at my shorts and T-shirt as I took Evan in my arms. His head cradled on my shoulder through the wracking coughs. Rasping, choking sounds, tearing him apart inside. He clung to me until the coughs subsided, then we stood still in the shallows, holding each other.

"Please tell me it's worth it," I whispered against his neck.

"It will be," he said, his voice a hoarse croak. "It will be."

CHAPTER 34

JO

The following morning, I woke with a heavy pall of dread in my gut. I'd had another dream about Lee. This time he'd been in our kitchen in Dolores, cooking up a batch of meth in the cast-iron skillet. His head was dented in and blood stained his collar.

"Don't test me, woman," he said. He dumped the contents of the skillet onto the floor and handed the pan to me, handle first. A blink or shift in time and we were in the living room. Lee lay face down on the cruddy green carpet.

"You're a liar," he said, his voice muffled. "I smell it on you. The lies." Then he sat up, grinning with his rotten, broken teeth. "Clean up your mess!"

I woke up swallowing a scream.

And then I knew. It came to me like one of Evan's dreams; distant and muted and then suddenly right there.

Dolores. The fire. Lee...

"I went down in the kitchen," I murmured. "I woke up in the living room."

And then that memory, in full Technicolor—cruddy green and blood red—emerged from the fog too. It hit me like a cold slug to the chest, but I'd known. Somewhere down deep I'd always known.

I rolled over and shook Evan awake, panic infusing my words. "I did it, didn't I? I killed him. I killed Lee. I hit him with the skillet. Not you. I woke up in the living room and he was dead at my feet. It was me, not you."

Evan came awake startled, then shook his head, as if saddened that I knew.

"It was an accident, Jo. You never meant to kill him. You were dazed from how he beat you, and you thought he was hurting me. You thought you were saving my life."

I nodded, flinching as I remembered the pan striking the back of Lee's head. Feeling his skull give...

"Oh god..." I looked at Evan, my eyes wide. "But...you told me you did it. You said you'd pay for it. But you didn't do it. You'd go to prison for me? For life? Evan, it was me..."

"Not you, Jo. Never you. You're not going to pay for Lee. Never."

"But..."

He clutched my face in his hands. "I told you, I'm going to keep you safe and I meant it. Okay?" He didn't wait for an answer. "Come on. We gotta get going."

I'll be safe and he'll be free.

I had half of that little puzzle now. But the rest?

I was sure I didn't want to know. The nameless feeling of some force coming to take Evan from me returned, and that dread hung over me while he showered and I packed up our stuff. We only had one bag now, his duffel. I rolled my lavender dress up tight and shoved it inside. My hand brushed something hard. Closer inspection showed an inside pocket with a rectangular object in it.

I unzipped the pocket and pulled out the burner phone I'd used to call Del in Oklahoma. I glanced at the bathroom door, puzzled. Evan had said he'd ditched it back in Wichita.

I turned the phone on and went to the screen listing outgoing calls. Three numbers were showing. The first number, the earliest call made, was Del's. It should have been the only number.

I made one call and then Evan threw the phone away. That's what he told me.

Yet a second call was above Del's. 411 information.

The third was a number with a 605 area code.

Eyes narrowed and my stomach rolling, I shot another glance at the bathroom door. The water was still going. I highlighted the 605 number and hit the call button.

Two rings, then a man's voice answered, "Rapid City Police, Detective Sams' desk."

I froze.

"Hello?"

"I…"

"Hello, can I help you? Is this an emergency?"

I hung up the phone and tossed it onto the bed as if it had burned me. Where was Rapid City? Why the fuck was Evan calling the police?

The water in the shower shut off and I quickly jammed the phone back into the duffel's inside pocket. Then thought about taking it out. Confronting him. Why not?

Because I don't want to know.

Evan came out, wrapped in a towel. I muttered something about him hogging the hot water, and slipped in without meeting his eye. I stood for a long time under the shower spray, pulling myself together.

I trust him. I trust him. I trust Evan with my life.

It was the truth, but the questions I hadn't been asking him and the oddities I'd brushed aside were now piled up so high, like that Jenga game, where you pull the wrong one—ask the wrong question—and the whole tower comes crashing down.

We dressed and packed up, said goodbye to Mary Ellen and left Franklin, Nebraska. I didn't demand any answers. The dread had gained weight. It pressed me down and made my jaw heavy. Evan was quiet as well, strangely subdued. I wondered if he felt the same unease, sensed the same unnamed something looming on the horizon.

I expected him to take us north—always north—but he drove Snowball onto 80 West, heading toward Wyoming.

I could ask him why, but knew he couldn't tell me.

Evan merged on to 26 West, driving across country that was remote and flat. An endless horizon of yellow and green with nothing to break it. We drove three hours in near-total silence, except for Snowball: she made a continual, high-pitched whine, as if she were in pain. When we stopped for gas and food, she stalled flat. Evan filled the tank with gas and the radiator with water. I doubted the car's ability to take us ten feet, let alone another mile. But she started up with a groan and we were on our way again.

Two more hours of flat, empty land and silence. Then a sign loomed ahead: Chimney Rock National Historical Site.

A mound of pale yellow rock rose some hundred feet in the air, an unusual, narrow jutting peak protruding from the top. The formation looked aptly-named, exactly as if someone had built a chimney on a rock mound. But to me it looked entirely different.

I knew why we were here.

Evan parked the car and I got out, glancing at a park sign. It explained the rock was a national landmark made of sandstone and clay. It had served as a landmark for the trappers and traders making their way on the Oregon Trail.

I didn't see rock or clay or sandstone or history.

I saw wet sand.

"It's a drip castle," I said, as Evan came to stand by me on the grass-swept plateau. "When I was five, my mother took me to Tybee Island. In Georgia. And we made drip castles on the beach."

He waited. Listening. I held my hand out to him and he took it.

"Instead of making walls and moats, or using buckets, you scoop up a handful of wet sand and let it drip from your fingers. It falls on itself like melted wax. You can make beautiful castles with tall spires."

I stared at Chimney Rock, the memory barreling at me in full color and light and warmth and sound as I pointed toward the formation.

"The best towers looked like that. Exactly like that. I'd make a mound first and pack it down hard, then I started the spire. It grew higher and higher, without falling over or crumbling under its own weight. My mother..." Tears stung my eyes, blurring the spire in front of us. "My mother laughed and said it was the best she'd ever seen. She said she was proud of me; said I might be an architect or an engineer someday. Maybe a sculptor or artist. Whatever I did, I knew she'd love me for it and be proud..."

My voice caved in. Evan didn't move.

"I remember," I said through my sobs. "I remember my mother, Evan. I can remember all of her. Her laugh, her smell. The way she looked right before her lights dimmed and her mood swung low. How that scared me. I remember the joy and relief when her lights came back on and she swung up high again. And I remember she loved me."

"Of course she did," Evan said hoarsely.

"I know now… I know she couldn't stay when she saw what Jasper did to me. It was too much for her. Even if I hadn't cut myself, if I'd just *told* her what he did to me, she still would've left. Because she wasn't strong enough to stay." I touched my scar with trembling fingers. "This wasn't why. This was only a telling. I've been wearing it all my life like a badge of shame. All this time, I blamed and punished myself. But she would've left anyway. Jasper killed her, not me. It wasn't me."

"No, it wasn't." Evan's voice sounded gruff. The wind snatched his words easily and bore them away across the plateau.

I sniffed. Then a half-laugh, half-sob erupted from me as a tremendous weight slipped off my shoulders. With the burden of the past gone, I could now see our entire journey to this place. Not a haphazard set of coincidences but a plan. First the Blue Whale. Then Joyland. Now Chimney Rock.

The impossibility struck me like a gale of wind. Swaying on weak legs, I turned and stared at Evan. As if truly seeing him for the first time.

My voice shook as I spoke. "You said when we reached the Center, I'd be safe."

"You will," Evan said, and I could see by the pain in his eyes he knew what was coming. "You'll be safe and—"

"You'll be free," I finished. "What does that mean, Evan? Tell me the truth. Tell me how you're doing this. How are you taking me to these exact right places to help me recover those exact right memories? And tell me what's going to happen at the Center. I know you'll be free. Free of what?"

He shook his head, his eyes dark. "Don't do this, Jo. Please. We're almost there."

"Almost where?" I cried. "And who will meet us when we get there? Detective Sams of the Rapid City Police Department?"

Evan scrubbed his hands over his face. "Jesus…"

"Why did you call the police?

"I had to."

"Why, Evan?"

"I don't know, Jo. It's part of the plan. But I don't know it until we approach the exit on the highway, or see the roadsign. I don't have the entire plan in front of me. I get in pieces, little flashes of dreams I can hardly remember. Or a feeling, an urge. Stop here. Go there. Make a left. Call this number. To the whale. To Joyland. To Chimney Rock. For *you*. Everything I've done is for you."

"But what about you? What about your freedom? What does that mean?"

Evan turned his gaze to the rock, the plateau. The wind whistled and blew his hair, stung his eyes.

"They'll never let me go, Jo." His voice sounded strangely hollow. "I could have salvaged something after Woodside, but after prison..." He shook his head. "I can't live my life looking over my shoulder, or try to build a life with you somewhere and wonder if it's all going to be ripped away again. I can't."

He turned to me, his eyes pleading. "I love you more than anything. More than my own life. No, that's not true. You *are* my life. You're in the marrow of my bones, Jo. In my dreams, my future, every particle of me. Now I'm begging you to hold on a little longer. To see this through. For me. The journey was for you, Jo. To give you your mother back. I see that now. But the destination...that's for me."

"I'm scared," I whispered, my words now torn away by the wind.

"So am I," Evan said, moving closer. "But we have to finish it."

"At the Center."

He nodded.

I looked to Chimney Rock, looming as large and solid and vibrant as the memories of my mother. Evan had given them back to me. This crazy journey guided by intuition or instinct or some other-worldy gift...it had given my mother back to me.

That same guide was waiting to take Evan where he needed to be, to set him free. I was scared for him—for us. Terrified. But how could I stop him?

I took his hands in mine. "Let's go."

CHAPTER
35

JO

385 North cut across flat land browned by the relentless sun. At a place called Rapid City, South Dakota, he guided the car onto another stretch of highway called the 90 West, but still it led north. Always north. Snowball wheezed and whined. As we merged onto 85 North, the car's temperature needle pushed into the red and stayed there. Evan didn't stop.

Snowball obliged us another six miles, then a terrible grinding sound came from under the hood. Smoke seeped into the car from the air vents and then tapered off as the engine died. We were six miles from the town of Belle Fourche, South Dakota.

We left Snowball on the side of the road and walked on the highway's shoulder, hand in hand, the sun starting to sink on the western plains.

Belle Fourche was situated on the northern slopes of the Black Hills, between two branches of the Redwater River. We crossed over the southern branch on our way into town, but Evan kept us walking north. Always north. One bag between us, no money and no car.

We walked through the center of town, passed shops and taverns, fast food places and country restaurants. As dusk fell, painting the sky purple and gold, we arrived at the Belle Fourche Visitor's Center where a commemorative plaque welcomed us. I read the words printed on it with a peculiar sensation that was half dread, half exhilaration.

Welcome to Belle Fourche
The Geographic Center of the United States

The plaque went on to describe how the inclusion of Hawaii and Alaska into the Union had moved the exact geographic center of the United States from Kansas to spot a little north of Belle Fourche.

Evan looked at me and I looked at him.

"Not just *a* center," I said, mustering a wan smile. "*The* center. Of the whole country."

Evan found a grin. "Go big or go home."

"I'll take home."

"Not yet."

We went inside the visitor's center, browsed the maps and models and displays. We learned Belle Fourche had been named by French explorers. "Beautiful Fork" was a trading post for ranchers and farmers settling the valley and miners digging deep in the Black Hills.

One display showed the Redwater River surging by the geographic center marker. The river was a popular kayaking and boating destination, although one section had been closed off. Too many drowning deaths, I read, where the waters turned unpredictable with deep, sucking currents and turbulent rapids.

A security guard had been watching us closely all this time. When he spoke into a walkie-talkie on his shoulder, I knew it was about us. I caught Evan's eye and he nodded.

We left the visitor center. Outside the wind was howling and the sky threatened a storm. A chill was in the air, and we stopped on a corner so I could put on Evan's plaid flannel, and he his jacket. A squad car approached the intersection. Anxiety tightened my chest and didn't let up, even when the cruiser turned and drove in the opposite direction.

We walked north out of town, across fields of dried grasses that grew rockier and greener the closer we came to the river.

Of course, the river. Water beckoned to Evan. He went and I followed.

The Center marker wasn't as decorative as the one at the visitor' center in town. Just a heavy iron plug in the ground with a bunch of surveyor's marks and symbols. We stood over it, the wind rippling our clothing and the first drops of rain falling.

"What happens now?" I asked.

"Won't be long," he said, looking over my shoulder. "It's almost over."

I turned. Police cars were turning down the dirt road running parallel to the river. One car, two, three. Four cruisers speeding in the darkening night. Coming toward us.

"Come on," Evan said.

We ran along the river that churned with white foam and roared against a high wall of rock. We picked our way to the shore, stumbling over rocks, our clothing snagging on bushes. I stared at the churning water. The rain was coming down hard now.

"This is it, Jo," Evan shouted over the roar of the river and the rain. "You're going to be okay."

"No," I cried, clutching the front of his jacket. This was the end but I couldn't take it. Cold terror shook me apart, rising up in me like a deadly tide. "We should never have come here. It's a mistake. A terrible fucking mistake."

"It's not a mistake. It's exactly right. It's how you'll be safe."

"Safe? From the police?" I cried. "They'll arrest me and I'll let them because I'm not letting you go, Evan. Whatever you're planning…"

"Then we'll never be together, Jo," Evan cried. "You have to let me take it; Lee and the fire…Let me take it with me, or there is no us. No little life. No going home."

In the woods behind us came sweeping cones of flashlight beams and barking dogs.

I stared at the churning water that looked so black and cold and merciless. "You'll be free," I murmured through numb lips.

"Yes." Evan pulled me closer. "They won't let me go, Jo. They'll never leave me alone. I'll never be what I want to be. You have to let me do this."

Lightning cracked the sky and the rain came in sheets. Beneath us, the river roared like a starved, caged animal. The lights were getting closer, casting wider nets in their beams. Evan moved closer to me, the rainwater dripping off his nose and chin.

"Remember what I said to you. What I swore to you?"

"Y-yes."

"Say it."

My heart jackhammered against my ribs as the rain collided with my tears. "You'll always come back to me."

"And it's still true," Evan said. *"I will always come back to you.* Tell me you believe it. Let me hear you say you believe me, Jo."

"Step away from the girl!" cried a man's voice. Out of the woods emerged a dozen men in uniform, leveling their weapons at us.

"Tell me, Jo," Evan cried over the roar of the water. "If you love me, tell me you believe. Tell me, please," he pleaded. *"Please."*

I nodded, my head bobbing mutely and then I found my voice. "I believe you."

His hands took my shoulders. "Then you're safe now. They have nothing on you. When you leave this place I want you to go home."

"Step away from the girl and put your hands up!"

The police were drawing closer, taking wide steps over rocks and brush, their weapons balanced on their wrists and crossed with flashlights.

"Go *home,* Jo." His fingers touched my scar. "Promise me."

Home.

The place where the river had cut the earth's face, made a scar wide and deep and beautiful.

"Let her go! Hands up!"

"I promise," I cried.

Evan smiled, relief flooding his face. "I love you, Jo," he said, pushing me gently away from the river's edge, away from him.

I refused to let go. "I love you. I love you, Evan. Please don't…"

The cops were done warning us. They surged forward and Evan's gentle push grew stronger, and I stumbled back a step. The muddy shore gave way beneath us, and Evan's feet slipped. He teetered over the water. I lunged for him, grabbing his jacket to haul him back.

"Jo, no!" Evan screamed, but I snagged his arm. He fell back into the churning river, taking me with him.

The water hit me like an icy slab and sucked me under. Cold, wet blackness enveloped me, pushing and pulling like a dog worrying a toy in its teeth. Under, deeper. I couldn't see the surface, couldn't see anything, only sensed I was being sucked further away from shore. The icy pressure squeezed my lungs. My legs kicked for the surface, numb and heavy against the water's relentless pressure.

Evan!

I nearly screamed, letting in a lungful of water as I fought the pulling tide. Then I felt it…A pressure on the back of my thigh, pushing me up. Evan's hand. Evan was pushing me up toward the surface while the water sucked him down.

I broke through with a gasp. Different hands hauled me out of the water. A scream tore from my throat as I scrambled to my feet and try to run toward the river. The police dragged me back. My eyes swept the rapids in a panic but saw nothing. No sign. Just white foam and whirlpools of swirling black water, greedily dragging and sucking the world into its depths. Taking everything I loved with it.

"Evan!" I screamed his name to the river. Screamed until something gave out in my throat. I fought like a wild animal toward the water, but the police held me back. Panic and terror tore at my mind, my thoughts, but Evan's words were bright in my mind.

I will always come back to you.

And I had told him I believed him. I promised. I had to let him go. And the police lining the river's edge. They needed to let him go too. They'd needed to see him vanish, and believe he was gone. They needed to watch the time tick by, the water giving nothing, until they gave up.

Because who could hold their breath longer than a few minutes?

Evan can. He's the only one. I have to believe…

I sagged into the arms of a cop, as if defeated though in truth my limbs were rubbery with terror. He was almost gentle as he led me back a few feet and helped me sit.

The rest of the police watched the water, their dogs roaming and sniffing the shore.

How long had it been now?

A minute? Two? At least two minutes. I started counting seconds, an imaginary second hand whirling around my brain.

Three minutes. Three was nothing.

Four. The cop slung his raincoat around my shoulders. I slumped within it, drawing my knees up to my chest.

Five minutes. He was good for five minutes.

Six. The cop stayed next to me, standing, his fingers tapping his service revolver.

Seven minutes now.

Flashlights scanned back and forth, casting yellow slants of light over black water.

Eight minutes. My voice collected itself, uncoiled and rose up in a tiny wail. It was time for us to clear out. I staggered to my feet, moaning softly. Grieving.

The cop helped me to stand, keeping a firm grip on my upper arm.

Nine minutes and a few police were moving down the river, following its current to see where it would cough up Evan or where he might try to emerge. But I heard them calling it a day.

Ten minutes and then I stopped counting.

They wouldn't find him. He was gone.

Evan Salinger was dead.

He was free.

PART III: DREAMCATCHER

The oldest and strongest emotion of mankind is fear. And the oldest and strongest kind of fear is fear of the unknown. —**H.P. Lovecraft**

CHAPTER 36

JO

Calhoun, Louisiana
One Month Later

Del's expert on false documents, James (last name not disclosed), didn't look seedy. Or skeezy. Or any other number of unsavory adjectives that popped to mind when I pictured a criminal of the underworld. He was young and leaning toward hipster with his groomed beard and horn-rimmed glasses. He looked *too* young if you asked me, but Del said he was legit and I trusted her. Even so, it took some will to slide over an envelope with five hundred in cash inside—the second half of the thousand dollars this job cost me.

Del was incognito today, wearing slacks and a button-down shirt and his birth name, Dellison Jones. He gave my hand a reassuring squeeze under the table as James counted the money without taking it out of the envelope. He nodded and tucked it into an inside pocket of his leather jacket. From a briefcase he pulled a portfolio case and withdrew a manila envelope.

"Your guy's picture looked like a mug shot," he began.

"It was a mug shot," I said.

James didn't blink. "Point being, I had to manipulate the background a little. Lucky for you, most DMV photos look like mug shots anyway. I don't think anyone looking hard will notice." He started to slide the folder to me, stopped. "The names are the names. I have to build an identity on your age, height, eye and hair color. Getting it all to match is my job, not creating the perfect alias. So don't bitch at me if you don't like the names."

My hands itched for the folder. Its contents were life. My life and Evan's.

"She doesn't care about the names, Jimmy," Dellison said. A wry grin split his face as he leaned over me. "But I do. I'll laugh my ass off if you're now Mildred P. Hufflestuff from Hoboken, New Jersey."

I opened the folder and studied the first set of documents—a social security card and an Arizona driver's license. The license that had my picture, my height and weight, and my new birthday.

"Amy Price," I said. "My name is Amy Price." *Hear that, Mama?* I thought with a small smile. *I was Jo and now I'm Amy.*

"Amy Price." Dellison said, trying it out. He sniffed. "Ain't nothing funny about that."

"I said no bitching." James sipped his rum and Coke.

I slid the second set of cards out of the folder. My heart clenched painfully and my eyes filled. I blinked hard, looking at Evan's handsome face. James had done an excellent job fading the background of the North Center Corrections Facility to the pale blue of a DMV shot.

"Justin Hollister," I murmured.

"That name ain't funny neither," Dellison said. "I was hoping for a Herbert or an Adolf."

I elbowed him in the side, and looked to James. "Thank you. These are perfect."

"I know," James sniffed. "One hundred percent legit. Clean social security numbers, laser perforation, functional bar codes and ultraviolet seals."

I nodded, marveling at the holographic image on my new driver's license. "And when we apply for jobs, the SSN's will work? No glitches?"

Jameson snorted. "My work doesn't *glitch*. This is your life now. Take it or leave it."

I took it. Took all four life-giving documents and tucked them into my bag, then clutched my bag as if some stranger were going to run up and snatch it away.

A week later I said goodbye to Del. She was dressed for work—glittering sequins and puffy hair—and she dabbed her eyes as I loaded up my pick-up truck.

I bought the truck with some of the money I'd won from the Midwest Poetry Journal's annual contest. The poem I submitted two weeks ago took first place: three thousand bucks. I'd burst into tears when the check arrived. An MPJ prize was a legit literary accomplishment, definitely something to crow about. But I cried more from relief. The money meant I could afford some transportation to make the trek west and still have some left over to find a place at Lake Powell.

"Go home," Evan said.

I shut the passenger side door. My entire life fit on the front seat: two bags' worth of clothes, a few books and my poetry journals. Taped to the dash was a photo of Del and I working behind the bar at The Rio.

I turned and looked at my best friend, my heart cracking. She'd not only given me a job, but let me live with her rent-free since my hearing a month ago.

The district attorney had tried to build a case, but the judge—over the loud, screeching protestations of Patty Stevenson—found insufficient evidence to charge me with the death of Lee Stevenson. The fire from Lee's home meth lab had destroyed anything that could incriminate me. The only solid piece of evidence in the whole case worked in my favor: Evan Salinger's confession to the murder, made via a burner cell phone to the Rapid City police department.

My attorney (appointed by the court) played the recording of the confession before the grand jury and I shivered to hear Evan's cold, lifeless voice, laced with the tiniest bit of mania. An edge of psychotic motive. It fit right with his record: the history of violence and mental problems, the assault conviction and incarceration at North Correctional. He escaped prison, stole a truck and drove to Dolores where he murdered my fiancé. Then dragged me across half the country before trying to drown me in the Redwater River. Only he wound up dead himself, sucked into the undertow and violent rapids at the curve of the river closed to the public.

It was a horrible, ugly twist on the truth, and it broke my heart to hear them talk about him like that. But he'd known they would. He'd lived his whole life in their ugly perception. And then he used it to break free. I was so proud of him, and that was how I kept my mouth shut and played along. To keep him safe.

"You sure about this, girl?" Del said now. "You know I love you. And I only keep asking *because* I love you."

"I know. I love you too. And I love him. I made him a promise and I'm going to keep it. I love him more than anything else, Del, so I'm following the plan. I'm going home and I'm waiting for him."

From the look on Del's face, I could've been a teenager claiming to have seen Santa Claus on the neighbor's roof. I'd told her about the road trip, leaving out the intimate details, and she'd reacted as I expected: concern laced with skepticism and a concern for my sanity. I began to understand how Evan must've felt all of his life.

Del studied me a moment more with her sharp, dark eyes. She sighed. "You do love him, honey. And that's all that matters, isn't it? Can't give up on love. Not never."

"Never," I agreed. "And a wise woman once told me that it was best to keep something in front of you. Something to hope for."

"I know it, baby, but what you're hoping for…"

She trailed off, but I could still hear her unspoken words. What I was hoping for was a miracle.

"I have to go," I told Del, hugging her tight. "I'll miss you. So much."

"I'll miss you too, honey," she said against my neck. "You call me every time you stop on the road. And you call me when you get to Lake Woebegone."

"Lake Powell," I said, drying my eyes on the heel of my hand.

"Whatever." She pulled me in for another hug. "You take care of yourself. I mean it. And God forbid if it don't work out—"

"Don't even."

"If it don't work out like you want, sugar, you come right back here, okay?"

"I will," I said, touched to the core by her offer and praying I'd never have to take her up on it.

I took US 20 West toward Dallas, the same route Evan took in our flight from Dolores. The drive to Lake Powell would take eight hours. I could've done it in one day, but I wasn't about to take any chances. I didn't think the authorities were still watching me, not after a month had passed, but better safe than sorry and all that.

Outside Dallas, I stopped at a small drugstore to buy a comb and scissors, then checked into a motel. After a meal of takeout barbecue and a Diet Coke, I stood in front of the bathroom mirror and cut my hair off.

I took it up to a chin-length bob, changing my appearance while still concealing my scar. It hurt seeing the tresses piling up in the sink, but only a little. When I thought of all that Evan sacrificed for me, some goddamn hair was nothing.

Besides, Jo March cut off her hair too.

Except I wasn't Jo anymore. I was Amy. But not Amy March. No, I decided if I had to be a literary Amy, I would be Amy Dunne from *Gone Girl*. On the lam, holing up in hotels.

I smiled at my reflection. "Hi, I'm Amy Price."

I offered a hand to shake. "Hi. Amy. Nice to meet you."

I didn't like it; it sounded wrong. Like a pen name I hadn't chosen for myself.

I'll be Jo for Evan, I decided. *I'll always be his Jo.*

I got an early start the next morning and made it to Page, Arizona before noon. The desert sand was the exact color I pictured it in my mind: a pale, burnt-orange that made the waters of Lake Powell vibrant, almost explosively blue.

Page was a small tourist city, its businesses geared toward the lake and the nearby Grand Canyon. Here, I set about constructing a life.

I'd planned to rent an apartment in the little town, or maybe find my dream lake cabin. But one day when I drove past Antelope Point Marina, with its rows of bobbing houseboats, I changed my mind.

Or maybe it was changed for me.

Evan would love a houseboat.

A home on the lake. Not by the water but *on* it. We'd fall asleep every night, rocked in its arms.

I found a houseboat realtor, Nick Burton, a rotund man with a sunburned face. He showed me around his inventory. Most were too big—two-story behemoths I couldn't drive, let alone afford. Then Nick showed me his smallest houseboat: twenty-four feet long, white with blue trim. It had one bathroom, one bedroom, a tiny living area and an outside deck with just enough room for two chairs. The kitchen and bath were outdated as hell—Nick said the boat was built in 1994.

"How much?" I asked.

"Twenty-five hundred."

I gaped. "That's it? Are you sure?"

Nick smiled. "I'd love to play poker with you sometime, Miss Price."

My cheeks reddened. "It's perfect. I'll take it."

But I couldn't *actually* take it since I was still very much unemployed. But I had five hundred dollars of my prize money to slap down as down payment, and that made Nick a little flexible. In his office overlooking the marina, he and I worked out a plan to let me rent the boat—and move in immediately—and then conclude the purchase after I could prove some source of income. He's also gave me a bunch of info on houseboat ownership and how to maneuver a vessel that size.

"Can I keep her docked here until I get the hang of it?" I asked as Nick walked me to the door.

"I'd recommend it. Slip fees are reasonable. And best to keep her here in the winter, for sure. But the rest of the year, take her out anywhere near the point. Lots of little swimming holes and coves. Fact it, soon as our deal is wrapped up, you can take her anywhere you'd like. She'll be all yours."

Mine and Evan's, I amended silently. Our home.

Living arrangements made, I set about finding work. It was June and the tourist season was in full swing. I quickly got a job running the register at a place called Lakeside Rentals. They dealt in kayaks, paddleboats and canoes. It wasn't the most enthralling job in the world but Marjorie Tate, the owner, was a sweet, boisterous gal in her mid-fifties with a silver braid down her back and a perpetual smile on her face. She was a far cry from Patty Stevenson and went out of her way to make me feel welcome. Though I felt her curious eyes on my face, she didn't ask me once about my scar.

"I had an accident," I finally said. "A long time ago."

I said it with a reassuring smile, indicating it was neither a secret nor a topic for further conversation. I didn't add *car* onto the accident or elaborate with dead uncles or an anguished mother. It was just an accident now. Something unfortunate.

On the lunchbreak of my second day, I took a walk around Page. Like Marjorie, the little city had a welcoming charm. I liked its southwest, touristy bustle in the middle of the silent desert. The lake to the north and the Canyon to the south. A Navajo reservation lay out east, Marjorie told me, and I saw several shops selling Native American art.

I stepped into one of these shops on a whim. The glaring dry heat of the desert—so different from Louisiana's wet, green smother—was immediately quelled by a whirring air conditioner and soft light.

The shop was a wonder of First Nation artwork and artifacts. I meandered along shelves of turquoise jewelry, gorgeous pottery and animals carved from wood or stone. On the wall hung small tapestries or rugs with simple but beautiful prints. From the ceiling hung dream catchers. Hundreds of them.

A dark-haired man with a leather-fringed vest and turquoise bolero called from the counter. "Let me know if I can help you with anything."

I smiled, about to tell him I was just looking, thanks, when I spotted a print on the wall above the register. I stepped closer, peering at a modern graphic of a man with his eyes closed. The details of his face only black lines against a smoky red backdrop. In the space above his eyebrows were shadowy figures holding bows and arrows, feathered headdresses spilling down their backs.

"This is beautiful," I said. "What is it?"

"Dream walker," the man said. "The sleeper is dreaming and the spirits who have crossed over are showing him a great battle that took place a long time ago."

"The sleeper is the dream walker?"

The man nodded, and when he spoke, his voice sounded old. Older than his years. "A man—or woman—in greater harmony with the realms that exist under the surface of our waking life."

"Under the surface," I mused. "Does one have be Native American to be a dream walker?"

The man rubbed his chin. "One only needs to be alive to sleep. And in sleep, we all dream. And if all of us sleep and dream, it stands to reason that many of us walk."

I thought immediately of Evan. I smiled. "I think so too."

My eyes raised to the dream catchers. One had a fine net like a delicate spider web, three feathers hanging down from strings of bright blue beads. Such a familiar blue. I hadn't planned on spending any money but I couldn't leave the shop without the dream catcher. After work, I took it to the houseboat and hung it over the bed. I lay looking up at it that night, rocked by the waters.

I'm here, I thought. *I'm home. Waiting for you. Come back to me.*

In that twilight place just before sleep, I imagined dream walkers in the skies above me, catching my words in their nets and walking them to Evan to guide him home.

CHAPTER
37

JO

Two weeks passed. I finalized the purchase of the houseboat and spent the remainder of the prize money filling it with everything a home needed: pots and pans, towels and sheets. I couldn't do anything about the dated fixtures, but I could add as many personal touches as my little budget could afford. I set every placemat or dishtowel or soap dish in its place like they were plugs in a dam, guarding a reservoir of optimism against leaks. Still, as the days passed in Page, my hope began to crack. Streams of *what if* trickled down the stone structure.

What if Evan's freedom came at the worst cost? What if I misunderstood his cryptic words? What if the river was too strong and didn't let him go? That was the biggest *what if* of all.

On good nights, I lay in bed, feeling the boat sway beneath me and listening for footsteps on the dock outside. I imagined the phone ringing. Pretended the harbormaster told me I had a visitor at the marina. I remembered Evan's promise to me and sent my silent call to the dream walkers until I fell asleep.

On bad nights, I called to Evan to come home with tears streaming down my cheeks, inching closer and closer to despair. The cold reality of that river was stronger than hope. The undertow had been too powerful. He'd been a fool to test nature. She always wins. I wept to sleep, then bolted from nightmares, a scream at the back of my throat and the feel of Evan's hand pushing me through the black water. I clung to those square inches of skin on the back of my leg, where the last sense memory of Evan's touch lived. I wondered if I'd ever feel his hands on me again.

By the end of the third week, the terrible nights outnumbered the hopeful ones. Fear was deteriorating into a panicked grief. The dam was sprouting more leaks than I had the will to fix. I spent my days off from work curled on my bed, crying until I turned inside–out, sometimes sick to my stomach from weeping. I had to force myself to shower and dress and eat. To keep up my end of the deal. Evan had never given up on me. I couldn't give up on him. But it was hard. So fucking hard.

One evening at twilight, I sat on the houseboat's tiny deck, wrapped in Evan's flannel shirt, sending my call into the skies. My eyes picked out all the blues of the lake, every orange and yellow in the desert stretching beyond. The sun slowly slipped away and I counted stars as they appeared.

I found Orion's belt, and Gemini, the twins. My mother pointed them out when I was six years old, and the vibrant color of the memory reminded me that anything was possible.

Anything.

Even footsteps on the dock. At this hour. When all the rented boats were docked and asleep in the rocking cradle of the lake.

I turned in my chair. A man was walking out of the east, the last of the sun's rays behind him, throwing his face into shadow.

Before my eyes could confirm it, my heart knew it was him. It stopped, then started again with a dizzying ferocity.

"Evan." My voice was hardly more than a whisper around his name.

He stopped and let the bag in his hand fall to the planks. I scrambled down from the boat and jumped onto the deck as he began to run. Twenty feet separated us. I closed the distance in seconds and crashed into him. Threw my arms around his neck, my legs around his waist and held on with everything I had.

His face pressed against my neck, bearded and scratchy. His arms wrapped around me, squeezing the breath from my lungs. His body shuddered against mine and then we stood still. Not speaking. Waiting to believe it was real.

He set me down and we stared at one another with hands and eyes. He cupped my cheek, then ran his fingers through my chin-length hair, over my scar, around my lips before bending to brush his mouth over mine in a tentative kiss. As if he were still trying to sort out if we were really here.

I clung to him, my fingers tangled in his hair that touched the edge of his collar, and kissed him hard. When he groaned and opened his mouth to take me in, I nearly slipped out of his arms in watery relief.

"Evan," I breathed. "You're here. You came back to me.'"

"I came home."

I led him inside. He stared in awe at our little houseboat, his eyes warm and full of questions.

But we needed each other first.

I pushed his jacket off his shoulders while his hands slipped under the worn flannel of his own shirt. My breasts curved into his hands. His palms were chafed with strange callouses and filled with the familiar greed for my skin. I could smell a journey on his skin: dirt and dust of the road, truck stops, cigarette smoke and burnt coffee. He broke our kiss, breathing hard.

"I need to wash it off," he said, as if he'd plucked the imagery out of my mind.

The shower was just big enough for us both to stand in. I soaped up a washcloth and scrubbed dirt and sweat off him, cramming my eyes with muscles that were larger than I remembered, skin that was darker with sun. He turned around so I could wash his back. My soapy fist swept over a small, black tattoo on his right shoulder blade. Two lines in a scratchy script.

11

"Why eleven?" I asked, though I was sure I knew.

"It's how long I was under," he said, his voice heavy. "I didn't usually time myself, but that night I needed to."

I closed my eyes. Eleven minutes in the black, cold water that tossed, churned, and sucked everything down deep. I couldn't imagine how he held his breath that long, much less counted the passing seconds. The ordeal would've driven me mad.

I pressed my lips to the tattoo. "I timed you, too. One month, two weeks, five days and sixteen hours until you walked up the dock." He turned in the slippery circle of my arms as the shower rained down on us. "Give or take five minutes."

"I love you, Jo." He hands moved slow over my skin. "I'll love you forever. I'll never stop."

I nodded, biting back tears. "I love you, Evan. I never said it enough. Not once in high school and only once on the riverbank. I love you. I'll love you forever and I'll never stop."

His mouth found mine again and he pressed his hard, rough body against mine

"There's no room to move in here," he said, his voice like a growl. "And we need to move."

I shut off the water and we stepped out. Two steps to the bed, dripping water over the gently rocking floor, then Evan lifted me and laid me down in a tangle of warm, wet limbs and sliding skin.

Evan kissed me like I was the air he needed to breathe. I clutched him like I was the gravity keeping him close. He needed no guiding hand to find the way. His palm slid to the small of my back, lifted and pressed me into his slow, grinding thrusts. He couldn't get deep enough. We'd never touch enough or kiss enough. But that night, we tried. Our cries rang out in the little houseboat, our home. At some wild moment, with my back arched and Evan bringing me to yet another crashing climax, I spied the dream catcher on the wall behind me. My tears mingled with the sweat of our greedy bodies and when we subsided, he lay curled around me, our limbs entwined. The houseboat swaying gently beneath us, the lake rocking us to sleep.

In sleep we dreamed. And in our dreams, we were together, still.

Epilogue

EVAN

Two years later

Jo packs up the lunch, stuffing sandwiches, chips, fruit, and thermoses of hot coffee into two backpacks. She also slips in a little bottle of champagne and two plastic cups, a soft smile touching her lips.

Today is a celebration. After two years of intense study—fire technology classes at the Page municipal building, and EMT courses at the local hospital—I'd taken my final exams in Mesa last weekend. I'd received the results in last evening's mail: a congratulatory letter with my test scores and an official certificate, the name **Justin Hollister** in bold print.

Jo—Amy Price to our friends and neighbors—howled with delight and put me in a chokehold when I handed her the papers.

"Oh my God, babe, you did it. You fucking did it!" Her face flushed and she fanned herself with envelope as she read. "The way you went on about the test being so hard. All that pacing around, worried you wouldn't pass. But you did…and just… Holy shit, I'm so proud of you."

She tossed the papers aside and began stripping out of her work clothes. I laughed, even as my body responded with a sudden rush of heat through my veins. "What are you doing?"

"Are you kidding?" Jo tossed her shirt aside and threw her arms around my neck, her bra-clad breasts pressed against my chest. "Firefighters are sexy as hell."

"I'm not a firefighter yet," I said, striding to the bed with her in my arms.

"Close enough," she said, kissing me softly, then deeply.

We celebrated all night. This morning, we head for the Canyon.

It's an hour's drive south. We know the route well: we make the trip as often as we can across the yellow and gold desert, painted with swaths of burnt orange. The skies, usually as blue as Lake Powell, are overcast and cold today. November chills have set in.

I look out the driver's side window, to the east and the Navajo reservation. I haven't been there yet. I don't know if I'll ever go. Something tells me not to. I have a new life now, this little perfect life with Jo. Maybe someday I'll head out there and maybe the road will open before me. I'll know just where to turn, what signs to follow, which street to take and which house to knock on the door.

Or maybe not. My old life died in the river with my old name. Cut loose from the anchor of Evan Salinger, I'm now truly free. A clean slate on which anything can be written.

Jo's been taking classes at the community college. She was offered a chance to teach poetry with their adult continuing education program. Strictly as a volunteer, but still, she was thrilled for the chance. I snuck once into the back of a classroom to listen to her teach. She stood in front of twenty people, forty eyes glued to her face and wondering about her scar. I alone knew the bravery it took for her to let herself be seen like that and the fiercest love and pride swept through me.

Just when I though I couldn't love her anymore, Josephine said or did something that stole my breath away. She'd waited for me. She watched me go under the black water and she waited for me to emerge. The wait nearly cracked her in two, but she held on. She believed in me. Trusted and loved me as much as I did her.

We park the truck and hike along the ridge. The Grand Canyon yawns open beneath us. The Colorado cuts through it like a small blue snake. The river seems so thin from up here, it's hard to imagine it could have split the earth like it did to reveal this beauty.

Jo and I stop at our favorite lookout spot. A family is there: father, mother and son. The boy looks to be about three years old. He's sitting on the father's shoulders. The father is gripping the boy's legs as they take in the gorge. The mother has her arm around the man's waist and she's looking up at her son. Smiling and laughing and talking about the Canyon. Telling him how big it is, how wide, how pretty and how old.

Her voice makes something flash through my brain.

A little tear in the fog of time.

I was up high once. I had a perch on a tall man's shoulders and his hands held my legs tightly so I wouldn't fall. My little index finger pointed at the tremendous chasm that opened the earth wide and deep. More breathtaking than a picture book, more exciting than an adventure story. A woman's voice, rich and full, told me amazing things about what I saw.

I can't make out the words. They're muffled and soft, as if coming from a great distance. But I know, with absolute certainty, that I was loved once. No matter what came after, what tragedy or desperate calamity tore me from my family, I was here at the Grand Canyon once. And the people who lifted me up and shared this moment with me loved me.

As quick as it came on, the memory slips away, back into the fog. The little family moves on and it's just Jo and me on the ledge.

I wrap her in my arms and rest my chin on her head. She holds me tightly and we watch the slow play of sunlight across the purples and oranges of the canyon rock.

"You ever get tired of coming here?" I ask.

"Never," she says. "And after this weekend, we might not get as many chances to come." Her hands give mine a warm squeeze. "You'll be busy saving lives and putting out fires."

"We'll make time," I say.

A chill wind whistles up and I move to hold her tighter. My hand slides across her sweater, over her belly. I linger there, but only for a moment.

She doesn't know yet but I do.

He's a speck of light in a safe, dark place. Not holding his breath in the water but breathing the water itself until it's time.

Instead of yearning for more memories of my lost childhood, I vow to make memories for our son. Someday he'll sit on my shoulders, here at the edge of the world. I'll hold his little legs tight while his mother tells him amazing things.

And he'll know he is loved.

THE

END

More From

Emma

Thank you for reading, and I'd love if you could take a moment to tell me what you thought. Any and all feedback is greatly appreciated!

For new releases and information please like my Facebook page: http://bitly.com/1yrzVvI or subscribe to emmascott.net
And follow me on Twitter at:
@EmmaS_writes

SNEAK
PEEK

Beside You in the Moonlight
Coming Spring, 2016

The year is 1970. Janey Martin, devastated by her first love's death in Vietnam, is sent to Paris by her parents to avoid prison for her part in destructive protests against the war. There, she keeps to herself, throws herself into her studies at the Sorbonne, and tries to leave everything and everyone from the States behind. Especially the agonizing memories of her lost love.

But the sound of American music from a small cafe/club is irresistible to her homesick heart. She ventures to La Cloche, a popular hangout with the local footballers. Janey meets Tristan Rousseau, a soccer playboy who seems like he has it all: cocky, rich, and handsome, with a new girl on his arm every night. Janey wants nothing to do with him, but when the group of footballers and their girlfriends pull her into their circle of friendship, Janey suspects there's more to Tristan than meets the eye.

Tristan has a secret he is desperate to keep, and a kinder heart than she ever suspected. With his gentle, patient help, Janey learns to let go of old pain that's been keeping her from loving again, and Tristan learns from her fiery passion how to fight for what he believes in. Together, they forge a love that heals their own broken hearts, and a partnership of compassion they seek to take into the world that is torn apart by war.

52721810R00165

Made in the USA
Charleston, SC
25 February 2016